A GOOD FAMILY

BOOKS BY MATT GOLDMAN

A Good Family

Carolina Moonset

Nils Shapiro Novels

Gone to Dust

Broken Ice

The Shallows

Dead West

A GOOD FAMILY

MATT GOLDMAN

TOR PUBLISHING GROUP
NEW YORK

A GOOD FAMILY

Copyright © 2023 by Matt Goldman

A Forge Book
Published by Tom Doherty Associates / Tor Publishing Group
120 Broadway
New York, NY 10271

www.tor-forge.com

Forge® is a registered trademark of Macmillan Publishing Group, LLC.

The Library of Congress Cataloging-in-Publication Data is available upon request.

ISBN 978-1-250-81017-5 (trade paperback)
ISBN 978-1-250-81015-1 (hardcover)
ISBN 978-1-250-81016-8 (ebook)

Our books may be purchased in bulk for promotional, educational, or business use. Please contact your local bookseller or the Macmillan Corporate and Premium Sales Department at 1-800-221-7945, extension 5442, or by email at MacmillanSpecialMarkets@macmillan.com.

First Edition: 2023

Printed in the United States of America

0 9 8 7 6 5 4 3 2 1

For my brother, Ken.

Keeping the beat. Baseball in the middle and west.
Freed via computer golf. Fellow skunkee on the streams of
Montana. Six on the floor in this day and age!

Thank you for always being there.

A
GOOD
FAMILY

· CHAPTER 1 ·

This, thought Katie. *This is what it's all about*. Family time. Sitting in the nook they'd built for these moments, informal and intimate, just the four of them isolated from the outside world in a cocoon of dark walnut benches and matching table. Filament-bulb sconces cast their warm glow against a wall of white beadboard. And the aroma of cooking drew them from bedrooms and basement along with Katie's texts on the family chat. *Dinner's ready! Wash your hands, please!* The nook created a sanctuary for conversation. *Tell me about your day.* Children's questions, jokes, teachable moments, and a sharing of opinions crisscrossed to form the emotional scaffolding called family that would support them in good times and bad. That was the idea, anyway.

"Nice job, Kaleb." This from Elin, a twelve-year-old vegetarian who trained herself for tween warfare by using her eight-year-old brother like an axe uses a sharpening stone. "You're eating the muscles and guts of cute animals."

"I am not. Mom, tell her I'm not."

"Well," said Katie, "you're not eating the guts. I promise."

Kaleb took that as a victory. Elin rolled her eyes and said, "Dad. Tell him."

Katie's husband, Jack, wasn't listening. He was lost in a spreadsheet on his laptop.

"No devices at the dinner table, *Dad*," said Elin in a voice both scolding and mocking since *no devices at the dinner table* was a rule laid down by Jack.

"Sorry, honey," said Jack. "Something's blowing up at work."

Kaleb leaned over and looked at his father's screen. "Whoa! That's a lot of numbers. Do you have to add all those up?"

Katie said, "Since when do you go over spreadsheets, Jack? You have people for that."

Jack looked at Katie over the screen of his laptop. His mouth was hidden but his eyes said *back off*. He was so touchy lately when it came to work. When it came to everything, really. Jack had his dream house now—he was supposed to be happy. Not angry. Not anxious. Not short with his wife. He had never given her a look like that before. And the kids had a point. No devices at the dinner table included Jack's devices, so Katie said to him what she often said to the kids. "It's okay to feel grumpy. It's okay to feel tired. It is not okay to be rude."

Jack dropped his eyes back to his spreadsheet, and Kaleb said, "Them's the rules, Dad."

"Yep," said Elin. "Them's the rules."

Jack sighed and shut his computer.

Imperfections aside, thought Katie, this was a moment for which they'd built the nook. It was the only element of the addition/remodel that Katie had insisted upon. "I want a nook in the kitchen for family time," she'd told Jack. "Like a booth in a restaurant for just the four of us." The addition/remodel itself was Jack's baby. He found the architect, the contractor, oversaw the budget, stopped by the house every day during construction. To keep his wife happy, one might say, or to keep her from weighing in on the rest of the project, another might say, Jack obliged her the nook.

The Kuhlmanns lived in Edina, Minnesota, in a neighborhood called Country Club on a street called Browndale in a house called perfect by friends and neighbors and drivers-by. Country Club had large homes best described as stately and lawns that looked like they'd all been mowed on the same day and, in the winter, sidewalks so free of snow and ice you'd think elves shoveled in the dead of night. Jack's architect and interior decorator and landscape designer worked with him to create a home so inviting you had to wonder who hadn't walked through to see the honed marble countertops and family photos, the five-panel doors and kids' artwork on the refrigerator, the blown-glass light fixtures and state-of-the-art laundry room complete with a custom-built wooden cage for the family's dirty clothes.

Two years ago Jack gave himself an obscene bonus after a fiscal year when his company developed a sodium-sulfur battery that solved two problems that had prevented sodium-sulfur batteries from powering electric vehicles. Jack's company eliminated the battery's corrosiveness and reduced its operating temperature from 300 degrees to 200 degrees, which is in line with the running temperature of most combustion engines. The big plus of making batteries from sodium and sulfur is that, unlike lithium and cobalt, the elements are plentiful and don't need to be purchased from countries that do terrible things to good people.

The new sodium-sulfur battery attracted huge investment in Jack's company from automobile manufacturers, public utilities, and organizations all over the world who had declared war on fossil fuels and human rights abuses. Jack's company raised over $1.2 billion, and the battery wasn't even on the market yet. But the money poured in and some of it built the house on Browndale. When they moved back in Jack said, "The only way I'm moving out of this house is when I'm carried out and loaded into a hearse."

Jack was proud of his new abode and he felt especially excited to show it off because that evening, after nook time with the family, the house would fill with neighborhood couples for book club—the first book club the Kuhlmanns would host since the remodel/addition.

Proud is not the word to describe how Katie felt about the house. Better words would be *undeserving, embarrassed, ashamed* even, because Katie Kuhlmann did not grow up with wealth. She married into a life of privilege, which made her life a hell of a lot easier for her than it was for most people. She worked hard as a mother and at her job at General Mills but this kind of extravagance was gifted from Jack, who grew up with old money, his family making their fortune in lumber when Minnesota was still just a territory. Jack built the remodel/addition as a fortress to preserve that gift, to keep the privilege inside and random cruelty of life outside.

It worked.

Almost.

· CHAPTER 2 ·

Katie first saw Jack at a University of Minnesota hockey game. She sat by herself in the student section wearing a white angora stocking hat. Two dark braids fell from her hat. She wore a powder blue turtleneck sweater out of which hung a silver pendant that looked like a small snowflake, and her lips shined like wet ice. When she stood to cheer Minnesota's first goal, Jack involuntarily said, "Who is that?"

He said these words to no one, but they were heard by Bagman, aka Adam Ross, who had earned his nickname after getting so drunk at a University of Minnesota football game that he passed out before the first half, and Jack and the guys put a paper bag over his head and left him that way for the remainder of the game.

Bagman disappeared down the concourse. Ten minutes later he emerged carrying three beers in a cardboard carrying tote. He approached Katie and handed her one of the beers then pointed to Jack. Katie held up her beer and mouthed *thank you*. By the end of the game, Katie and Jack had made a date for the following Saturday night.

"Who's ready for ice cream?" said Katie. She slid out of the nook and removed two bowls from the cupboard and ice cream from the freezer and, while she scooped, watched her husband violate the sanctity of the nook by reopening his laptop while his children, his precious children, *their* precious children, sat unobserved and ignored as if they were decorative plastic fruit.

"What's happening at work, Jack?" said Katie.

"Nothing. It'll blow over."

"Really? Because you look like you're about to throw up."

"Yuck!" said Kaleb. "I'm getting out of here!"

"I am not going to throw up," said Jack. "I just have to iron out a few hiccups."

"You can't iron hiccups," said Elin. "You iron wrinkles. You get rid of hiccups by holding your breath or by getting them scared out of you like this: Boo!!!!!!!!!!!!"

Kaleb jerked and knocked over his juice glass. Jack yanked his precious laptop out of the wet, slammed it shut, slid out of the nook, and stormed out of the kitchen. And then the thought came—it came so clearly Katie wondered if she'd said it out loud.

Jack's hiding something. My husband is hiding something from me.

· CHAPTER 3 ·

Book club started in the living room with spouses commenting on whatever book they were supposed to have read, then the women lingered upstairs as the men traipsed down to the basement for the built-in mahogany bar and red-felt billiards table and eighty-inch TV.

The living room was the jewel of the newly added space to the Kuhlmann home and was now the home's second living room, the original being renamed the sitting room though no one, in Katie's recollection, had ever sat in it. The new living room had ten-foot-tall ceilings and eight-foot-tall windows. They went all around, one after the other like matching glass tablets on three walls. They might have called it the sunroom if they didn't already have a sunroom. The space was large enough to host three sitting areas, each defined by an area rug over the hardwood floor. The room also featured two fireplaces and a grand piano. Not a baby grand—a concert grand, a seemingly odd choice since both Elin and Kaleb had abandoned lessons two years ago. But when you have to fill a space you have to fill a space.

The day when the family moved back in and Katie saw the space completely finished and furnished, the word that came to her mind was *obscene*. Jack had promised a tasteful home but Katie felt like he'd delivered an embassy. If they wanted to fill the house with friends, they'd run out of real friends and have to dip into Facebook friends, the kind you have but who aren't really friends or even acquaintances—they just accumulate on your page like unpaired socks in an overflowing sock drawer.

The main seating area was a three-sided sectional that easily sat five on each side. Two winged armchairs guarded the open end like sentries. The whole thing was anchored by a coffee table the size of a small bedroom. Three silver platters sat on the table, one covered in lemon bars, one in chocolate turtles, and one in tiny jars filled with butterscotch budino. There was also a cup of dessert spoons, a stack of plates, and paper napkins edged in silver.

The women looked like they belonged in Katie's new space more than she did, like they'd picked their outfits from display windows in downtown Edina or at the upscale Galleria mall. Katie tried to shop those beautiful stores but couldn't stomach it. She considered Nordstrom Rack a luxury. Otherwise it was outlet malls or Marshalls or the J.Crew Factory store. Maybe it was because she grew up with little money or maybe because she enjoyed bargain hunting but she couldn't keep up with her Country Club friends when it came to clothing and felt self-conscious as if she were wearing a sandwich board that said 50% OFF!

Katie had opened a bottle of port and brought out tiny stemware. The female half of the club discussed which book they'd read for January (the women mostly did read the book and they always skipped December because, you know, the holidays). The January book club was scheduled to be hosted by the Ackermans, who were not in attendance for the November book club—they had driven up to Roseau for their daughter's hockey tournament.

That's when Sandra (don't call me S-and-ra, it's S-ah-ndra) Dahlstrom said, "I heard the Ackermans are getting divorced."

Sandra had long hair that vacillated between blond and brown and looked twenty years younger than Sandra herself, whose beauty shouted *forty-four!* next to her hair that lied *twenty-four*. She wore yoga pants too often but believed one should highlight their best traits, which in Sandra's case were her legs. Sandra worked as an executive coach but currently had no clients because she was taking a break to rebrand.

"No," said Katie. "The Ackermans can't be getting divorced. They're so . . . normal."

"Their son is in Hannah's class," said Sandra, reaching for a lemon bar, "and he told Hannah that his parents are getting a divorce, and his dad sleeps in the basement, and after they talk to the therapist some more he's moving into an apartment."

The cluster of eleven women sat silent for a moment, all of them thinking the same thing: If it could happen to Terri and Richard, it could happen to them. Well, almost all of them were thinking that. Not Katie. The idea of her and Jack splitting felt impossible. Sure, things weren't great between them lately, but Katie had built her life with Jack. She'd been with him since the night they met at the University of Minnesota hockey game. They were a couple. A team. All of the growth they'd each experienced in the last twenty-four years was interwoven. Together they were a basket that held life. Apart they'd be nothing.

"Excuse me, ladies." This from Sandra's husband, Lucas, a forensic accountant who wore a camel cardigan over a white dress shirt and pants so pressed each crease could be used as a weapon. No one had ever seen him wear jeans, even when mowing the lawn, which he did twice a week whether the lawn needed it or not. He kept his hair so short he might as well have been bald even though he wasn't, and his scalp shined as if it had been waxed. Lucas said, "Sandra, honey. Hannah just called because the dog threw up. I'm going to run home and take care of it."

Sandra Dahlstrom looked at her husband for what felt like a full minute, pushed her long sometimes blond, sometimes brown hair back over her lined forehead and said with great flatness, "Have fun."

Lucas laughed. "I'll try. See you soon, ladies. And save me a budino!"

Sandra watched her husband exit the living room then turned back to the women and said, "According to Hannah, the Ackerman's son—I can never remember that boy's name—he said Terri and Richard called a family meeting and said the two of them had simply grown apart and that they still love each other as people, whatever that means, and they'd remain good friends but it would be better if they were no longer married. They are still going to celebrate family birthdays and holidays together and—".

Miriam Friedman shook her head of gray curly Johann Sebastian Bach hair and said, "Bullshit." She owned a handful of foodie-grade delis around town called *Deeeeeelish!* As Miriam refilled her tiny glass with port she said, "Never going to happen."

"Probably not," said Latisha Nicolaides. "Not once the lawyers get through with them. I should know—I'm a lawyer. But it sounds like maybe they really have just grown apart. It happens."

"As opposed to?" said Katie.

"As opposed to someone cheating," said Miriam.

Jane Hansen nodded as if this was common knowledge. Jane was the oldest of the book club members and wore her hair short and gray over her thin face.

"I know half a dozen couples who have broken up because someone cheated," said Miriam, "and first of all, in four of the six it was the woman who strayed, so let's just keep that in mind. And second of all, I don't condone cheating, but with every one of those couples, the cheating was a symptom of a dying marriage and not the direct cause for the divorce. I mean, that's what I think. And yes, I'm drunk and yes, I talk too much when I'm drunk and yes, I will stand by that statement when I'm sober. And for the record, I drink too much at book club because it's always within walking distance and who are we kidding anyway? It's why we do this. Pass the lemon bars."

Latisha Nicolaides lifted the silver tray, extended it toward Miriam and said, "I don't know what happened between Terri and Richard, but every night before Peter goes on a business trip I make sure we have some quality naked time. Even if I'm not in the mood and especially if he's not in the mood." A few women laughed but most knew Latisha wasn't joking. She had jet black hair and brown skin and glacier-blue eyes. She worked as in-house counsel for Cargill and intermittently as a plus-size model. Katie adored Latisha but found it strange to see a neighbor stripped down to her underwear in Target's Sunday circular.

Latisha said, "Because the last thing you want to do is send a good-looking, successful man to another city with an expense account and a hotel bar and his balls full. And I do it all over again the night he gets back." She picked up her chocolate turtle and took a bite to punctuate her point.

"It's like training a dog," said Jane Hansen. "Reward good behavior with a treat." Jane Hansen was, in fact, a professional dog trainer.

The women laughed though Jane wasn't joking, either.

Miriam said, "What do you think the chances are that the guys downstairs are having this same conversation? Think any of them worry about us when we go on business trips? Or when leaving us home while they're away on one?" Miriam poured herself more port and said, "As if it's only possible men could feel sexually unsatisfied or just plain promiscuous or so unloved they look elsewhere to fill the void. Holy shit, what year is it? 1900? I don't expect equality when it comes to children and housework because our husbands' double-barrel shotguns of entitlement and laziness are always loaded, but everywhere else, I damn well expect equality. Boardroom, bedroom, and I will kick any of their asses in a 5K."

"Hear, hear," said Latisha Nicolaides.

The women clinked their cordials and drank and laughed. Katie's mind wandered to a place she did not know or understand but she felt she was about to burst into tears.

· CHAPTER 4 ·

The guests had left, and the foyer was free of shoes. Elin and Kaleb were asleep in their rooms upstairs. Jack sat on the sectional finishing the last of a bottle of Shiraz, and Katie plopped herself down next to him and said, "Want to break in the new living room?" She put her hand on Jack's thigh.

"Honey, I'm wiped and I have a 6:30 breakfast meeting tomorrow. I think I'd better just call it a night."

Katie kept her smile, found Jack's hand and squeezed it. "Okay, hon. Get a good night's sleep."

"Thank you," said Jack, who kissed the top of her head then rocked himself up and off the couch exhaling something between a sigh and a groan. "I'll turn on the alarm on my way up."

Katie went into the kitchen. A few cabinet doors were open, a sure sign Jack had been in there recently. The man seemed incapable of closing a cabinet door. Katie shut them and washed the wine glasses by hand and set them on a drying rack next to the sink. The house was dead quiet, partly because everyone else was in bed and partly because the interior walls were stuffed with blown-in insulation and covered in 5/8-inch Sheetrock, which made them virtually soundproof. And the dishwasher was so damn quiet it projected a red light on the floor just to let you know it was running. Katie found the silence disconcerting. It was unnatural. And it provided the perfect backdrop to scare her half to death when the doorbell rang.

One of the book club guests had apparently forgotten their phone. Or keys. Or purse. Or—

Katie heard Jack's footsteps on the stairs. Apparently he wasn't *that* tired, and then she heard the door open.

"Holy shit," Jack said. "Unfuckingbelievable!"

Then Katie recognized a voice she hadn't heard in decades.

It was in the form of laughter. Loud, boisterous laughter.

Katie walked out of the kitchen and into the front hall and then to the foyer.

"Katie!" A large man practically ran toward her, and before Katie could react, he embraced her in a bear hug. "Look at you! Still beautiful!"

"Bagman?"

Bagman, aka Adam Ross, was Jack's best friend from college. He had bought Katie a beer and pointed toward Jack, which resulted in Jack asking Katie out on their first date. A few months later he dropped out of college and moved back to Florida. They'd neither seen nor heard from him since.

Katie, Jack, and Bagman went into the kitchen and sat in the nook, the *family* nook, but not before Jack poured three low-balls of rye, and Katie laid out a spread of cheese and crackers assembled from vestiges of book club. Adam Ross had not aged gracefully. His olive skin managed to look pale, his hair was in full retreat and what remained had turned from black to gray. Puffy, purple half-moons hung under his eyes and his neck had given way to a collar of jiggly jumble. His body had changed from a carrot to a pineapple.

Katie said, "Can I hang up your coat, Adam?"

Bagman wore a butterscotch, thigh-length waxed cotton jacket with green corduroy cuffs and collar. "No, thanks," he said. "I'm comfy. My blood has gone thin. Twenty-four years," said Bagman. "You don't call. You don't write. I thought you were my friend." This with a twinkle in his eye and a hunk of cheese in his mouth and more of a Brooklyn accent than Katie had remembered.

"I couldn't find you!" said Jack. "I tried. Right, Katie? It killed us we couldn't even invite you to the wedding. I asked all our old friends. Checked with the fraternity alumni association. It's like you disappeared."

"Got to keep a low profile. Too many old girlfriends trying to track me down."

Jack and Bagman laughed.

Katie said, "Why am I hearing New York in your voice? You're from Florida."

"Have you been to Boca?" said Bagman. "It's Coney Island with orange trees."

"Seriously," said Jack, "I could not find you. How many times did I try, Katie? A hundred? Every time the internet invented a new site, I looked. First on AOL. Then MySpace. Then Facebook. Instagram. Twitter. Those websites that find people. I tried everything. And now you just show up out of nowhere? How is that possible?"

"Simple," said Bagman. "I got in my car and drove north. Three days later, here I am. Sorry I showed up unannounced and knocked on your door so late. But I thought I'm here—what the hell." Adam patted Jack on the shoulder.

"But why Minnesota?" This from Katie, who was feeling like a third wheel. She was thrilled to see Bagman. He was one of those lovable disasters—the kind of person you don't envy but whose friendship you cherish. Katie only knew him less than a year before Adam left school, but he had always been kind to her. He was easy to talk to. And those first months Katie dated Jack, when she was introduced to Jack's world of expensive cars and vacation homes, Adam helped Katie navigate her awful feeling of not belonging.

"Yeah," said Jack, as if the question could only be answered if it came from him. "What are you doing in Minnesota?" Jack was beginning to slur his words. His sentences stumbled from one to the next, his eyes off kilter, and with resignation in his posture.

Bagman reached for a cracker. His unzipped jacket separated, and Katie saw a leather strap over his shirt and the chrome butt of a pistol.

Katie had probably been around dozens, even hundreds of people carrying concealed weapons, but had never known it. To know was different. Why would Adam Ross feel the need to arm himself? Katie thought, *Well, that's Florida for you. Craziest state in the nation.*

The gun felt discordant to Adam. Katie had always seen him as a gentle soul. A calm presence. At twenty years old, Adam didn't seem to have the explosive energy of most young men. His blood didn't simmer just under the boiling point. He took life in stride. But looking at Adam, Katie wondered if life did not take Adam in stride. It had taken its toll on him—his eyes had dulled in his puffy face.

Bagman reached across the table, placed his hand on the back of Jack's head and pulled it toward him. "I missed you, man. Sorry I've been out of touch. Three wives. Four jobs. A couple of pounds, maybe. Time got away from me."

Katie looked at Adam Bagman Ross for the truth. It had been twenty-four years since he dropped out of college and moved back to southern Florida where he'd grown up. She could never understand why anyone from Florida would go to school so far north if they weren't offered a scholarship. Bagman definitely did not have a scholarship. He had been enrolled in the University of Minnesota's General College, which was designed for remedial students. Maybe that's why he went north—he wasn't accepted anywhere else. Or maybe, like a lot of people, he just wanted to get far away from his family. Back when they were in college Katie asked why he went to school in Minnesota and his answer was always the same, "For you, Katie, my dear. For you."

Bagman made himself another cheese and cracker sandwich and shoved the entire thing in his mouth.

"Doesn't matter," said Jack. "You're here now. Are you in town on business?"

"What else? Need to keep the money coming in. You know what it costs to look like this?" laughed Bagman. "I sell industrial insulation products. Mostly heat shields for furnaces and boilers. Not glamorous but it's a job." Bagman looked around the kitchen. Custom cabinets, marble countertops, two Sub-Zeros, one refrigerator and one freezer. The Wolf range and double built-in ovens. Copper pots hanging from a rack. An espresso machine built into the wall and a wine fridge under the kitchen island. "Looks like you two have done well for yourselves."

"Got lucky," said Jack. "Right product at the right time."

Katie said, "How long will you be in town, Adam?"

"TBD," said Bagman. "Just got assigned Minnesota. We're expanding north. I'm thinking at least two months of cold-calling and shoe leather. See if I can open this market."

"You could have told us you were coming," said Jack.

Bagman smiled and swirled the rye in his glass. "And spoil the surprise? What fun is that?"

Jack said, "Where are you staying?"

"The Hilton downtown."

"Forget that place. Stay with us."

Katie felt anger and fear. Angry because Jack hadn't consulted with her first before inviting Adam to stay with them. Afraid because Bagman might accept and then there'd be a gun in the house. It was one thing if she or Jack had decided to keep a gun in the house. They could lock it up to their satisfaction. Make it inaccessible to the kids. But how do you enforce a guest meeting your safety standards?

"Nah, thanks" said Bagman. "I'm comfortable at the Hilton. Besides, a day or two, you'd love me. After that, you'd be spiking my booze with arsenic."

"We have a ton of room," said Jack. "Right, Katie?"

Katie felt herself nodding in agreement.

"We built a mother-in-law suite over the garage. It has a kitchen, a full bathroom, a separate entrance. It's like an apartment up there. You can buy groceries and cook. You'll have a home base—hotels get old fast. Plus underneath we have room for three cars so you can keep your Florida-mobile out of the cold and snow. All that space is just sitting there unused. Tell him, Katie."

Katie told him.

· CHAPTER 5 ·

About a month after Jack and Katie hosted book club, Sandra (it's S-ah-ndra, damnit) Dahlstrom called Katie and said, "Knock off work a little early and meet me at Wirth today?"

It was early December and snow had yet to stick to the ground. But the week had been cold enough for Theodore Wirth Park to make snow and groom Nordic ski trails.

Katie said, "Classic or skate?"

"Skate," said Sandra. "Four o'clock? Or should we say a 3:30 meeting out of the office?" Sandra giggled at her own joke then added, "Don't blow it off. You work too hard."

Katie put her gear in her Volvo wagon, slipping skis and poles through the fold-down port in the backseat. She had waxed her skis the night before in accordance with the weather forecast, dug out her merino wool top, stretch pants, lobster mittens, hat, and goggles. She tried to stay in shape in the off-season by roller skiing around the city lakes and lifting free weights, but there is no substitute for actual skiing, and with each passing year the first outing of winter grew more painful. Katie promised to meet Sandra for a few laps after work to get the pain out of the way so winter fun could begin.

She shut the tailgate on her Volvo and, before plopping herself behind the wheel, checked the weather forecast on her phone. Not that she had time to scrape the wax off her skis and apply a different wax, but to satisfy her compulsion of wanting to know what to expect.

The forecast had changed overnight. The temperature would be a few degrees warmer than previously predicted, well within her applied wax's range. However, the forecast for precipitation had changed. Last night her phone said there might be a dusting of snow during late afternoon. Now it said there would be two to four inches. Not a dumping, but enough to coat the ground and trees. And that would be lovely.

She felt a child's excitement both for the snow and for her first ski of the season. The trail had always been good to Katie. Like life, it presented her with challenges, but unlike life, Katie could meet those challenges unencumbered. There was no subjective gatekeeper telling her she could not climb that hill. There were no corporate policies that forced her to slow down because the person in front of her couldn't go faster. Cross-country skiing had gifted Katie peace of mind and peace of heart when she was a child. And it helped her love winter in Minnesota, which isn't always easy to love.

Katie got behind the wheel, started the car, put it in reverse, and was assaulted by a tirade of *BEEP-BEEP-BEEP*. She slammed on the brakes and saw four mittens pressed against her rear window.

Elin and Kaleb had missed the school bus. Again. She unrolled her window and said, "Get in."

They did without a whisper of shame or regret, Elin sitting in the passenger seat and Kaleb jumping in behind. Seatbelts clicked as Kaleb said, "When I'm big enough, I get front seat every day."

"When you're big enough," said Elin, "I'll have my own car and I'm never driving you anywhere."

"Mom—"

"I heard," said Katie, who backed into the street and put the car in drive. She glanced in the rearview mirror to see Kaleb using his fists to stamp tiny footprints in the fogged window. "Guys, why'd you miss the bus?"

"Dad forgot to tell us it was time to leave." This from Elin, who at twelve, knew exactly what she was doing.

"Is it Dad's responsibility to know when you should leave, or is it your responsibility?"

"You told Dad, make sure we leave for the bus at 8:30." Elin changed the radio station on the car stereo. "So according to you, it's Dad's responsibility."

Damnit, thought Katie. Why did I read her all those books when she was little? She's too young to be this smart. Or maybe it was just her generation and all they had access to. YouTube and TikTok and anything else their phones desired. And why didn't Jack remind them it was time to leave? How much could he screw up in one day? He drank with Bagman until who knew when and overslept and didn't have time to shower before his breakfast meeting so he came back home to shower. Just how hard was it to keep an eye on the time when it's broadcast from three screens in each room, another on your wrist and another in your pocket?

Katie said, "Well, from now on, it's your responsibility to leave the house on time."

"Can Bagman drive us to school sometimes?" said Elin.

Adam Bagman Ross had been living over their garage for a month but was so busy that Katie sometimes forgot he was there. "His name is Adam. And no, he can't. He has a job. And you have a school bus. That's how you're supposed to get to school."

"He's so funny," said Kaleb. "He can make fart sounds with his hands. He said he'd teach me."

"I want to get in on that," said Elin. "Next time he comes for dinner. Why can't we visit him in the apartment over the garage?"

"I've told you," said Katie, "Adam needs privacy. It's rude to encroach on a guest." This a half-truth because Katie had yet to have the gun conversation with Adam. She tried to discuss it with Jack but he waved her away as if she were a gnat.

"Mom?" said Kaleb, writing his name on the fogged window under the tiny footprints he'd just made.

"What honey?"

"How come squirrels get hit by cars like every day, but you never see a dead bunny by the side of the road?"

Typical boy brain, thought Katie, thinking about a different topic and asking a question irrelevant to the conversation.

"I don't know, Kaleb."

"I do," said Elin. "It's because squirrels can't make up their mind. They start to cross the street. Then they stop and turn around. Then they stop again and decide to go for it. By the time they figure it out, a car comes by and *splat*. But rabbits, first of all, they have eyes on both sides of their heads so they're already looking both ways."

"So do squirrels," said Kaleb.

"Yeah, whatever," said Elin. "But bunnies don't change their mind. They just go for it. And they're faster than squirrels anyway. And the ones that aren't fast get eaten by cats when they're babies. So yeah. That's the answer to your question."

"I think Elin is probably right," said Katie, and she meant it. Wavering never did a person or squirrel any good. Better to just make a decision and go for it even if you're wrong. Worst case, you learn something new. But if you waver, you may not get a chance to learn something new. You may get *splat*. Katie felt unnerved. What did it say that Elin, at only twelve, had surpassed Katie in intelligence? Not just book smarts, but street smarts, as well.

Katie's anger over the missed school bus gave way to calm. Happiness even. Because the answer to Katie's question was that she was a good parent. Who wants a child less intelligent than themselves? So what if Elin passed her a few years earlier than most kids pass their parents? Good for Elin. Good for the whole damn family. She felt a rush of love for her children. All of the buses they've missed, their strep throats, their fighting, Kaleb's tendency to hide food under his bed, Elin's rabid depletion of toilet paper and its resulting clogs and overflows—none of it made a dent—no, none of it even made a scratch in her love for them.

She pulled into the line of cars queued to drop the kids in front of the school and said, "Do not miss the bus after school."

"It doesn't matter if we miss the bus," said Kaleb. "We can just walk home."

"Not without talking to me or Dad first. Got it?"

"Yes."

"And if you ever do walk home, Kaleb, promise me you won't walk across frozen ponds. Ever, ever, ever. Or the creek. You can't trust the ice."

"Even if the pond has a hockey rink on it?"

"Yes. Even if the pond has a hockey rink on it. People some-times think the ice is safe when it's not."

"Dumb people," said Elin.

"No," said Katie. "Even smart people. This goes for you, too, Elin: no walking across ponds or the creek. It gets deep in places and you never know. And don't miss the bus after school. We can't give you a ride home today. Dad will be at work, and I'll be at work or cross-country skiing."

"Duh," said Elin, "we see your skis."

"Very observant. But not polite. You have to work on that."

"I'm super polite to regular people."

"I'm not regular people?"

"No," said Kaleb, "you're our mom."

Katie's eyes glossed over. Her kids felt safe enough and loved enough to misbehave at home. How many kids did she know, back when she was a kid herself, who were scared to death of their parents? They walked a narrow path at home and acted like raging idiots out of the house. She reached over and placed a hand on Elin's shoulder.

Elin said, "Are you crying?"

"A little."

"Because I'm only polite to regular people?"

"Yes."

"Weird."

"That's your mom."

A car honked behind them and Katie instinctively threw up her hand to give the driver the finger. Oh no, she thought. Not in the school drop-off line. But she was still wearing mittens, and her offensive gesture was interpreted as a friendly wave. She pulled forward under the school's overhang, and a yellow-vested volunteer opened both the front and rear passenger doors.

"Have a good day," said Katie. "I love you guys."

"Love you, too," said Elin as she ran out of the car.

Kaleb was still strapped in.

"Time to go, honey."

Kaleb didn't move.

"Is something wrong?"

"I forgot my lunch."

· CHAPTER 6 ·

Kaleb entered the house through the three-car garage because he forgot his lunch *and* his key. When the garage door lifted, Katie saw Jack's car—he still hadn't gone to the office. She wondered if he'd fallen asleep or wasn't feeling well. She called to see if he was okay but he didn't answer. Maybe he was in the shower. Maybe he was talking to Kaleb. Maybe he was on a conference call.

She looked to her right and saw Jane Hansen walking three golden retrievers in perfect formation. The dogs didn't pull or lunge at squirrels, and Jane walked as easily as if she were walking alone. Jane offered a friendly wave, and Katie returned it, but seeing her reminded Katie of last month's book club and the divorcing Ackermans. Jane Hansen had been married forty years, and Katie wondered if Jane's success had anything to do with controlling her husband the way she controlled her dogs.

When Kaleb returned to the car, Katie said, "Did you see Dad inside?"

"Yeah," said Kaleb.

"What was he doing?"

"He was in his office looking at a lot of numbers and yelling at someone on the phone."

"Do you know who he was yelling at?"

"Nope. He just yelled, *You better fix it and fix it now!* I don't think he saw me."

The missed bus and forgotten lunch made Katie half an hour

late to General Mills, but she worked through her lunch thanks to an energy bar and protein shake and encouraged her team to leave by three o'clock because the roads were sure to be slick with snow. No one objected.

It was a fifteen-minute drive to Theodore Wirth Park from General Mills even with the snowy roads. About seven minutes into it, Katie received a text from Sandra. Her phone's robotic voice read the text through her car's speakers.

So sorry! My marketing consultant requested an emergency meeting. Can't make it. Ski for the both of us!

So like Sandra, thought Katie. Make plans—guilt Katie into participating—then bail. Katie decided not to let Sandra's flightiness deter her. She continued to the park, changed into her ski clothes and boots in the chalet and tossed her work clothes in a locker.

The snow fell in quarter-sized flakes, each riding its way down with grace and patience. The ground and trees turned white, and the air was so dense with snow that it absorbed color—the landscape faded to sepia tone, quiet and beautiful in its muted state. Katie heard the sound of her own breath, her skis sliding on snow, her poles planting and releasing with a faint squeak. The air smelled of pine.

She felt she was clipping along when she heard a voice behind her say, "On your left." It's what skiers said when they wanted to pass. Katie, who was more than a bit competitive on the ski trail, hated getting passed. If it were later in the year she'd kick it up a gear, but she wanted to go easy on her first ski of the season. Tomorrow was Saturday—she could ski two more days in a row if her muscles weren't sore with lactic acid.

Katie stepped to her right, out of the track, and looked back to see who had the nerve to pass her. She recognized the body first, not such a hard thing to do since cross-country skiers, at the least the competitive ones, wear skintight tops and bottoms.

Or even a one-piece outfit worthy of a superhero. She raised her eyes to see the face and his jaw confirmed it.

Noah Byrne wore a tasseled hat and yellow-lensed goggles but his square jaw was as identifiable as a fingerprint. Katie couldn't see his eyes, but his head angled toward her, and the tightly clenched mouth of a serious athlete yielded to a serious smile.

"Katie!" said Noah. "I wondered if that was you." He hopped out of the track, stopped, and leaned on his poles.

Katie said, "Noah?" As if there were any doubt.

Noah Byrne took a moment to catch his breath. "Sorry. I'm on my fifth lap."

"What are you doing in town? You're New York, right?"

"Was New York." He took a few more breaths. "Moved here a couple of months ago." Steam rose from Noah's head and shoulders. It wasn't steam, of course, it was sweat evaporating into the subfreezing air, condensing to appear like steam. Katie knew that but still thought of it as steam. She wondered, *What else in my life appears to be something it's not?*

· CHAPTER 7 ·

The Birkebeiner is the largest cross-country ski race in North America, attracts skiers from all over the world, and is only a three-hour drive from Minneapolis. That's where Katie and Noah met last winter. After the race, in the recovery tent, Katie and her girlfriends found themselves at a table with Noah and his friends. The two groups chatted and when one of Katie's friends and one of Noah's friends realized they'd graduated from Tufts the same year, an invitation to dinner was offered and accepted.

The New York guys, as Katie and her friends would soon call them, had rented a four-thousand-square-foot log McMansion just north of Hayward, Wisconsin. The log mansion was fake. Not the square footage but the logs. The exterior was sided with quarter-logs split the long way, as was the interior. The long slivers sandwiched traditionally constructed walls of studs and Sheetrock. Katie saw those walls as obvious fakes but she saw Noah Byrne as uncommonly real.

One of the New York guys was a professional chef and prepared a feast. The liquor flowed and the evening got real flirty real fast. Katie found herself on the patio with Noah and a roaring fire and whiskey maple sours shaken with egg whites. Their cocktails were topped in foam drizzled with bitters and the stars shone in northern Wisconsin's black sky. The elements swirled into a concoction of perfection. Heat from the fire and the cold air complemented each other like sweet and salt. It was just the two of them on the patio. They sat in Adirondack chairs that tilted them back to face the stars.

"I don't want to know what's happening inside," said Noah.

"Neither do I," said Katie. She had come with two carloads of ski friends including Sandra Dahlstrom, Miriam Friedman, and Terri Ackerman, the last of whom would, nine months later, miss November book club and have her failing marriage gossiped about.

"We're at that age," said Noah. "Marriages start to fail under the stress of jobs and kids. But whatever's happening in there isn't going to help."

Katie looked at Noah. His eyes on the stars, not her. Their chairs were next to each other but not close enough for him to reach over and touch her. It felt safe. Noah felt safe. Even the notion that something untoward might transpire between them felt impossible.

"Your marriage is good?" said Katie.

"I think so," said Noah. "It's certainly more about function than intimacy lately but how could it not be? We have big jobs and teenage daughters. It's a lot. Sometimes just figuring out the what and when of dinner feels like a major undertaking. What about you?"

"I think it's good. The day-to-day of raising a family, that's what we chose, right? Tough to complain about getting exactly what you wanted. I hear the romance returns in your fifties. Something to look forward to."

"I'll drink to that," said Noah. He extended his cocktail toward Katie, and she extended hers toward him. They breached the gap and clinked glasses.

Noah still looked upward then felt Katie's eyes on him and looked over to offer a smile in the firelight. A kind smile, full of respect and—what was that Katie saw in Noah's eyes? Sadness? Or maybe just resignation. What an interesting man, thought Katie. And then she felt what she'd seen in Noah's expression. It wasn't sadness. It wasn't resignation.

It was loss.

· CHAPTER 8 ·

A couple of skiers passed the sidelined Katie and Noah. Katie said, "Finish this lap and then catch up in the chalet?"

"Yes, please," said Noah. "Go easy on me."

"Go easy on you? You just yelled, 'On your left.' You go easy on me."

Katie didn't know if Noah was taking it easy on her or if adrenaline had kicked in because she stayed within ten feet of him for the remainder of the loop. She thought the first run of the season would be something to suffer through, but following Noah, Katie felt a magnetic pull like when she was a child getting out of bed on Christmas morning.

She tried to remember what she knew about Noah. He lived in New York City. He'd attended St. Lawrence University in upstate New York and skied for the Nordic team. He was a lawyer. He was married and had two kids a bit older than Elin and Kaleb. Twins. She couldn't remember how much older. And his ethnicity was . . . what was that word he'd made up for one-quarter Asian and one-quarter African American and one-half Irish? Some combination of Blasian and Blire-ish . . . She couldn't remember. She'd have to ask.

They walked into Theodore Wirth Park's old chalet made of timber and large stones—it looked like a building you'd see in Yellowstone National Park. Katie excused herself to go to the restroom. She took off her hat and pushed and pulled at her sweaty hair, dark and perfect as if she were twenty years old. She'd been dyeing it for years and promised herself she'd stop. Katie didn't want to end up looking like Sandra with young hair and an old face. She hoped Noah wouldn't think of her that way and knew that meant something but she didn't want to know what. Katie returned to discover Noah holding two hot chocolates. They found a seat upstairs looking out on the white, rolling hills.

"Tell me everything," said Katie.

"Well," said Noah, "I don't know if you've seen the news in the last few years . . ."

"Once or twice," said Katie. She smiled.

Noah returned the smile and said, "Then you know that Minneapolis has become a hotspot of civil rights litigation and, no offense, but there's a dearth of non-white attorneys in the great white north. So my firm thought it would be a good idea for me to open an office here."

"That's exciting," said Katie.

"It's a big change," said Noah. "It was just me for the first month or so, but I've hired a few associates and some support staff and business is good. Tell me what's new with you."

"You must miss your family terribly."

Noah hesitated then said, "I do but the girls are in college. I'd miss them anyway."

"What? I thought they were only sixteen."

"They were when I met you last winter. Now they're seventeen. They started kindergarten a year early and despite my parenting, never flunked a grade. So they went in August. Carly is at Michigan and Samantha is at Vanderbilt."

Katie shook her head. "That blows my mind. College seems so far away for my two."

Noah said, "When my partners asked if I'd consider opening a new office in Minnesota, they threw money at me including a big relocation fee. I held them off for a while until they bettered the offer. I finally relented and said, 'Well, if it's in the best interest of the firm . . .' Truth was I jumped at it. My wife was traveling all the time for her career, and I had twins headed to college. Not cheap."

"You should have called me," said Katie. "I could have showed you around and introduced you to people and—"

"I wanted to, but I couldn't remember your last name."

"Kuhlmann. What's your phone number?"

Noah told her, and Katie sent him a text. "There. Now you have my name and number. So how often do you go back to New York?"

A woman sitting at the table next to them stood to photograph her slices of pizza, walking around the table to capture it from different angles. She ate with another woman, both about Katie's age. The women might be her and Sandra if Sandra hadn't flaked on skiing.

The woman said, "Sorry. Instagram." As if that excused her. She took a few more pictures then headed to the restroom.

Katie and Noah volleyed questions and answers back and forth, and one hot chocolate led to two. Katie texted Jack and the kids. *Ran into old friends at Wirth. You okay ordering a pizza? Would like to stay a little longer to catch up.*

Old friends. Noah was neither an old friend nor in the plural. Katie knew that. She wasn't stupid. She wasn't obtuse. But she did not acknowledge what it meant.

"And I'm psyched to experience a proper winter," said Noah. "Manhattan gets its share of cold and snow but nothing like upstate New York or here. I have nothing else to do when I'm not working, so I'll be in the best shape I've ever been at this year's Birkie. Are you going?"

"Every year," said Katie. Her phone lit up. "I'm sorry. My daughter's calling. I just want to make sure she's okay."

"Of course."

Katie picked up her phone. "Hi, honey."

"We can't find Dad."

"What do you mean?"

"He was in the basement watching TV. Then the pizza came and we went to get him and he's gone."

"Did you try calling him?"

"Uh, duh. His phone is on the kitchen counter. His car is here. His shoes are in the mudroom. The alarm is on. The TV is on in the basement and his drink is on the table but he isn't down there."

The Instagram woman from the adjacent table returned from the restroom, looking down at her phone, Katie assumed, to see how many likes her posts had received. When the woman looked up, Katie saw her face clearly and thought she recognized her. Katie tried to remember where she'd seen her. Probably a parent of one of the kids' classmates or teammates.

Katie said, "Elin, did you check all the bathrooms?"

"Mom, I'm not stupid. Dad was in the basement. We were in the kitchen. He didn't come up the basement stairs or we would have heard him. The basement doesn't have a door to the outside. He just disappeared. Now Kaleb is crying because he thinks the ghost of the laundry chute got Dad."

"Okay, honey. I'm on my way. Let me talk to Kaleb, please."

Noah was gracious and understanding when Katie left him at the table with her hot chocolate. She drove along Wirth Parkway then headed west on the highway. She felt no alarm. No concern. There would be a simple explanation for Jack's disappearance.

· CHAPTER 9 ·

Katie pulled into her garage and parked next to Jack's car. She felt the hood. It was cold. Adam's car was not in its garage stall. She entered the mudroom. Kaleb ran to her crying. Katie knelt—he was too big to jump into her arms like he used to. She pulled him close as he wept into her turtleneck and said, "Dad's gone!"

Elin leaned on the doorjamb that led to the kitchen. "Dramatic much?"

"I am not!" This muffled from Katie's shoulder. "I couldn't find Dad, so I searched my feelings to find him just like Luke Skywalker, and my feelings didn't tell me anything!" Another loud sob.

"I poured him a bowl of Count Chocula," said Elin, "then he was fine. He was playing the puzzle game on the back of the box. He totally forgot—"

"Any word from Dad?" said Katie.

Elin shook her head. Katie saw fear on her daughter's face. The poor thing, thought Katie, had stepped up to parent her little brother, remained strong for him, now her shield was crumbling.

Katie said, "Come on. Let's go in the kitchen and make some calls. We'll find Dad." Katie stood and kicked her shoes toward the shoe pile. Kaleb held tight, and Katie lifted him off the ground, his arms wrapped around her neck and his feet dangling down to her knees. They followed Elin into the kitchen and heard, "How was skiing?"

Jack Kuhlmann emerged from the basement, an empty low-ball in his right hand, his dress shirt untucked, and his ample crop of hair tousled. The gray emerged more in its unkempt state, as if the universe was trying to counter his boyish charm.

Kaleb dropped from Katie and ran to Jack, who knelt to embrace his son.

"Where were you?" said Elin.

"What do you mean?"

"We looked everywhere and couldn't find you!"

"I was in the basement."

"We *looked* in the basement." Elin sounded more angry than scared. More accusatory than relieved. Katie saw that. Jack did not. He smiled and rubbed the top of Kaleb's head. Kaleb laughed.

Elin looked embarrassed. Katie knew her daughter. Elin did not call for help unless it was absolutely necessary. If Elin said she searched everywhere for Jack, then she had. Elin shared Katie's competitiveness and Katie understood that Elin felt she'd lost by looking for Jack and not finding him. By calling her mother to come home and Jack just appearing moments after Katie walked in the door. Like Elin had been tricked. Like someone had forced her to go back in time to be a little girl again. "The kids called me scared to death, Jack. They couldn't find you anywhere."

Jack smiled. "Sorry. I just changed the filter on the central vacuum. I must have been in the mechanical room when you looked for me."

"I looked in the mechanical room," said Elin.

"Then I must have been in the storage room getting the new filter or in the laundry room throwing the old filter in the garbage. I'm sorry, guys. I didn't mean to scare you."

Katie pictured the geography of the basement, half of it finished as nicely as the aboveground part of the house and half of it unfinished—concrete floors with poured concrete walls and ceilings open to the joists above. Katie did the math—could Elin have missed Jack? She didn't see how and according to the expression on Elin's face, neither did she.

Jack said, "Anyone up for pizza?" He retreated into the kitchen. Kaleb bound in after him.

Elin spoke in just above a whisper, "He wasn't down there."

Katie didn't know what to say so she put an arm around Elin and pulled her tight. "Thank you for calling me. That was the right thing to do."

Elin's eyes filled with tears. "I. Looked. Everywhere. I promise. I was going to call Bagman to help me look but his car wasn't in the garage."

"I believe you."

"Then is Dad a liar?"

"I don't know, sweetie. What I do know is it's not your fault you didn't find Dad. It's a big basement—it's possible he was in the furnace room then walked into the laundry room right before you looked in the furnace room or something like that."

"But I called his name. I yelled for him. He would have heard me."

"That's a good point, Elin. That's a very good point."

That night, Katie lay in bed next to Jack, who snored softly, their backs facing each other as the red numerals on her nightstand clock read 2:34 A.M. She always seemed to notice when the clock landed on 2:34 or 1:23 or 4:44 or most significantly, 12:34 or 11:11. They were tricks, thought Katie. Arbitrary semblances of order. Just numbers assigned to represent the changing from one minute to the next, illusions of order and stability when, of course, there was no order, no stability. Katie wondered if her life was like that, too. The marriage, the house, the family, all illusory constants like consecutive or matching numbers on a clock.

Not the kids, thought Katie. Not Elin and Kaleb. They were

real. Take them away and she would die. But Jack and the house? She had invested so much in both and both could go poof and she would not die. That couldn't be right. She waited for the feeling to change. For common sense to kick in. But it did not.

· CHAPTER 10 ·

On Saturday morning Katie found Jack in the basement watching golf on TV. She sat next to him, wanted to press her shoulder into his, but felt it wasn't safe to do so. Was *safe* the right word? Yes. Not dangerous to her physical safety but to her emotional safety.

She said, "Why are you watching down here?"

Jack said, "I like it down here."

"It's like you have your own apartment." The words came out less playfully than Katie had intended.

"I'm never living in an apartment again. Maybe a condo. A condo someplace warm. Where I can play golf in the winter. Just for a few months a year. Then right back here where I belong."

Katie noticed Jack said *I*, not *we*.

"We've never talked about being snowbirds. Where are you thinking? Arizona? Florida?"

"Cabo."

"We've never even been to Cabo. You should cross-country ski. You'd like winter more."

Jack didn't respond. He just sat there watching golf as if he were looking at a painting. The hypnotic voices of the golf announcers droned on for a full minute.

Katie said, "Both kids will be gone to their sleepovers by 5:30. Dinner date?"

"What?" said Jack from a distant place.

"We have the house to ourselves tonight. Want to have a date?" Katie laughed. "With me?"

Jack kept his eyes on the television. "Tonight's the Edina-Minnetonka hockey game. I told you last week. I'm going with Reed and Tom and Charles and Mike."

Katie thought for a moment then said, "It's a high school hockey game. You're not in high school. Our kids aren't in high school. Maybe skip it to wine and dine your wife?"

"Honey. Edina and Minnetonka are ranked number one and number two in the state. Missing the game is not an option. The guys would kill me. The tickets were impossible to get."

Katie did not know how to respond. She sat through commercials for Mercedes-Benz and Charles Schwab and Federal Express then stood and walked away without saying a thing. She thought Jack might call her back for a reassuring word or hug. Tell her to wait up for him. Or that they'd have a morning date instead. Maybe breakfast and a walk. Katie made it halfway up the stairs before giving up hope of hearing Jack's voice.

She checked the garage and saw Adam's car was in its stall, so she climbed the steps in back leading up to the guest suite and knocked. Adam Bagman Ross opened the door wearing an apron. The place smelled of cooking oil and potatoes and the vent hood over the stove roared.

"Katie!" said Adam. "Come in. You're just in time."

"For?"

"I'm frying up some latkes. You can be my taste tester."

"Uh," said Katie. "All right."

Katie entered and sat at the table, sure she'd have to shower after she left to get the smell of grease out of her hair. Adam brought her a plate of freshly fried latkes with sides of sour cream and applesauce. "Have you ever had latkes before?"

"I don't think I have."

"They're potato pancakes. I'm courting a potential customer who invited me to a Hanukkah party tonight. You can buy these frozen at Trader Joe's, but nothing's better than homemade.

Here." Adam cut a piece of latke, forked it into the sour cream and then the applesauce and handed the fork to Katie.

Katie put the latke into her mouth and said, "Oh my God, Adam. This is delicious."

"I'll make up a batch for the family. The kids will love them."

Katie finished another bite, set her fork down and said, "Adam, I'd like to ask you a favor."

"Anything."

"Something's going on with Jack."

"What do you mean?"

"He's cold. He's distant. He's short-tempered. Even with the kids. And especially with me. He won't tell me what's bothering him. So I thought maybe you could talk to him. See if he opens up to you."

Adam smiled. "Sure thing. I'll take him to a whiskey bar. Buy him the good stuff. That'll get him talking."

"Thank you, Adam. I really appreciate it."

"For you, Katie. Anything."

"There is one more thing . . ."

"What's that?"

"Adam, that first night you showed up, when we were all sitting in the kitchen drinking . . ."

"Yeah?"

"Well, you didn't want to take off your jacket. But you unzipped it and once, when you leaned forward, I saw the butt of a pistol holstered against your body."

Adam said nothing. The twinkle in his eyes went flat. He couldn't even manage a courtesy smile.

Katie said, "You have a legal right to carry a gun. Minnesota is a concealed carry state. They probably all are by now. But I'm not comfortable with a gun in the house."

"I took a safety course."

"I'm sure you did. But what if one of the kids wandered up here?"

"I always carry it on me."

"Adam, I'm not comfortable with a gun in the house. You'll need to find another place for it. A safe-deposit box. Something. Thanks for understanding."

Adam Bagman Ross stared at Katie and said, "You're a good mother, Katie. I always knew you would be. Even way back when. I'll ditch the gun."

Katie smiled, and the tension eased between them even though she left the apartment over the garage absolutely sure Bagman would not ditch the gun.

CHAPTER 11

Jack dropped the kids at their sleepover parties then went straight to dinner with the guys before the hockey game. Noah popped into Katie's head. She rationalized it would be okay to text him, say something innocent about her sore triceps and quadriceps from yesterday's skiing. She picked up her phone to do just that when she felt the vibration of an incoming text.

Terri Ackerman had a rough day. Join us for wine therapy?

The text was from Sandra Dahlstrom. Twenty minutes later, Katie walked halfway around the block and sat in the Dahlstrom living room with Sandra, Latisha Nicolaides, Miriam Friedman, and Terri Ackerman. Even Katie, who had never gone through a girl-crush phase, thought Terri was stunning. A tall Norwegian with a neck long enough to be categorized as a limb, naturally blond hair, and light gray eyes, wolflike, that Katie had never seen on a human being before.

On the coffee table: two bottles of red wine, two bottles of white wine, a platter of hors d'oeuvres and another of tiny cakes. Katie wondered how Sandra pulled all this together so quickly after learning Terri Ackerman had had a rough day, but Katie hadn't eaten dinner and was grateful for the spread. She'd just bitten into a piece of puff pastry topped with Parmesan and asparagus when Terri spoke.

"This is so nice of everyone," said Terri. "I feel terrible. You gave up your Saturday night."

"We feel terrible," said Miriam. "We had nothing else to do on a Saturday night."

The women laughed.

Terri said, "Richard and I had our first big fight about the divorce today. Then he took the kids to the hockey game and all of a sudden the house was so quiet and . . ." Terri picked up her wine and pushed her finger around the rim of the glass. ". . . that's the way it's going to be half the time. Seven days with them. Seven days without them. I don't know how I'm going to do it."

Katie imagined herself in the same situation. Every other week of not tucking her kids in at night. Not seeing their faces first thing in the morning. Not eating dinner with them. Not helping with homework. Impossible.

"I'll tell you how you're going to do it," said Sandra, pushing back her blond-brown hair, "with old wine and young men and a whole gaggle of married neighbor ladies asking what it's like to be single again."

"That is true," said Miriam, who was on her second glass of wine. "We don't mean to make light of your situation, Terri, but we do look forward to receiving reports from the outside world. Being in a marriage for damn near twenty-five years is a bit like living in North Korea, only with nicer homes and cars and more colorful clothes. I have read a few blog posts about life after marriage, but frankly, I don't believe most of it. They make it sound like it's a lovefest out there for people in their forties and fifties. That everyone's bed-hopping. One-night stands. Friends with benefits. Open relationships. We really do need some firsthand reporting to corroborate . . ." Miriam tailed off. She had intended to cheer up Terri, but saw it wasn't working. Terri seemed to be in a bubble of despair, and Miriam's words bounced off without effect.

Terri pressed her back into the couch and said, "I think Richard and I will get through this amicably. As long as I don't fight fifty-fifty custody. It's just so damn hard. And so sad. I mean, is it too much to want romantic love in your life? And that's not a rhetorical question. Because maybe the answer is yes. Maybe romantic love is just the grease to help the species procreate. But if that's true, why have I been so lonely in my marriage?"

Latisha's glacier-like eyes glowed blue in Sandra's blue-themed living room. It's too bad they weren't real, thought Katie. Knowing they were contacts wrecked the fun. Latisha was more beautiful without them. Latisha said, "It's not for a lack of effort, Terri. Don't forget that you tried to save your marriage. The counseling. The romantic vacations. The books you've read. You really have made a hell of an effort. It's not your fault it didn't work out. Sometimes people just grow apart. It's luck, really. Getting married in your twenties is a roll of the dice. We weren't adults then. The closer our kids get to that age, the more I realize we were just kids when we committed to one person for life. We didn't know who we'd become. Life hadn't had its whack at us yet."

Katie listened to Latisha as if she were the Dalai Lama or Oprah. Her own marriage felt like it was falling the way of Terri's, though she hadn't shared this with her friends. Once the word got out, the gossip would create its own reality the way a forest fire creates its own weather. People would look at her oddly. Other parents and kids would think of Elin and Kaleb differently. They'd be met by whispers and a quick changing of the subject wherever they went.

Latisha finished with, "You'll never be alone, Terri. We promise."

"Thank you," said Terri. "That means a lot. More than a lot."

"My wine cellar is your wine cellar," said Sandra. "Seriously, ours is getting so full we'll have to expand into the bomb shelter. Can you believe people built bomb shelters in the 1950s? As if it would actually protect you from a nuclear bomb? The point is, Terri. We have wine. Lots of it because Lucas likes to collect it faster than I can drink it."

Katie wondered why Sandra seemed only able to make light of the situation. Maybe things between her and Lucas were not good, and Terri's impending divorce made Sandra's problems uncomfortably real. That, Katie could understand.

"And remember what you said," said Miriam, "you can only see the dark side today. Wait until your sex life takes off—that'll brighten things up."

Always with the sex, Miriam is, thought Katie.

"I'll drink to that," said Terri.

The women clinked wine glasses. Except for Katie who sat motionless, staring off into nothing, drifting into another world. Then her phone buzzed. She picked it up hoping one of the kids had changed their mind and felt like coming home from their birthday party. But the text was not from one of her children.

It was from Noah Byrne: *Beautiful snow tonight. More tomorrow. A few laps at Wirth after work Monday?*

Katie responded: *Definitely!* And immediately regretted the exclamation point.

Noah responded with a thumbs-up Memoji that looked like him. Katie would have to ask Elin to tweak her Memoji into one that resembled her more. She stared at Noah's cartoon likeness. It stirred something in her. What did that mean at forty-five years of age? After she'd had children? One's biological clock doesn't tick until the battery is dead and then tick again, does it? Katie set down her phone to hear Latisha relaying what her daughter had told her about dating sites, presumably for Terri's benefit, then Katie drifted away again.

Latisha was saying something about how Terri shouldn't trust the free dating sites because you get what you pay for, and then Katie interrupted by saying, "No."

"No, what?" said Sandra.

"No to Terri's question," said Katie. "It's *not* too much to want romantic love in your life. Every human being deserves to get what they need. Food. Shelter. Health care."

"Please don't make this about politics," said Sandra.

"It's not about politics," said Katie. She broke from her stare and looked at Sandra. "It's about decency. People deserve dignity. Everyone. In their personal relationships. In their work. In the opportunities life presents them. And people deserve romantic love if that's what their heart desires. To be denied that in your marriage is humiliating. And cruel."

The room grew quiet. Terri seemed to avoid eye contact with Katie. She looked down and with sadness in her voice said, "You're singing my song, sister."

Katie felt a disharmony in the room. Something awkward. Something tragic. Then:

"Listen," said Miriam, who was on her third glass of wine, "marriages are like snowflakes. No two are the same and they all eventually melt and turn into mush. It's all about managing expectations. For both parties. What do they want their marriage to be? Because what makes a marriage work is wanting the same thing. Whether it's passionate knock your knickers off love or just a second income and driver to tote the kids to trombone lessons. I sowed my wild oats in my twenties. Left no stone unfucked. Had a cornucopia of lovers. Experimented. Did everything I could think of and then some. Fell in love. Fell out of love. Had my heart broken. Broke a few hearts myself." Miriam swallowed more wine. "The point is, I have no regrets. I love Harlan. He loves me. But honestly, we both love Netflix more. And that is why our marriage works. We have sex, but it's not a regular thing. I'd say it's more along the lines of birthdays and our anniversary or one of us tapping the other on the shoulder and saying, 'Hey, would you mind?'"

"That's not my marriage," said Latisha. "Peter and I still can't get enough of each other. He's all over me. And that is not a complaint."

"It's that free lingerie Target gives you for modeling," said Sandra. "The man has inexpensive tastes. Plus he sees you every Sunday in the Target ad. How's he supposed to control himself?"

The women laughed and Katie thought Miriam was right. Marriage was about wanting the same thing. She knew what she wanted, but apparently Jack wanted something different. What exactly, she didn't know. Maybe Bagman would find out.

"Oh, look," said Latisha. "It's snowing. How beautiful."

It was beautiful. The neighborhood looked Christmas card perfect. Lamplight, picturesque homes adorned with holiday lights—yes holiday, not just Christmas because the Friedmans had them, too—the lights cast their glow into the falling snow. The temperature was just below freezing, so the white fluff gathered on everything it touched: trees, roofs, and birdhouses to add to the Hallmark-esque scene.

The view out Sandra's window lightened Katie's heart. The beauty lifted her. What did that say about life? she wondered. You can't see real beauty unless you feel real pain? Or maybe you just can't appreciate it without the change. The way you can't appreciate thirty degrees unless you're coming out of a week that didn't get above zero.

Usually the first to leave a party, Katie stayed until the end, walking out of Sandra's at midnight with Terri Ackerman, their bodies warmed with red wine, their spirits lifted by six inches of fresh snow. They said goodnight and again, Terri avoided looking directly at Katie, then Katie started her walk around the block.

She was in no rush to get home. Elin and Kaleb were at sleepovers. Jack was probably still out with his friends. She hoped so. Katie didn't want to be alone with him in that big house. Not tonight after all that talk of divorce and child custody. Not tonight after seeing firsthand that divorce was like stripping the insulation off live electrical wires—nothing good could come of that.

Katie fell asleep alone, and when she woke, Jack slept soundly next to her.

She checked the weather for Monday's forecast then descended to the basement to wax her skis for tomorrow's trek with Noah Byrne. She texted him to see if he could meet her at 3:30. That would allow her to beat the post work/school rush and to get home in time to make the kids dinner.

Katie finished her skis and checked the garage. Adam's car was gone. That must have been one hell of a Hanukkah party. She left the house at 10:30 A.M., and Jack was still asleep. What was going on with him? She picked up Elin and Kaleb from their sleepovers, took them to Chipotle for an early lunch, then dropped them at home so they could get started on homework. She went to REI to buy new Nordic clothing—she'd been wearing her current garb for fifteen years—then stopped at the Edina Galleria, an upscale mall sandwiched between a regular mall and a Target, and purchased new bras and underwear, also long overdue. She was considering hitting the bookstore to peruse the section written by PhDs and had books with *marriage* or *relationship* in the title when her phone rang and Elin's picture popped up on her screen.

"He disappeared again," said Elin.

· CHAPTER 12 ·

"Dad disappeared?" said Katie.

"Yes, Dad. Who else would I be talking about?"

"I'll be home in fifteen minutes."

Katie pulled into the garage. Again she felt the hood of Jack's car. It was cold. Bagman had not returned. She dropped her shopping bags in the mudroom, and Elin entered.

"He was in the basement and Lily Nygaard called to see if I could come over, so I went down to ask Dad and he wasn't there. So I yelled for Kaleb to come down and he did and he guarded the stairs while I searched everywhere and Dad's not down there. And there's no way he could have come upstairs while I was looking and no way he could have gone in or out of the house because the alarm is set to chime and so yeah . . . he just disappeared."

"And you tried—"

"Calling? Yes. His phone is downstairs and his keys are right there on the hook."

Together, Katie, Elin, and Kaleb searched the entire house. All 6,700 square feet of it. They did not find Jack. They finished the search in the owners' suite, checking the walk-in closets and bathroom just to make sure, but no Jack. They were headed back down the stairs when Jack appeared on the landing.

Jack said, "What's going on?"

Elin yelled, "We looked everywhere for you! Where were you?!"

Katie saw fear on her daughter's face. Not fear for Jack but fear for herself. For her sanity. For her ability to distinguish real from fantasy.

Jack said, "I was in the basement putzing around. You should have come into the workshop."

"I! Did! Come! Into! The! Workshop!" And with that Elin stormed up to her bedroom and slammed the door.

"Kaleb," said Katie, "would you like a frozen Charleston Chew?"

A frozen Charleston Chew candy bar for Kaleb was like a bully stick for a dog—it could keep him occupied for some time. Katie sat Kaleb down in front of Nickelodeon with his impromptu treat and insisted Jack join her in the sunroom.

The walls were made of windows on three sides. The ceiling—beadboard. The furniture was overstuffed and upholstered in natural cotton canvas. Jack sat in the loveseat. Katie took an armchair.

Katie said, "Why have you been hiding from the kids?"

"I haven't been."

"Your behavior has been more than odd lately. You've been cold and distant and short with me. All of a sudden you're no longer interested in sex. You're drinking every night. And you're hiding from your own children. What is going on with you?"

Jack smirked like a twelve-year-old boy being scolded by his mother.

"It's not funny," said Katie. "Elin is upset. She's scared. You're gaslighting your daughter and it has to stop. You have to go up to her room right now and tell her the truth about where you were. And then you can come right back down here and tell me."

"Oh," said Jack, "I think I know what happened. There's a crawl space under the sunroom. I went in there to look for my goalie mitt. We're playing a pickup game in the park tomorrow night."

"The kids are in that crawl space all the time. It's their fort. They looked for you there."

"I don't think they did."

"So that's it?" said Katie. "You're going to let your daughter think she's crazy because you won't own up about where you were?"

"Hey," said Jack, brows furled with a tremolo in his voice and a finger pointed at Katie. "I was in the basement. I'm sorry she couldn't find me. I'll go up right now and explain again. But I'm not hiding from anyone and maybe we built this house too big for young kids, so I'll try to remember to keep my phone on me so if it happens again they can call. End of story. So just get the fuck off my back."

There was a long silence in the over-insulated house. Katie let it hang like fog, fog that wouldn't burn off anytime soon. She touched her necklace and felt the points of the small pendant that looked like a snowflake. After a minute she stood and said, "You have never spoken to me like that before." And she walked out of the room.

"I'm not a liar," said Elin. "But Dad is making it look like I'm a liar."

Katie sat on the bed and placed her hand on Elin's head, dark hair splaying on the pillow, half covering a face streaked with tears.

"I know you're not a liar, honey. I believe you."

"You do?"

"One hundred percent."

"Then where was Dad? It's like we were playing hide-and-seek and he found the best hiding spot ever, only we weren't playing hide-and-seek and he made it sound like he was there the whole time and I just didn't see him, which is not true."

"I think Dad thinks he's playing a joke on you."

"It's not funny."

"No. It's not funny. And I've talked to him and asked that he not disappear anymore." Katie's concern for Elin gave way to anger. Whatever Jack was up to, one thing was certain: he was neglecting his children. They were not old enough to be left alone, and in a house this big, retreating to the basement *was* leaving them alone. She would have to initiate that conversation—it was one thing for Jack to go cold on her, but he could not do that to Elin and Kaleb. Katie would not allow it.

The next morning, Katie gathered her ski equipment and clothing she'd purchased at REI. Both kids had basketball practice after school. It was the Friedmans turn to pick up and drop off, which left Katie free to ski guilt-free. She had just loaded all her gear into her Volvo next to Bagman's Lexus, and was about to leave for work when a car pulled up in front of the house.

A woman got out. She looked about thirty years old, had long straight black hair, made-up eyes and lips, and wore a red wool coat that fell to mid-thigh. "Excuse me," she said. "Is this the Kuhlmann residence?"

"Yes," said Katie, wondering if she should have volunteered that information. The woman looked like she might be selling something. Based on the way she was dressed, Katie guessed interior decorating services. "Can I help you?"

"I'm looking for Jack Kuhlmann."

"I'm sorry. He's not here right now. Can I help you?"

The woman smiled. Knowingly. Confidently. She said, "I'll try back another time."

"Do you want his cell number?" said Katie.

"I have it, thanks. Are you his wife?"

Katie hesitated. Then, "What is this about?"

"Thank you," said the woman. "Have a good day." She turned, walked back to her car, and drove away.

· CHAPTER 13 ·

What was *that* about? wondered Katie. *Who* was that? The woman was beautiful. And young. She had intelligence in her eyes and in her mannerisms. Katie's hair hadn't shined like that in over a decade. Katie thought that if Jack was sleeping with her, it certainly would explain why he'd lost interest in Katie.

She got in the car and headed toward General Mills. She merged onto Highway 100 and began to cry. Not just because Jack might be sleeping with another woman, but because Katie knew she could not stand for it. She would never be one of those wives who stood by her misbehaving man for the supposed benefit of her family. Jack might be one of those misbehaving men who, if caught, would apologize and beg for forgiveness and do anything he could to keep his family intact. But Katie knew she would not forgive him. Could not forgive him. She would not set that example for her children, especially Elin. So she cried for the end of her beautiful family. Cried for going the way of Terri Ackerman, Elin and Kaleb traveling back and forth between parents, their little backpacks stuffed with books and clothes. Katie cried over the anguish of not seeing her kids for days at a time. For whole holidays. The smashing of their perfect bubble. Their innocence. Their trust.

And yet who was she to not forgive? She didn't know if the woman asking after Jack was his lover. She might have been an employee. Or a want-to-be employee. Or a competitor who wanted to discuss something without either her company or his company knowing about it. And who was Katie to be so high and mighty after she had conveniently not told Jack about running into Noah Byrne? She was doing the same thing today—lying by omission. Off to ski after work. Like she had done for years. But she did not mention she'd be skiing with Noah. Jack did not even know that Noah Byrne existed.

Work crawled. An hours-long meeting with the Fruit Roll-Up department over next year's holiday-themed flavors. The Yellow Box Cheerios division, which accounted for half of all General Mills business, was making noise about wanting more square footage, and some tool from operations asked Katie if she'd mind moving her division off campus. She replied that she did mind. Vehemently.

Finally, at 3:30, she met Noah outside the Theodore Wirth chalet. High blue sky and a sinking sun bouncing off the snow. Noah wore dark lenses and a bright smile. They skied for an hour then sat in the chalet, hair pasted to their heads with sweat, noses in need of frequent blowing. Katie found their compromised physical states comforting. It felt raw and vulnerable and implied familiarity. They sat together without pretense. Without putting on a show.

Noah surprised her by sneaking in a bottle of pinot noir which, under the table, he poured into Styrofoam cups pilfered from the hot chocolate machine. They exchanged small talk about the laps they just skied, plans for February's Birkie, work and kids.

Katie said, "So, how's your wife doing with you two being in different cities? What's her name again?"

Noah forced a smile. "Tana."

"Tana," said Katie. "Right."

Noah bobbed his head back and forth and said, "Things with Tana are . . . complicated."

"Oh," said Katie. "I'm sorry."

"Thank you. We're taking a break."

Katie stared into her cup of wine and said, "How does that work, taking a break?"

Noah said, "Awkwardly." He smiled. "Truth is, it's been a long time coming. Longer than either of us wanted to acknowledge. We're college sweethearts. Been together our whole adult lives. Tough to admit we made a mistake."

Katie felt a droplet of sweat trickle down her spine. It burned like ice. She rounded her shoulders to squish it against her sweater.

Noah said, "We were about to separate when I got the offer to open the office here. Sorry I didn't tell you that last time."

"That's okay. You barely know me."

"Still. I only told you part of my story." Noah sighed. "The move couldn't have come at a better time. It solved my marriage problem. Instant, distant separation."

Katie said, "How are you doing? With the separation?"

"Actually . . . well. There's no talk of reconciliation. Our conversations are about the girls. Tana sounds better. I feel better."

Katie said, "You seem good."

"Thank you."

Katie envied Noah's peace. She felt like she was sitting in a cauldron of water that was about to boil and she didn't know how to get out.

Noah said, "Careers and kids, the news always on TV. We didn't make the relationship a priority—we took it for granted. You see a person as the cornerstone of your life and all of a sudden that person is gone. Not dead gone. But gone for you. From you. Everything else is there. Your job. Your kids. I have a great relationship with my daughters—at least I think I do. You'd have to ask them for an honest assessment. And I have a decent relationship with Tana. It functions anyway. We don't fight. We're lucky we both have jobs so we're not battling over money. And we're lucky our kids are in college and will turn eighteen soon so there are no custody issues." Noah looked off at nothing. His eyes were somewhere else but his mouth smiled. "I flew back to New York for Thanksgiving. The four of us ate together. It was fine. Almost too fine."

Katie studied Noah. Dark eyes behind round lenses. Stubble on his square jaw. His straight hair fell nearly to his shoulders. Strong shoulders. He looked more advertising or graphic artist than lawyer. Maybe that was New York or maybe she knew only corporate lawyers. She said, "What does that mean, that everything was almost too fine?"

"It was like any other Thanksgiving. We ate at the apartment. I cooked. Turkey and our usual side dishes. Tana and I cleaned up together. One apple pie. One pumpkin. Culinarily nothing had changed. And emotionally nothing had changed because our marriage had died a long time ago. I suppose the ho-hum of it all was an indicator that splitting up was the right thing to do. But one thing had changed. I stayed at a hotel and . . ." Noah trailed off and looked down.

Katie said, "And *what*?" She couldn't help herself. She wanted to know. Know everything. About Noah. About his marriage. About any marriage, really.

Noah looked up. "I found out Tana had been having an affair."

"Oh, Noah. Shit. I'm so sorry."

Noah said. "It's amazing what you don't see if you don't open your eyes. What you won't see."

Katie wanted to ask how Noah found out about Tana's affair but said, "Ugh. What a gut punch."

Noah took Katie's cup and refilled it with wine under the table. "After turkey and pie, I left the apartment. I stepped out onto 129th, and saw a guy sitting in a Land Rover and I just had this feeling. My hotel was in midtown. I started south toward the train. Couple of blocks later I circled back up to 129th, went up to the apartment, walked in and there he was. Claus. Serving a second dessert to my wife and daughters."

"Yuck."

"Yeah. I acted like it was no big deal because in a way it wasn't. We're separated. We're not priests. We're not monks. The twins were meeting him for the first time. They felt terrible and awkward. Tana called me later that night and told me she'd been seeing Claus for two years. *That* was a shock." Noah exhaled. "So . . . It's over. I tell people we're separated but it's . . . We're just waiting for the rubber stamp from the court. *We*? That's a hard habit to break. *I*. There is no more we. *I* am waiting. And *I'm* here in Minnesota for the foreseeable future."

"That's too much change at once." Katie said it without thinking. It just came out and she regretted it. "I'm sorry. That's me being judgy."

"Don't apologize. You're right. It is a lot of change. But it's okay." Noah smiled. With his mouth and his eyes this time. "I grew up in Poughkeepsie. Far different from Minneapolis but the weather's similar. And the trees. The light. In a way, I feel like I'm reconnecting with my childhood. I'm in a town I don't know, so I have that feeling of exploration. Every time I go to a new neighborhood it's an adventure. A kind of excitement that anything could happen. I could discover something wonderful."

"Or *someone*," said Katie.

"Yes," said Noah. "Or someone. I'm just starting that process. FYI, the dating world has changed."

Katie felt herself falling into an unfamiliar place with nothing to hold on to. Unfamiliar and yet familiar because she'd been falling for a long time—she just hadn't admitted it. Katie Kuhlmann had been thick like the earth's crust, calm and beautiful on the surface masking the fire and destruction below. Reconnecting with Noah changed that. It changed everything.

She sensed the most unbearable sense of doom. She shook it

off and said, "Hey. What was the name you created for yourself? For being Black and Asian and Irish?"

Noah laughed and said, "You remember that?"

Katie turned her eyes to Noah. "I remember the word exists. I don't remember what it is."

Noah set down his cup and said, "Blaserish."

"Yes!" said Katie. She smiled. "I believe you're the only Blaserish person I know."

"There aren't a lot of us. It's never listed on forms when they ask your race. I have to check *Other*, which isn't validating at all."

Katie said, "Why do you think you stayed in your marriage so long? You must have been unhappy."

Noah nodded. "There's this saying my father taught me. *The perfect is the enemy of the good*. I think it's Voltaire."

"I've heard that saying."

"There's no such thing as a perfect marriage. But still—that saying popped into my head whenever I felt dissatisfied with my marriage. I mistook not perfect with disastrous. I'd bury my dissatisfaction and pretend it was normal." Noah finished his wine. "So now you're caught up on my calamitous life. What's new with you?"

Katie felt like she was standing on a precipice. She could turn around and walk back to safety. Or she could step forward and tempt fate.

CHAPTER 14

Katie had told no one of Jack's withdrawal from their marriage, from her. About his erratic behavior. To tell Noah, at least for her, would move their friendship into a more intimate space.

Katie said, "I don't want to burden you with my life. You have enough going on."

"Like I burdened you when I told you about what I've been going through?"

Katie sipped her wine. "You didn't burden me."

"There you have it," said Noah, producing a baggie of cheese, crackers, and prosciutto.

Katie said, "You smuggle in dessert, too?"

"You'll find out. Now talk."

"Well . . . I am grateful for all that's good . . . my kids, my job, my house, everyone's health . . . I don't want to be a complainer—"

"How Minnesotan of you."

"Yes, I suppose. But things with Jack have not been good."

"What kind of things?"

Katie told him about Jack's distance, emotionally and physically, disappearing on the kids, frequent nights out with the guys, reluctance to talk about work, reluctance to share anything with her, really. She told Noah about Bagman coming back into their life. And she told him about the smartly dressed beautiful young woman who showed up at the house that morning looking for Jack.

Noah listened. He must have had his lawyer face on because he gave away nothing. When she was done he said, "I'm sorry."

"Thank you. You're a guy," said Katie. "What do you think Jack's behavior means?"

"Do you really want to know?" said Noah. Katie nodded. Noah said, "He's hiding something from you. Could be personal. Could be work-related. Those disappearances from the kids—he might have snuck out for phone calls he couldn't risk being overheard."

"Wherever he went, he didn't take his phone with him."

"He might have two phones."

"I hadn't thought of that." Katie bit into some cheese, cracker, and prosciutto. She sipped more wine. She said, "Do you think I should just straight out ask him what's going on?"

The chalet had grown crowded with after-work skiers and Nordic teams from around town. Kids chased each other and squealed. Skiers stamped the snow from their boots.

Noah took Katie's Styrofoam cup and refilled it again under the table. "You could. Chances are his answer won't be honest. You'd have a better chance of finding out what's going on if you . . . well . . . maybe I'm not the right person to ask."

Katie leaned forward. "I'd have a better chance of finding out what's going on if I did what?"

"Okay. Remember. I'm a civil litigation lawyer. This is going to sound weird to you but it's part of my everyday life."

"I have no idea what you're talking about."

"I'm talking about a private investigator." Noah stacked meat and cheese on a cracker. "That's what private investigators do. Find out what people are up to. Give you a report. Maybe with pictures. If I'd been paying even a little attention to Tana, I would have learned of her affair a long time ago and not wasted two precious years of my life hoping things would get better."

Katie bound her hair in a ponytail behind her head. "You think I should hire a private investigator?"

"I know that sounds crazy. Maybe you should talk to mine first."

"Your what?"

"My private investigator. Technically, she's a legal investigator. The firm just hired her full time. But she was private before that and has a ton of experience with this kind of thing. Tell her what's going on—she'll tell you what a P.I. can and can't do. What you might learn. Then it's your call. Worst-case scenario is you'll spend an hour talking to a smart, insightful person. She's great."

Katie thought for what felt like a long time then said, "She'd do that for me?"

"Yes. Partly as a favor to me—"

"Her boss."

"Correct. But mostly because she's a justice freak. If she thinks you're being wronged, she will get into it. Can't help herself. It's her nature. That's why she quit being a cop. Too many rules. Too many bad guys released on technicalities. As a P.I., she can get to the truth without all the red tape. And civil litigation requires less burden of proof than criminal prosecution, so she sees the wrongdoers punished more often. Believe me, Makeena Chandler is someone you want on your side."

Katie thought over Noah's suggestion. Noah waited.

Finally, he said, "Are you all right?"

Katie nodded. "I have some emotional triggers when it comes to families splitting up. My parents and brothers were killed in an automobile accident when I was ten."

"God," said Noah. "I'm so sorry."

"They were lovely. My brothers were five years younger. Twins. Holy terrors. But I adored them. And my parents. So kind. We had no money but we more than made up for it with love. So much love. And togetherness. When I met Jack, he was present. And I thought, he's here so he must love me." Katie twisted her lips into an expression of dismay.

Noah waited for her to say something else and when she didn't he said, "Yes."

"Yes, what?"

"Yes, it's easy to mistake presence for love."

Katie and Noah sat in a bubble of silence surrounded by a cacophony of middle and high school kids letting off after-school steam. They retreated into separate but connected thoughts and lingered there.

"Okay," she said.

"Okay?"

"I'll meet with your private investigator. What's her name again?"

"Makeena Chandler." Noah picked up his phone and texted Makeena's contact information to Katie. "I'll tell her to expect your call. Do not be put off by her directness. She doesn't suffer fools. She doesn't waste time. She won't care if you like her. But she's hardworking and honest and über-capable and if she thinks you have a reason to be concerned, she'll recommend a course of action."

Katie stared at the contact info on her phone then looked up at Noah. "So when are we skiing again?"

They made a plan and said goodbye in the parking lot. There, Katie could not help herself and hugged Noah goodbye. "Thank you," she said.

"For what?"

"For making me feel not crazy."

· CHAPTER 15 ·

On the way home, Katie picked up a rotisserie chicken, a baguette, and salad greens, and the four Kuhlmanns ate dinner in the nook. They paired off by gender, Katie and Elin sitting on one side of the table and Jack and Kaleb on the other. Katie noticed Elin's coolness toward Jack, who seemed too preoccupied to care.

Elin said, "Where's that Adam guy? He's been here forever and we've barely seen him."

Jack had his face in his phone.

Katie said, "He has a meeting tonight."

"During dinner?"

"He's a salesman. Salespeople take customers out to dinner because they think the people will be more likely to buy stuff if they've had a good meal."

"Sounds like a real hard job," said Elin. "What college do I go to for that?"

Kaleb said, "My wrist bent too far in basketball and now it hurts."

"Maybe we should ice it," said Katie.

"I think it'll get better if we flush it," said Kaleb.

Elin rolled her eyes. "That's not a real medical thing. It's for babies."

"Nuh-uh," said Kaleb. "It works."

"Such a baby," said Elin. And then, "I guess the no phones at the dinner table rule is officially over, Dad."

"Sorry, honey," said Jack. "I have an emergency at the office."

Katie wanted to ask Jack then and there about the woman who'd come to the house looking for him but thought it would be easier for him to lie in front of the kids, for their benefit presumably, than it would be for him to lie to only his wife.

Kaleb said, "Can we flush my wrist now?"

Elin said, "During dinner? Gross."

Elin had a point. When the kids were younger, the pain from bumps and sprains could be eased by flushing them away. Stub a toe. Put your naked foot in the toilet and flush. The pain went down with the porcelain-cool water. Bump a knee. Bend it into the toilet and flush. Hyperextend a thumb? Toilet bowl and flush. Katie always followed the procedure with a good scrubbing with anti-bacterial soap. But still. During dinner?

Katie said, "After we eat, Kaleb."

"Fine," said Kaleb, resigned.

After dinner and chocolate chip cookies and Kaleb's wrist pain being flushed down the toilet, Katie found Jack in his home office, staring at side-by-side-by-side monitors filled with what looked like one big spreadsheet.

Katie did not ease into the conversation. She leaned on the frame of his open door, folded her arms, and said, "Someone came by the house looking for you this morning."

Jack kept his eyes on his screens. "Oh yeah? Who?"

"A woman."

"What's her name?"

"She wouldn't tell me her name."

Jack heard something unpleasant in Katie's voice. He swiveled his chair around and faced her. "What did she want?"

"She wouldn't tell me that, either."

"Was she selling something?"

Katie shrugged her shoulders. "Didn't say."

Jack said, "What did she look like?"

"Pretty," said Katie. "Maybe thirty. Long black hair. Petite. Asian. Well-dressed. Who is she, Jack?"

Jack looked confused. "How would I know?"

Katie kept her arms folded. "You tell me."

Jack shook his head. "I would if I could. She didn't leave a number? Email? Anything?"

"No. She spoke with an East Coast accent. Fast and to the point. Intelligent. And she was only interested in talking to you."

Katie's words bounced off Jack, as if she'd just said, *Parka, orange juice, typist.*

"Well," he said, "I guess she's a mystery."

"She sure the hell is."

Katie turned away from Jack and went into the kitchen, poured herself a glass of red, and called Makeena Chandler. She followed the call with a text. *Thx, Noah. Having lunch with Makeena tomorrow.*

After tucking in the kids, Katie poked her head back into Jack's office and said, "If I go for a walk, will you promise not to disappear? In case one of the kids wakes up?"

Jack kept his eyes on his screens. "I promise not to disappear."

"Thank you. Appreciate you going above and beyond."

Jack seemed too absorbed in his work to notice his wife's sarcasm.

Katie texted Sandra Dahlstrom to ask if she was interested in taking a stroll for a decaf latte then walked halfway around the block to wait for her. Sandra's husband, Lucas, stood on the front step shoving spruce tops into the concrete planters on either side of the door. He wore a wool peacoat, wide-wale corduroy pants, and a woolen herringbone newsboy cap. Katie thought Lucas looked like he'd dropped out of the 1920s.

"Hey, Lucas. A little nighttime decorating. Looks good."

Lucas looked up from his work, a spruce top in one hand. "Thank you, Katie. Sandra wanted me to switch out the mums with the spruce tops before Thanksgiving, but I've been just so gol darn busy during the day. I'll get the lights strung through 'em and the Dahlstrom family will have done their part to give the neighborhood some holiday dazzle." Katie stood there and smiled. Lucas smiled back. Then he said, "Can I help you with something?"

"Oh," said Katie. "Maybe Sandra didn't tell you. We're going for a walk. Just waiting for her to come out."

"No," said Lucas. "She didn't tell me." He paused and Katie could see a sourness in his expression. He thought for a moment, then his good little soldier smile returned. "Well, I hope you girls have fun. Beautiful evening for it."

"Thanks."

"Say, did Sandra tell you we're redoing the kitchen?"

"No."

"Big operation," said Lucas. "We're keeping the cabinets but getting new doors. And new countertops. I just can't decide between granite and quartz. They both have their plusses and minuses, I'll tell you that. Plenty more research to do before we pull the trigger."

"Well," said Katie, who had recently redone an entire house and found the topic beyond boring, "you can't go wrong with either. Whichever you choose will work great."

"From your mouth to God's ears," said Lucas.

Katie had to restrain herself from saying, *It's a countertop. It will be okay.* Then Sandra emerged from the front door.

Lucas said, "I understand you and Katie are going for a walk."

"Is that all right with you?" said Sandra.

"Sure! Sure thing. Just try to stay out of trouble." Lucas laughed at his joke. Not because it was funny but because he was nervous. At least that's what Katie thought. When he realized he was the only one laughing, he stopped.

"See you later, Lucas," said Katie. "And keep up the good work."

"Will do," said Lucas as he jabbed a spruce top into the planter's frozen dirt.

"If Lucas was as good at arranging spruce tops as he was analyzing numbers," said Sandra, "we'd have the best-looking house on the block."

"That's the dang truth," said Lucas. "Everyone in the neighborhood asks for my advice on financials. No one asks for my advice on spruce tops."

Lucas laughed and Katie thought, *Why are you laughing? That's not a joke. It's just the truth.* Katie glanced at Sandra who was less than amused. Katie said, "Ready, Sandra?"

More holiday lights were up—the Country Club neighborhood glowed and shimmered. The sidewalks were free of snow, the banks about shin high, and patches of virgin snow that had not been trampled by dogs or children or letter carriers glistened like powdered diamonds.

Sandra said, "This is a nice surprise. Especially during peppermint mocha season."

"Don't tempt me," said Katie. "I'm in training for the Birkie. Have you signed up yet?"

"No. My knees took a pounding during pickleball over the summer. Too much of a good thing. I'm not sure I'll race this winter."

"You have to," said Katie. "It's tradition. I heard they can inject a rooster's comb into your knees. It's supposed to work like cartilage or something and make your knees feel better."

"What about the rooster? How does he feel?" They turned the corner toward France Avenue and Sandra said, "Did you think Terri was acting weird the other night?"

"You mean other than the weirdness that comes from going through a divorce?"

"Yes."

Katie said, "Terri did seem a bit awkward."

"Exactly," said Sandra. "Awkward. I definitely noticed it."

"Good," said Katie, "because I was worried it was just with me. Glad you felt it, too."

"Oh . . . ," said Sandra. But that's all she said. They crossed Drexel and turned toward Fiftieth Street. An inflatable snowman stood twelve feet tall, lit up from within.

"Oh, what?" said Katie.

"Terri wasn't awkward with me. I noticed she was awkward with you. That inflatable snowman is a bit garish, don't you think? Totally Edina West. We're more classy on the east side. Or at least we're supposed to be. Who let these people move into the neighborhood?" Sandra laughed but Katie wasn't sure if she was joking.

"We'll pick up a plastic knife at the coffee shop," said Katie, "gut him where he stands. So you really thought Terri was only awkward with me?"

Katie had not told Sandra about her troubles with Jack. Nor had she told Sandra about running into Noah. She had the strongest feeling to guard that secret, as if not telling anyone about Noah made him a fantasy who didn't threaten her real life. Yet all she had to do was look at their exchange of texts to know Noah Byrne was not a fantasy—he was very real.

Sandra said, "Did you and Terri have an argument about something? Or did the kids get in a fight?"

"Not that I know of," said Katie. "Maybe I should ask if I've done something to offend her."

They started toward the glow of high-end retail establishments and restaurants. The entire area glimmered with warm white Christmas lights in bare naked maples. Winter was beautiful.

Until it was not. That usually happened sometime between February and March when the snow lost its luster and the cold began to hurt.

Sandra said, "Maybe don't confront Terri. She's going through so much—she might feel like she's getting beat up on. See if she acts awkward with you next time. Could have been a fluke."

"I hope so," said Katie. "Is the liquor store still open? Maybe we should get some peppermint schnapps for our mochas."

"Now you're talking, lady."

They bought a flask-sized bottle of schnapps from the liquor store and mochas from Starbucks and mixed them in the parking lot like teenage girls. They meandered home, weaving through the Country Club neighborhood, admiring the lights and decorations, making a few snide comments about less traditional choices and the LED lights that were so white they're blue.

"They look like the lighting in Walgreens," said Sandra. "No one looks good in that light. It's how they trick you into buying makeup."

Katie was drunk by the time she got home, sipping the mocha down and refilling it with schnapps so by the end she was mostly drinking schnapps. But she was walking, not driving, and at forty-five years old felt entitled to get drunk once in a while. She checked in on the kids, who were sound asleep, and Jack, who was out cold, then slipped out of her clothes and under the covers where sleep came fast and hard.

· CHAPTER 16 ·

Katie met Makeena Chandler for lunch at Yum on Lake Street. Katie ordered chicken noodle soup and a turkey sandwich and sat across the table from one of the more beautiful women she'd ever seen.

Makeena had dark skin and long dark hair woven into tiny braids. She was tall—maybe five-feet-ten—curvy and wore gold, teardrop wire-rim glasses and looked at you through calm, caramel eyes. She had an ingratiating smile that Katie found comforting, but thought it was probably a tool of the trade.

"Thank you for meeting me," said Katie. "I really have no idea what if anything is going on with my husband, and Noah thought you'd be helpful."

Makeena smiled. "How long have you known Noah?"

"I barely know him. Met him at a ski race last year then bumped into him on the trail here. We've talked a couple times since then and that's it." Saying it out loud, Katie realized it was true: she barely knew Noah. They had no friends in common. The only person she knew who could vouch for him was sitting across the table from her now.

"So tell me," said Makeena, "what's going on at home?"

Katie told her.

Makeena said, "When's the last time you and your husband had sex?"

"Noah warned me that you're direct."

"We're not talking about him now. When was it?"

"A little over three months ago."

"But who's counting, right?" Makeena laughed. "And did he perform?"

"I'm not sure I underst—"

"You understand the question. Did his hydraulics work? Did he complete the mission? Did he pull the trigger too soon? How was it?"

"It was . . ." Katie gathered her thoughts and said, ". . . fine."

"Fine?"

Katie stirred her soup that did not need stirring. "We've been together a long time," she said. "We have a routine. It's not a bad routine, it's just . . . routine. No surprises. Nothing special. But he had no problem with his plumbing or whatever you called it and everything was . . . fine. Why do you ask?"

"Plenty of times, a husband or wife thinks their spouse is cheating but it turns out the spouse just lost interest in sex. If it's a man, that loss of interest is often related to performance anxiety. But sounds like that isn't a problem for your husband."

Katie swallowed. "So he's having an affair?"

"Maybe. Is three months an unusually long time for you two to go between encounters?"

"Yes. We were more in a once- or twice-a-week pattern, then about a year ago it started to taper off. Jack says he's too tired. Or preoccupied with a problem at work. We used to be about fifty-fifty when it came to initiating things, but lately I've been initiating more. Come to think of it, I've been initiating every time. Or at least I've tried to."

Katie hadn't wanted to admit that to herself. Now that she had, she felt unwanted. Unloved. Belittled. Humiliated even. It's not that she'd never felt those things in her life—she had—but she'd never much cared until now. A marriage is supposed to be a safe haven from a cruel world. Not the source of it.

"And Jack's rejected you?"

Katie nodded.

"Well," said Makeena, "the good news is, you're not crazy. Something's going on. Whether it's romantic or otherwise, as the wife, it's best you find out what it is."

Katie set down her spoon. "And how do I do that?"

"One of three ways. The first is ask him. You know I'm a believer in being direct. Sit him down. Ask if he's having an affair. He might be honest. He might lie. What he can't deny is that he's been distant. And cold. Ask him about that. And do not let him off the hook until he talks. Then you listen. If he's feeling guilty about something, he might want to relieve himself of carrying that burden."

"What are the other two ways?"

"Hire someone like me. They'll follow your husband. Give you a log of his whereabouts. Probably include pictures. Maybe bribe the cleaning crew at his office to hand over the contents of his garbage can. Things like that."

"And the third way?" said Katie.

"Do some snooping yourself. Try to look in his phone. See if you can track it with your family plan. Or if he uses a device to find his keys like a Tile or Apple AirTag, switch it with one you can track—he won't know, they all look the same. Or sneak one into his stuff. Maybe hide some cameras in the house to see what he's up to when you're not home. But even carefully hidden cameras are easy to find if you're looking for them. Just turn out the lights and shine a flashlight around the room. The lens will reflect back at you. Or borrow a friend's car he won't recognize and follow him. Let's say you do that. He leaves work and goes to a strange house or maybe to a bar. You can't follow him in—he'll recognize you. But later that night, at home, act casual. Ask where he went after work. See if he tells the truth. Whoa. Hold on."

Makeena pulled out her phone to take a picture of Katie. "Smile for me real big like I'm taking your picture."

"You are taking my picture. Why?"

"Smile for me, Katie. Go on. Like it's your birthday. And I'm not taking your picture. It's of a gentleman over your left shoulder. That's why I asked you to meet for lunch here. I can get a little work done. Smile. Smile big. Our firm has a case against a suburban city manager, and he just might be having lunch with someone he claims to have never heard of."

Makeena turned the phone around to show Katie. The pictures were, indeed, not of her but of a man in his mid-fifties who sat behind her. "Now," said Makeena, "let's get back to you. If I were you I wouldn't confront your husband directly. Not yet. See, once you do that, he'll be more careful. Right now, he thinks you don't have a clue what's going on. Let him think that. No one suspects they're being surveilled. They assume whatever they're up to is their secret. Just like that fool behind you. People don't get careful until they're accused of misbehaving. Until they know someone is suspicious."

Katie considered the three options, and Makeena's phone rang.

She answered it. "Hey, baby . . . Yeah, hold on. I'll text you what I got." She did, then said, "Let me know if that works for you . . . Good. Will do. Now quit bothering me." Makeena ended the call, looked up at Katie, and said, "Noah says hello."

Did Makeena answer the phone, *Hey, baby*? Katie was almost sure she had. Did that mean . . . ? Katie didn't want to think about it but she couldn't stop herself. Makeena was beautiful. Noah was obnoxiously handsome. It made perfect sense they'd be together, even with their dicey boss-employee relationship. But Makeena didn't give off an employee vibe. Katie couldn't imagine Makeena being a subordinate and certainly not subservient to anyone. She was her own person, Makeena. The kind who could work for a company but by sheer force of personality carve out her own space. Independent and strong.

Katie said, "I don't want to take up any more of your time. You've been incredibly helpful."

"You're not taking up my time. I'm eating lunch. And surveilling my subject. So what are you going to do?"

"If I hire a private investigator, could it be you?"

Makeena shook her head. "Can't. I'm contractually obligated to the law firm. I can give you some names. And here—take my card. You can contact me anytime. Seriously. You might have nothing to worry about, but you might. You can always talk to me. My advice: prepare for the worst."

Katie managed a smile. "I don't even know what the worst would be."

"That's interesting."

"Is it?"

"I just said it was. Let's do a tiny thought experiment. Let's say you hire one of my colleagues and that P.I. follows your husband around day and night for a month and comes up with nothing. Turns out your husband's just working hard. Or is worried about a merger or takeover or keeping his customers happy. There's no other woman. There's no anything. How would that make you feel?"

Katie set down her spoon and stared into her soup. She thought through the question Makeena has just asked, and the answer filled her like smoke.

· CHAPTER 17 ·

Adam Bagman Ross continued to be a non-intrusive house guest. He used the separate entrance to the apartment above the garage, a set of stairs out back, and the Kuhlmanns hardly saw him. Katie's concern over Adam's concealed pistol had waned, mostly because he was rarely in the house, and the kids never went into the guest apartment over the garage.

On Sunday night, Adam ordered take-out Italian for the whole family and entertained the kids with stories about manatees and alligators and pink flamingos.

"See this stomach," he said, pointing to his belly, "if I eat enough baked ziti, it'll get bigger, and the manatees will let me swim with them."

"Whoa," said Kaleb.

"He's joking," said Elin.

"Am I?" said Bagman. "Because if I can gain enough weight and float on the surface of the water, the manatees will look up and see a shape that looks exactly like them. That's how I'll get invited to spend some quality manatee time. If it works, I'll put in a good word for you two, and maybe—I'm not making any promises—maybe the manatees will let you swim with them, too."

"Mom, can I?" said Kaleb.

"If Dad goes with you," said Katie.

"Will you, Dad?"

"Sure," said Jack, "if we ever visit Florida."

"We have to," said Kaleb, "because of the manatees."

"And after that," said Bagman, a forkful of ziti hovering near his mouth, "we'll wear pink tights and stand on one leg and see if the flamingos join us."

"You're a funny dude, Bagman," said Elin. "I'm surprised you're friends with this guy." Elin motioned toward Jack.

"You don't think I'm funny?" said Jack.

"I know you're not," said Elin. "Not anymore. You used to be when I was little but you've lost your sense of humor."

Katie and Bagman looked at Jack with raised eyebrows. How would Jack respond to that? Elin had teed him up for a witty response, but Jack just shrugged his shoulders then looked away. There was an awkward silence until Katie broke it.

"You're so good with kids, Adam," she said. "I'm surprised you don't have any of your own."

Bagman said, "Tough to have a family in my line of work."

"It's tough to have a family when you sell industrial heat shields?"

"I'm on the road eighty percent of the time. The road is my office. And sadly, the road is my life. I can't tell you how much it means to settle down in a real house with a real family for a while. It'll be a sad day when it ends." Adam opened a container filled with cannoli. "Now this, Elin and Kaleb, this is how I'm going to join the manatees."

One week passed. Katie had stopped her attempts at initiating sex, and Jack didn't seem to notice. Christmas was ten days away. Katie shopped and decorated. The family trimmed the tree together. Bagman loaded it with presents. Katie insisted he join them for Christmas Eve and Christmas Day.

Jack's brother owned a cabin up in Nisswa. He and his wife

invited Jack and family north for bonfires with s'mores, ice fishing in a deluxe shack, hot tubbing, the sauna followed by a traditional roll in the snow. Katie declined. She was jammed at work and had too much to do before Christmas. Jack told his brother he would go up Saturday afternoon. Elin and Kaleb chose to go up Friday after school with their cousins.

Friday after work, when the kids were headed up north and Jack was still at the office, Katie met Noah at Wirth to cross-country ski. After eight intense laps plus extra hill work, rather than cooling down and catching up in the chalet, Katie asked Noah if he would trade cars with her for a few hours.

"I have finally got up the courage to follow Jack and today's my chance." She unzipped her top at the neck to help her body heat escape. "The kids are up north. Jack should still be at work so I can tail him from there."

"Tail?" said Noah. "Have you been reading private detective books?"

"That's what Makeena called it. This is her idea. She also said I need a car Jack won't recognize. Is it all right if we switch?"

Noah wiped his damp hair off his forehead and sighed then cleaned his goggles with the hem of his quarter zip. "Yeah. I'll trade cars."

"Why did you hesitate?"

"Did I?"

"Yes."

"Okay, okay. I hesitated. But I only did that because I was trying to figure out how to invite myself on your stakeout."

"Really? You want to go with me?"

"Yes, really. I'm not doing anything else tonight. Plus I have New York City driving skills. You can ride shotgun. It'll be dark in ten minutes. No one will be able to see inside the car. And . . ." Noah removed his shell. ". . . it would be an adventure."

"That's not what you were going to say," said Katie.

"True. I was going to say, if you find out bad news, it might not be a bad idea to have a friend with you."

Katie thought about that and said, "Okay. But if I'm sitting in a car with you for a few hours, I'm showering first."

She went home and showered, and an hour later, Noah opened the gate to the underground parking of his apartment building. The garage was warm and smelled of fresh concrete. Noah surprised her with a bag of take-out dinner, or as he called it, "stake-out" dinner. They swapped cars, leaving Katie's in Noah's parking spot, and headed west. Jack's company was in Eden Prairie's industrial park, a modern sprawl of boxy buildings and big lawns. They parked on a wide street, and Noah turned off the 4Runner's lights.

Electro-North 45 occupied a modern, industrial-looking building. The exterior walls were made of concrete and opaque blue glass. Floodlights lit the grounds and façade, and the name ELECTRO-NORTH 45 glowed in white letters above the front entrance.

Noah said, "What's the 45 stand for?"

Katie said, "The 45th parallel. Minneapolis is smack on it."

"And how do you know Jack's still at work?" said Noah, distributing cardboard clamshells of chicken tikka masala, onion naan, basmati rice, tandoori shrimp, and vegetable samosas.

Katie looked at her phone. "I hid an AirTag in his backseat."

"You're like a spy."

"Makeena suggested it. Jack's car is still here. There's only one way out of the parking lot, so we can just sit here on the street. Sorry if this takes a long time."

"I don't mind," said Noah, handing Katie plastic flatware, napkins, and more food. "You're a decent hang."

"Such the flatterer."

It was 6:30 and dark as midnight. Traffic was light. Most people in the industrial park had gone home. Noah said, "Don't let the compliment go to your head. So what's your listening pleasure? News? Alt rock? Alt folk? Classical? Smooth jazz? Oldies? Show tunes?"

"You pick," said Katie. She looked at Noah in the dim glow of the dash. He offered her a sad smile. She returned it and said, "Thanks for dinner."

"Nothing's too spicy," said Noah, starting a Radiohead Essentials playlist. "I've lived in Minnesota long enough to know heat scares the locals."

Katie didn't know if Noah was being literal or metaphorical or both. She had just bit into a samosa when she saw Jack's car. "There he is. The silver BMW."

"On it," said Noah. He let Jack get a block away, then turned on his headlights and pulled away from the curb. A few minutes later, Jack headed north on Highway 169. Noah let a car fill the gap between them. He and Katie drove in silence.

Katie's phone rang. She looked at the screen. "It's him." Noah muted the music. Katie answered the call on speaker. "Hey."

"Hey," said Jack. "How was skiing?"

Katie wondered why Jack was calling. They seemed well past the checking-in part of their relationship. He'd been cold and distant and a terrible father, lately. A terrible person, really. But she answered his question. "Skiing was good. Pushed it today. Heading home now."

"I just left the office. I'm going to hit the gym then may catch up with Bagman if he's working late."

"All right. Hope you guys have fun."

"Thanks. I'll see you back at the house."

"Sounds good." Katie ended the call.

They drove in silence for another minute then Noah said, "That sounded awkward."

"Yeah. Probably because he's lying."

"Jack's not going to the gym?"

"We passed that exit five minutes ago."

· CHAPTER 18 ·

Katie and Noah followed Jack into downtown Minneapolis. He got off on the Washington Street exit, pulled in front of the Hewing Hotel, took a ticket from the valet, and entered the hotel. Any feelings of adventure had faded. The mood in the 4Runner was somber. Katie didn't know what Jack was up to, but she knew he'd just lied to her. Badly. Going to a swank downtown hotel was far different than going to the gym.

Noah pulled in front of the hotel, behind another car, and said, "I'll follow him in. Is that okay? He has no idea who I am."

Katie took a breath and shut her eyes. "Okay. I guess you should. Thank you." She found a picture of Jack on her phone and showed it to Noah. "This is him."

Noah pulled the car forward, and the valet approached. He rolled down the window. "Hi. We're staying at the hotel, but I'm not going to valet the car. Is it okay if I leave it here while I check in?"

The valet waved him forward.

Katie said, "You're an excellent liar."

"Only to valets and other lawyers."

Katie smiled, hoping that was true.

Noah got out of the car with an ingratiating smile. He tipped the valet for his cooperation, then headed into the hotel. Katie waited. Or tried to. She looked through the glass doors and into the hotel. It was an upscale collage of brick and timber with a north woods theme. One of the hipper hotels in town, the clientele was on the young side. The bar and restaurant were full. People came and went. Katie couldn't get a clear view. So she pressed her back into the car seat and waited.

Outside, everything flowed at normal speed. Cars came and went. People entered and exited the hotel. Pedestrians strolled the sidewalks and crossed the street. But inside the 4Runner, time seemed to have stopped. That's what it felt like to Katie. Time stopped. Her life stopped. Her heart stopped.

The driver-side door swung open. Noah sat behind the wheel and pulled out of the parking space. He put on his seatbelt and said, "I'm going to drive around the block and show you what I saw."

Katie turned toward him. "Show me?" Noah handed her his phone. She saw a picture of Jack sitting in the lounge with a pretty young woman with long, dark hair. Katie said, "That's her. The woman who came to the house asking for Jack." Her heart began to race and her stomach twisted.

"Flip through the next few pictures," said Noah. "Look at Jack's face."

Katie did. And at the woman's. They did not look in love. Or lust. Whatever their conversation was, the woman looked like she had the upper hand. She looked confident. Strong. At ease. Jack looked shaken. The casual observer wouldn't see it, but Katie did. And Noah had. Jack's usual rich boy, never-had-a-problem-in-his-life swagger was gone. He tried to look sure of himself. He smiled. He kept his chin up. But his eyes betrayed him. He was scared. Nervous.

Noah said, "It doesn't look like a comfortable conversation."

"No, it does not. How old do you think that woman is?"

"Thirty," said Noah. "Give or take a few years. My question is, what do you want to do?"

"What do you mean?"

"Do you want me to continue around the block so you can

go in and confront Jack? Pretend you just happen to be there? Admit you were suspicious so you followed him? Do you want to catch him in whatever's going on so you two can face it?"

Katie said, "No. No, I don't want to make a scene. I will talk to him at home. The kids are up north tonight. It's the perfect time to have this out."

Noah said, "I think that's wise. I'm sorry you have to go through this. It sucks."

Katie managed a smile. "Thank you for saying that."

"I'd be a monster not to say that."

They were quiet for a minute, then Katie said, "You might be the most emotionally intelligent man I know."

"You might be the only person who's ever said that to me," said Noah.

Katie smiled. "I think emotional intelligence is learned. You have to go through some shit to acquire the knowledge. I have. Losing my whole family. You've gone through some shit, too."

"I suppose I have," said Noah.

"Not to mention losing your wife to a guy named Claus."

Noah laughed. "Claus. Who the hell has named their kid Claus since World War II?"

Katie laughed and thought how wonderful her evening with Noah had been. *I've tried with Jack,* she thought. But Jack's more comfortable in his emotionally unintelligent world. He's a grown man who hides from his children and prioritizes high school hockey games. *And I don't have to justify driving around with Noah. Jack's the one sitting with a beautiful young woman in a hotel bar.*

They had just pulled into Noah's garage when he said, "You want to come up for some fortification juice?"

Katie had been lost in thought. Lost in wonder. She didn't remember the drive back to Noah's or even descending into the underground garage. She snapped out of it when hearing his voice and said, "I'd love some fortification juice, but I shouldn't drink here. I need to drive myself home."

"Yeah," said Noah. "You probably shouldn't drink here." Kindness in his voice. Understanding. And a hint of something lost.

Katie said, "I'll text you later tonight or maybe in the morning to let you know how the confrontation went."

"Whenever you're ready." He stared into her deep brown eyes, then turned away and exited the car.

· CHAPTER 19 ·

Katie returned home. Bagman's car was not in the garage. He sure worked strange hours, thought Katie, wining and dining potential customers. Out at all hours. Is that why he carried a pistol?

She texted with the kids, helped herself to a glass of wine—one glass of wine, she needed her wits—and sat in the nook—the *family* nook—and waited for Jack to return home. Katie ran the conversation over in her head, explored the different roads it might take. Then, shortly after ten P.M., Katie heard Jack walk into the mudroom. He entered the kitchen, walked straight past her and into the pantry, and returned with a bottle of rye. He uncorked it and poured it into a glass without ice or water.

Katie said, "Jack?"

A delay. And then, "Yeah?"

"Are you going to say hello?"

"Sorry. I'm tired."

Jack downed his rye and poured himself another.

Jack said, "What's up?"

"Have a seat." Katie saw concern in Jack's eyes. Not fear. Not cowardliness. Just concern.

Jack sat in the nook opposite Katie.

Katie said, "We need to talk."

"I'm listening." Jack looked exasperated. He squirmed in his seat. Like he knew what was coming.

"I got a call tonight from a colleague at work. You've met her at a party but you wouldn't remember her. She's in my office a lot and sees your picture on my desk. Anyway, she said she saw you at the Hewing Hotel tonight, drinking in the lounge with a woman who she described as the same woman I met yesterday morning outside the house. The one who was looking for you. And I thought, Huh. That's weird. Jack told me he was going to the gym then maybe meeting up with Bagman. Sounds like you did neither. Want to explain?"

Jack bit his lower lip and nodded then said, "Are you accusing me of something?"

"I'm accusing you," said Katie, "of not going to the gym and meeting up with Bagman. You want to tell me what you were doing?"

"Sure," said Jack. He crossed his arms and tucked his chin into his chest. "The woman's name is Rebecca Wong. She's a reporter for *The Wall Street Journal*. If you don't believe me look her up. She's doing a story on Electro-North 45."

"That sounds like a good thing. Why did my friend say you looked terribly upset during your conversation?"

"Because this particular *Wall Street Journal* article is not a good thing." Jack morphed from offended and unjustly accused to solemn and believable. "The article they're planning to write, well, it's not flattering. I had been avoiding Rebecca Wong. Ignored her calls. She even stopped by the office, but I wouldn't see her. She came to the house probably hoping to catch me with my guard down. But my in-house lawyers told me it would be in my best interest if I got my side of the story out there. Right after I told you I was headed to the gym, she called me on my cell. She said she was headed back to New York soon, so I met with her and told her my side of the story."

"Oh," said Katie. She felt small and distant and oh so very stupid. She would google Rebecca Wong as soon as the conversation ended but she already believed Jack. If he had work problems, that could explain his distance. Maybe even the disappearances. His regressive behavior. And yet something didn't feel quite right. She looked at her sulking husband and said, "Is the company in trouble?"

"Yes. *The Wall Street Journal* is planning on writing an article saying our new electric vehicle battery's specs aren't what we claim. It's serious."

"You mean Electro-North 45 can't produce the new battery at scale?"

"I wish it were that simple. They're accusing us of falsifying the data from early trials, data that attracted significant investment and fueled our stock price."

Katie thought over what Jack had just said. The house was so quiet. It had in-floor heat. Long coils of flexible tubing through which hot water flowed, warming each room from the ground up. So there wasn't even the soft whisper of forced air heat, or the knocks and clangs of radiators. It was too quiet. Katie said, "When you say 'they're accusing' you, who do you mean by *they*? *The Wall Street Journal*?"

Jack looked like a little boy who had just got caught throwing a baseball through a plate glass window. He said, "Yes. Their investigative reporting has uncovered quite a lot in the last few years. And if they go through with this story, if they actually run it, the Securities and Exchange Commission won't be far behind."

Katie said, "How much trouble are you in, Jack?"

"I don't know yet."

But Katie saw that he did know. He just wasn't being honest about it. Jack was in big trouble. She wondered what it would be like if he were forced to resign. To leave the company he founded. To lose that big paycheck and stock options and all the perks that went along with running a company. And Katie was surprised by her reaction. If Jack lost his job, she'd feel relief. Relief and hope. Hope that he'd return to her and the kids. Even if it meant selling the house and moving out of the Country Club neighborhood. Who cared how much money they had if they were happy with each other?

Katie said the only honest thing she could think of: "Well, I hope everything turns out okay."

"Thank you," said Jack. "I hope so, too."

Jack poured himself another drink and disappeared into his office. Katie went upstairs and texted Noah that she felt like a fool. She would explain it all to him tomorrow. She was almost asleep when Jack came in and slipped under the covers and turned his back toward her. Katie put her hand on Jack's back. Rubbed his shoulders. He did not respond.

Katie opened her eyes and saw the clock on her nightstand. It read 2:34 A.M. 2–3–4. There it was again. The Universe playing tricks on her. 2:34 was just a moment like any other moment—it had no significance. She turned over on her other side and saw the same thing. 2:34. Only it was on Jack's clock, and she saw the numbers because Jack wasn't there.

She got out of bed. Jack wasn't in the master bathroom. Katie put on her robe and checked the alarm panel on the wall. The alarm was on. Jack's wallet, phone, and keys were on his nightstand. She felt his side of the bed. It was cool. Katie thought, *Where is my husband now?*

· CHAPTER 20 ·

Katie couldn't find Jack anywhere on the second floor. She didn't know why, but she checked all the upstairs bathrooms and bedrooms and, of course, the common area at the top of the stairs. He wasn't on the main floor. Not in the kitchen, the living room, the sitting room, the pantry, the sunroom, the powder room, the music room, nor was Jack in the mudroom, home office, or the front entry.

She stopped to listen, hoping to hear a TV somewhere in that big house. But she didn't. She returned to the kitchen and poured herself a glass of water partly because she was thirsty and partly because she needed to hear something. Anything. Even if it was water streaming into a glass.

Katie checked the doors—they were all locked. Jack didn't take his keys, and he couldn't have taken one of the kids' keys because she made sure the kids had taken them up north in case they returned when she wasn't home. Finally, Katie approached the door to the basement. The stairwell was dark, as was Jack's billiards room at the bottom of the stairs. She turned on the lights for both and started down.

Jack was not in the billiards room. Not crouched down behind the bar. Not in the mechanical room, the storage room, the laundry room. Not in the little crawl space under the sunroom. He was not in the house.

Katie remembered thinking, *I guess you never know what goes on in someone else's house* when hearing about the Ackermans' impending divorce. Now she thought, *Someone else's house? I don't even know what's going on in* my *house.*

Katie returned upstairs and turned off the alarm. She opened the door to the garage. Jack's car was there. So was Bagman's. She entered the garage and felt each car's hood. Jack's was cool. Bagman's was warm. Maybe Jack went to visit Bagman in the apartment over the garage. Bagman's car was also spotless—he must have had it washed. She tried to look inside the car but the windows were heavily tinted. She supposed that had something to do with Florida's intense sunshine. The windows' opaque appearance sparked Katie's curiosity. She turned on her phone's flashlight, pressed it against the driver's side window, and looked inside the car.

She saw nothing out of the ordinary. Light gray leather seats. Dark polished wood on the dash and around the gear shift. A half drank bottle of water in the cup holder. She moved the phone to the rear window on the driver's side. There, she saw a garbage bag behind the driver's seat. Plastic. Black. Secured with several wraps of duct tape. Katie felt a chill, turned off her flashlight, returned to the house, and went back to sleep.

The clock read 6:19 when she woke. Nothing special about those numbers. When Katie sat up, she noticed Jack was asleep next to her. She thought of waking him and asking where he was last night but decided to let him sleep. She went downstairs and made coffee, sat in the sunroom and read the news on her iPad, and was startled by a knock on the window.

Bagman stood in a frozen flower bed with a big smile and a white box. From the grease stains, Katie guessed it contained something sweet and fried. She motioned for Bagman to go to the back door, where she invited him in.

"Trade you some coffee for one of whatever's in that box," said Katie.

"Deal."

They sat at the kitchen table with donuts and coffee and a friendship half rekindled. Their conversation leaned perfunctory until Katie said, "Did Jack come visit you last night?"

"Not that I know of," said Adam. "I didn't get home until late. If you don't mind me saying so, there are some very beautiful, age-appropriate women in this town."

Katie smiled. Same old Bagman. "Did you see Jack last night?"

"Your Jack? No, ma'am."

"Have you and Jack had a chance to talk?"

Bagman shook his head. "Other than coming and going in the garage, I've only talked to him when I'm in the house with you. Every time I ask if he wants to grab a beer or see a game, he says he's busy. Love the pad above the garage. Very grateful. But I'm starting to think he doesn't like me."

"Oh, that's not true. The night you showed up is the happiest I've seen Jack in a while."

"Well, I've tried to talk to him. Find out how he's doing. Like you and I talked about. Maybe I just need to wait for him to come to me."

"It's a shame," said Katie.

"What's a shame?"

"That Jack's not making time for you. You two used to be inseparable."

"Yeah," said Bagman. "But people move on. And apparently Jack has moved on from me."

Katie was about to say, *That makes two of us.* But Katie stopped herself. Instead she said, "More coffee?"

Bagman seemed to read Katie's mind and said, "I take it you're not seeing much of him, either."

She shrugged. "Jack has a lot on his plate lately."

"See, that's why I don't have a family. Or a wife. If I did, she'd be eating donuts and telling some guy how she never sees me."

Katie laughed. Bagman always had made her laugh. "So how's it going breaking into the Minnesota market?"

"Rough," said Bagman. "Because I'm an outsider. Everybody here seems to have lived here their entire lives. Their whole family is here. Their friends are the same friends they've had since they were in third grade. Just like when I went to school here."

Katie smiled. "Maybe Jack can introduce you to some contacts. He knows everyone in this town."

"I was hoping the same thing," said Bagman, half an eclair in his cheek. "I'll ask him if I ever see him."

· CHAPTER 21 ·

Katie texted Sandra Dahlstrom to ask if she wanted to ski. Sandra declined—she promised to take her daughter holiday shopping. Katie then texted Noah, who said he'd meet her at ten o'clock. At 9:30, Katie went upstairs to tell Jack she was leaving, but he was still asleep. She let Jack be and texted him:

Headed out for a ski. Have a safe drive north. Hug the kids for me.

Katie and Noah skied hard for the second day in a row. After skiing, they went to Kramarczuk's for lunch, a Polish deli near Noah's apartment, where Katie told Noah everything. About the woman at the Hewing Hotel being Rebecca Wong, a *Wall Street Journal* reporter. About Jack's concern that if *The Wall Street Journal* continued investigating Jack's company for falsifying test results for their new sodium-sulfur battery to attract investment and inflate the stock price, the SEC would get involved. About Jack's odd disappearance in the middle of the night followed by him sleeping in like a rock star.

"He must have left the house," said Noah.

"How?" said Katie.

"Maybe he turns off the alarm and resets it before he goes. Maybe he has another key."

"I'd hear the alarm chime, if not when he left, certainly when he came back. And even if he somehow did sneak out, his car was in the garage. He'd have to walk to wherever he was going."

"Or Lyft or Uber," said Noah.

"Not in my neighborhood. Every neighbor makes it their business to know everyone else's business. If some insomniac noticed Jack get into a strange car, the entire block would be talking about it the next day."

"That sounds like it might be an exaggeration."

"I'll invite you over in May. You'll see."

"Why May?"

"It's dandelion season. When you drive over, you'll see dandelions the entire way. In every lawn, park, and boulevard. Until you get to the Country Club neighborhood. Then, no dandelions. Not less. Not a few. None. The whole neighborhood has banded together to train as lawn care specialists to ensure that everyone has a perfectly coiffed green carpet in front of their home. I'm telling you, the Country Club neighborhood is a fortress of conformity. There are no secrets. What is that dubious expression on your face?"

Noah forced a smile and said, "I believe you." But he didn't sound like he believed Katie.

Katie said, "Do you think Makeena could moonlight for me?"

"No," said Noah. "Not now. I'm sorry. She's working fourteen-hour days on a class action suit. It's our biggest piece of litigation. But I can find you another investigator."

"I don't want another investigator. I like her."

"We all like Makeena."

Katie opened her mouth and could not stop herself from saying, "Do you like her, like her?"

Noah laughed.

"What's so funny?"

"That's such a seventh-grade question."

"Sorry," said Katie. "Do you, young man, have romantic inclinations toward Makeena?"

Noah said, "I'm her boss."

"I didn't ask if you were her boss. That, I know. I'm asking if you're dating? Do you whisper sweet nothings to each other in the copier room? Or do you just hook up?"

Noah said, "I'm uncomfortable talking about my dating life with you."

"Why? I thought we were friends."

"We are friends . . ." Noah trailed off. He looked away from Katie. He might have been looking at the glassed-in carousel of desserts spinning in the distance, but he might have just been avoiding Katie's eyes.

Katie said, "What?"

"Nothing."

"Nothing? Now who's being a seventh grader?"

Noah pushed his goulash around with his spoon. He ripped off a piece of potato roll and soaked up the liquid, took a bite, and set the roll back on his plate. "I don't like discussing my dating life with you because if all this meshuggaas with Jack—"

"What's meshuggaas?"

"Craziness. It's Yiddish. Very common in New York. Apparently, not in Minnesota. Anyway, if whatever's going on leads to you and Jack splitting up, and I'm not saying it will—and believe me when I say for your sake, I hope you don't split up—but if you do, I would, whenever you're ready, throw my hat into the giant pile of suitors' hats." He paused. "Suitors who would be pursuing you."

"Oh," said Katie.

"And if I talk about my dating life, you might use some of that information to pick my hat out of the pile and hand it back to me and say, 'Thank you but no thank you, good sir. Be gone.'"

Katie did not know how to respond. She looked into Noah's eyes. Kind eyes. Hazel and warm, Irish green shimmering behind brown irises. She could see that he saw her. Being seen felt thrilling and terrifying, validating and scandalous.

Noah said, "You don't have to say anything. Moving on to the next topic."

Katie said, "I would not hand your hat back to you."

"Oh," said Noah. "I didn't expect that. That's nice. Thank you."

Noah's admission knocked Katie off her game. She wanted to ask more about him and Makeena, but the question seemed moot. If Noah wanted to pursue Katie one day, whatever was or was not going on between him and Makeena must not be important. She felt flattered. And a bit in awe. And wobbly.

· CHAPTER 22 ·

When Katie returned home, she found Jack working in his office and said, "Why are you here?"

"Nice to see you, too," said Jack, his eyes on three monitors, never on Katie.

"I meant. You're going up to the cabin. Why haven't you left yet?"

"Eh," said Jack. "I decided not to go."

"You can't do that," said Katie. "The kids are waiting for you."

"Sorry. I have too much work."

It was one thing for Jack to disappoint her, thought Katie, but it was unforgivable for him to disappoint Elin and Kaleb. "Well, maybe you could have done that this morning if you hadn't slept in. Where were you last night?"

"What do you mean?"

"Jack, don't. Just don't. It's bad enough you do it to the kids."

"Do what?"

"Disappear. I woke up last night. You weren't anywhere in the house. The alarm was on. Your car was here. Your wallet and keys were here. Where were you?"

Jack stared at Katie. His eyes went cold. His mouth grew small. Katie felt something she'd never felt in all the years she'd known Jack Kuhlmann. She felt threatened.

He said, "Where were *you*?"

"What?" said Katie.

"Where were you?" said Jack, folding his arms.

"I was here. Looking for you."

"Where were you earlier last night? Were you with your boyfriend? Were you two following me? Is that how you know I was talking to the *Wall Street Journal* reporter?"

"I don't have a boyfriend," said Katie. She heard her voice shake. She'd lost her bearings and didn't know what was happening.

"Then who is he?" said Jack. "The guy you've been skiing with. And hanging out with in the chalet."

Katie's heart raced. How did Jack know about Noah? She told herself she had done nothing wrong. She had not cheated on her husband. Physically. Or emotionally. Well, maybe in her daydreams. She was guilty of one thing: lying by omission. She said, "You mean Noah?"

"Is that his name?"

"He's a ski friend. From the Birkie. We train together sometimes. And yes, once in a while we hang out in the chalet after."

"Why haven't you told me about him?"

"There's nothing to tell. Just like I don't tell you about everyone I meet at work."

Jack held up his phone. On the screen, Katie saw a picture of her and Noah in the chalet, smiling, drinking hot chocolate. Jack said, "This doesn't look like nothing."

Katie said, "Where did you get that?"

"Does it matter?" said Jack.

"That's from the day I ran into Noah. I didn't even know he'd moved to Minneapolis. So yes. It matters. Because from the looks of it, Jack, you were having me followed. How dare you?"

"No," said Jack. "I wasn't having you followed. A friend was there, saw you, and sent me this. Sound familiar?"

Katie remembered the two women sitting near her and Noah. She thought they were Instagramming their meals. She'd recognized one of them but couldn't remember from where. She said,

"Noah is a ski friend. Nothing more. And I don't believe you—you had me followed, and I'm beyond insulted. I've given you no reason to mistrust me. I mean, what is going on, Jack? You barely look at me anymore. You won't touch me. You disappear all the time. Is it all because of the *Wall Street Journal* reporter? Rebecca Wong? Is that why you've been behaving so strangely?"

"The *Wall Street Journal* story is nothing," said Jack. "Forget I even mentioned it."

"What?" Katie felt like she was in a dream. Nothing made sense. "What are you talking about?"

"You know," said Jack, looking down at his desk, "I have a shit-ton of work to do."

"I'm sure you do." Katie turned and left the room. She was shaking.

She went into the kitchen and tried to piece together what had happened but could not. She took a few minutes to calm down, then called Elin. "Dad's not coming up there. Would you and Kaleb like me to come get you or would you rather spend another night and come home with your cousins tomorrow?"

Elin said, "You sound weird."

"I'm feeling weird."

"Is everything okay?" said Elin.

Katie said, "I'm having a bad day."

"Sorry."

"Thank you. I'll be okay. Is Kaleb there? Do you want to ask him?"

"He went sledding with Dylan."

"All right. Do you want to call me back after you talk to him?"

"Okay. And Mom, will you please tell *Santa* I changed my mind about the beanbag from Pottery Barn Teen."

Katie could hear Elin's eyes roll on the word *Santa*, feeling, at twelve years old, she still had to play the game. Katie said, "Oh, you don't want the beanbag anymore?"

"I do. But I want the white hairy one instead of the pink hairy one."

"Okay, honey. I'll tell *Santa*."

A labored "thank you," from Elin.

"I love you, sweetie," said Katie. "I love you so much."

"Me, too."

Katie ended the call. She couldn't bear to be in the house with Jack, so she left for Pottery Barn Teen.

Katie drove straight to the Galleria, checking her mirrors to see if anyone was following. How ridiculous, she thought, that she was not only suspicious of being followed but had done some following herself. She pulled into the parking lot, found a spot, and her phone rang. It was Elin.

"Hi, honey."

"We're going to stay one more night and come back with Uncle Dougie and Aunt Hope tomorrow."

"Are you sure? I'm happy to come get you."

"We're sure. We're making our own pizzas for dinner and we can put whatever toppings we want on them and then we're watching as many *Toy Story* movies as we can before falling asleep."

"That sounds like fun."

"Yeah."

"Don't stay up too late. You'll be grumpy when you get back."

"It's almost winter break. I can sleep in for ten whole days."

"That's right. I forgot. Oh boy, this month. Okay, honey. See you tomorrow. I love you."

"I love you, Mom."

"Is Kaleb nearby?"

Katie listened to Kaleb's tales from the sledding hill, reminded him to brush his teeth and shower, told him she loved him and ended the call.

She grabbed the pink hairy beanbag from the rear of her car and entered the Galleria. Katie walked past a quartet of Dickensian carolers, quaint and benign, and wondered how her life went from quaint and benign to murky and untethered. Her husband was cold and distant yet accused Katie of having an affair, backed by pictures of her and Noah in the chalet. How did that happen? Something didn't make sense. Maybe everything didn't make sense. The first time Katie saw Noah, it was happenstance. She had made no plan to meet him on the trail. She didn't even know he was in town. She ran into him unexpectedly. So . . . a friend of Jack's noticed her and Noah in the chalet and took a picture of them together? Seemed unlikely. Jack must have had someone following Katie. But why would Jack do that? Katie had never given him any reason to distrust her. What could he possibly be up to?

Katie decided she would go home and talk to Jack. Come completely clean about her friendship with Noah, and hopefully get to the root of Jack's weird behavior. He wasn't having an affair with Rebecca Wong. But still, things were odd. Terribly odd. And messy. Living in this big bowl of spaghetti, where one strand twisted into the next and there seemed to be no start and no end. Living like this could not continue.

Katie exchanged the hairy pink beanbag for the hairy white beanbag then drove home. Jack was not there and neither was his car. She showered and took a nap. When she woke it was late afternoon and she found Jack in his office, poring over spreadsheets again.

"Can we talk?"

Jack looked up from his bank of monitors. He hesitated, pushed back from his desk and said, "Sure."

"I want to tell you about Noah Byrne."

"That black guy is Irish?"

"He's black. And Irish. And Chinese."

"Okay."

"I met him last year at the Birkie," said Katie. "More accurately, my group met his group. They invited us over for dinner then we all went our separate ways and that was that. Never heard from him or saw him again. Until I ran into him at Wirth when I was out for my first ski of the year. He'd moved here a few months before that. He's a civil rights lawyer. Anyway, we ended up skiing a few laps together and then I texted you that I'd run into friends and we were going to grab a bite. I lied. It wasn't friends. It was a friend. Noah. And because he's a man, I felt guilty about it. Whoever sent you that picture of us together, it was taken right after skiing. We had drinks, the drinks being hot chocolate."

"Uh-huh," said Jack.

Katie remained standing. Jack sat behind his desk. She felt like she was in a superior's office and didn't care for the imbalance.

"I swear to you that's all it was. And all it ever has been." Katie sat in Jack's Eames lounge chair, his favorite piece of furniture that he bought after receiving his first large year-end bonus. She put her feet up on the ottoman and said, "I wasn't honest with you about Noah because I felt strange skiing alone with a man. Just the two of us. The second time I didn't tell you about Noah because I didn't tell anyone about him. Yes, you're my husband and I should have told you. But life has seemed, well, a bit claustrophobic lately. Like the walls are closing in. And it felt like a relief valve to have a friend who didn't know my family or friends or neighborhood or work environment. And I've wanted to keep that friendship to myself. Not because he's a man but because he's an outsider."

"So it's ongoing. Your friendship with Noah Byrne."

"Yes. And I'm sorry I wasn't forthcoming about it. But I am being forthcoming now." Katie knew that was only partly true. She had lied by omission before, and she was doing it again. Noah had helped her follow Jack to the Hewing Hotel for his meeting with Rebecca Wong. She felt attracted to Noah. She had developed romantic feelings for him. Last night's talk about what they'd do if they were both available . . . Well, the important thing, rationalized Katie, is that she hadn't acted on those feelings.

She had put her marriage first. Katie had been trying with Jack. He had rejected her. Over and over again. Katie said, "So now you know everything that's going on with me. Why don't you tell me what's going on with you?"

Jack pushed his chair all the way back to his credenza, V-ing his eyebrows, the blood rushing to his face. "I told you what's going on with me. *The Wall Street Journal* is circling Electro-North 45. I'm the CEO. I'm responsible for every stupid mistake made by every stupid employee in my company. The liability falls on me. I'm sorry if I'm a bit preoccupied. I'm sorry if that inconveniences you."

"I don't accept your apology," said Katie. "You keep changing your story. You're worried. Then you're not. Now you are again. And why are you cutting me out of your life? You have no interest in making love to me. You disappear with your friends, or worse, into some cranny in the house. You've withdrawn from the entire family. We're here for you, but how can we support you if you shut us out?"

"I am not withdrawing from the family!" Jack's shouts died in the heavily insulated walls. He took a breath. And then another. "I'm trying to keep my head above water. The *Journal* story is going to break in the news any day and then it'll be a total shit show. The stock will plummet, and as you know, Katie, we own a hell of a lot of Electro-North 45 stock. I can't dump it because I know it's going to tank and the SEC would be all over me. So maybe I just need a little fucking space to deal with this shit because I'm drowning in it!"

Katie waited to make sure Jack had said all he had to say. She refused to lower herself to his level. In a calm and steady voice she said, "Talk to me like an adult, Jack. Your temper tantrum isn't becoming. Nor is it constructive."

"I'm a little worked up," said Jack. "Anyone in my position would be."

"I don't agree. You're acting like you personally misled investors. Did you know the battery's trial data was cooked from the beginning?"

"Of course I didn't," said Jack.

Katie knew her husband. Knew him better than anyone. And she was certain he was lying. She said, "I mean, isn't there some kind of quality control test that would flag something so basic as false data?"

"Yes, but—"

"So they caught it. And told you. And you said lie? Then held a big press conference touting Electro-North 45's great new electric vehicle battery of the future?"

Jack looked like he had not only fallen out of love with his wife but that he hated her. Hated her with more passion than he'd ever had when loving her. He said, "Forget I ever told you anything about this."

"What?"

"You're my wife. They can't make you testify against me. So just fucking forget I told you anything. About *The Wall Street Journal*. About the sodium-sulfur battery. About any of it."

Katie said, "You wouldn't have even told me if you didn't have to explain away Rebecca Wong."

Jack said nothing.

"I'm trying to be honest with you, Jack. I'd appreciate if you did the same with me."

"Don't worry about you. You'll be fine. You have your friend-who's-just-a-friend, Noah Byrne. You can always fall into his arms."

"He is just a friend, Jack. I am not going to have an affair with him. I wouldn't do that. Just the idea of it is impossible."

"You don't know that," said Jack. "You don't know what you're capable of."

"I think I do know. I won't have an affair."

"No," said Jack. His anger had ebbed. Now he was just distant. Cold. Like his quarter of a century with Katie didn't exist. "You don't know what one step in the wrong direction can lead to."

Katie said, "What are you trying to tell me, Jack?"

"I am trying to tell you, Katie, about human nature. That's all."

"Are you having an affair, Jack?"

"No."

"I'm not sure I believe you."

"Believe me or don't. I have to get back to work."

· CHAPTER 23 ·

Katie left the house to run more Christmas errands but took a detour from her usual route. She drove through her childhood neighborhood to see the house where she spent the first ten years of her life. The suburb was called New Hope, but for Katie, it should have been called Old Hope. A hope that she could return to the happiness of her youth. She was so happy with her family who had nothing. So happy until they were taken away because she had a sinus infection and couldn't join them on that trip.

The duplex still looked much like it did forty years ago. A single-story structure on the west end of Lions Park. The Ecklunds' half of the house was 850 square feet. Tiny for a family of five. Katie shared a bedroom with her younger brothers, Neil and Blake, and there was one bathroom for all five of them. Katie was the oldest child, and there had been talk of building her a bedroom in the unfinished basement. A space of her own. She could not believe her good fortune when her parents discussed the idea with her, as if her own bedroom was just falling out of the sky. She had no idea that her parents wanted her to have her own space for privacy—she'd soon be going through physical changes that would be torturous with Neil and Blake in the same room.

She needed a space where she would be free from her bed-jumping, bed-wetting, perpetually wrestling little brothers. Neil and Blake. Twins. Their names were so 1980s. She could barely remember what they looked like. She found herself going back to old family photos so she would not lose their images. Looking at their school portraits, hair forced into place and held there with her mother's hairspray. Teeth too big for their mouths. Or missing. Big gaps in their smiles. Wearing their special-occasion shirts with collars and buttons and without stains. The photographs misrepresented who Neil and Blake were but their smiles were genuine. The merriment in their eyes.

Lions Park had two baseball fields facing each other, two tennis courts, a hockey rink—the boards were up year-round—a large, flat round depression that was flooded in winter for a recreational rink, and a warming house. Katie's family had no money, but right across the street was heaven for an active kid, and Katie and her brothers were active kids.

She was content then, happy, even when fighting off Neil and Blake, pounding on the door for bathroom time only to finally get in there to see one of them had peed all over the toilet seat. But those were good times. Honest times. She held a hand to her heart and hoped Elin and Kaleb felt the same about their childhoods.

Katie pulled away from her former tiny house and headed back toward the city. Her phone rang. The caller ID on her car screen said SANDRA DAHLSTROM. Katie pushed the answer button on her steering wheel and said, "Hi Sandra. What's up?"

"We need to talk."

· CHAPTER 24 ·

They met at Patisserie 46 for coffee and delights glazed with tempered chocolate and festooned with gold flakes.

"I'm worried sick about her," said Sandra, spooning whipped cream from the top of her caffeinated concoction. Her blond-brown hair was pulled back tight, revealing a full face, which Sandra had buried under more makeup than usual. "Terri has tried to keep her chin up with her whole 'we just grew apart' routine. I think there's more to it than that."

"What do you mean?" said Katie. She drank tea, unsweetened, and limited herself to one cube of dark chocolate. The Birkie was on her mind. She was focused on breaking her personal record this year. Not because she cared more about cross-country skiing than she had in the past, but because she needed something on which to focus. Something to quiet the chaos in her life.

"Well," said Sandra, "I don't think Terri's being honest with us."

"About what?"

"Just between us, right?"

Katie nodded.

"I don't blame her for this—I really don't. But I think the real reason the Ackermans are getting divorced is because Terri has been seeing someone else."

"What?" said Katie. "Why do you think that?"

"She's so up and down. I mean, who wouldn't be down if their marriage was ending. If they were looking at fifty-fifty custody? If they had to move out of Country Club? Can you imagine?"

Katie could imagine. Had imagined. It was easy to do with Elin and Kaleb up north for a couple of days. She had lost one family and the idea of losing another, even half the time, was unthinkable. And yet that's where Jack was pushing her. Her only hope was that if they divorced, he'd be too lazy and self-centered to spend much time with his children. Not the best situation for Elin and Kaleb but, selfishly, that would be ideal for Katie.

"So I understand her being down," continued Sandra. "But what I don't understand is why sometimes she's so up. Like giddy. Like—"

"She's in love?" said Katie.

"Yes. Like she's in love. And sometimes, she disappears."

Katie set down her half-eaten cube of chocolate. She swallowed and felt her face flush and said, "What do you mean, Terri disappears?"

"The other night, Lucas's cell rang at 10:30. It was Richard. He asked if Terri was with me. Lucas always has his volume cranked up, so even though he didn't have his phone on speaker, I could hear Richard clearly. Lucas told him no, Terri wasn't at our house or out with me. And then I heard crying."

Katie sipped her tea. She thought she knew where this was going, and it terrified her but she kept the terror buried deep, far from Sandra's radar.

"Richard was actually crying. A grown man. It was . . . uncomfortable. Then he told Lucas that Terri just leaves the house at random times, mostly at night, and says she just wants to go for a walk. Or a drive. Or needs something at Walgreens. Richard said Terri is super protective of her phone. She won't let Richard or the kids touch it. Richard's sure she's been having an affair."

"Maybe," said Katie. The words came out casually, but now she felt hot in her feet and her hands, as if her body was trying to tell her mind something it didn't want to know.

"Maybe? What else would explain that behavior?"

"I don't know," said Katie. "Terri's going through a major life change. Everything she knows is getting ripped out by the roots. She seemed so down last time we saw her, and depression can lead to all sorts of unusual behavior. Maybe Terri really does need to go for a walk or a drive. Maybe she texts her therapist a lot and that's why she doesn't want anyone near her phone. Or maybe Terri sees a therapist who is only available by text. That's a thing. Some people still stigmatize mental health issues and want to keep it as private as possible. Or maybe . . ."

Katie kept talking. She used one part of her brain to form words and sentences into cohesive thoughts. Anything to explain away the possibility that Terri Ackerman was seeing another man. And she used another part of her brain to consider that if Terri Ackerman was having an affair and was disappearing at odd times for trysts, she was doing so with a person who might also be disappearing from home at odd times. And in odd ways.

The likelihood of coincidence faded. There was so much she did not know about the strangeness in her house as of late. But she did know a few things: First, Jack disappeared at odd times. She didn't understand how he managed to wriggle out of the house, past locked doors and the alarm system, but he did. Second, Jack had not wanted to tell Katie about Rebecca Wong, the *Wall Street Journal* reporter, and her investigation into Electro-North 45. He had said he regretted telling her. He told her to forget about it. Jumped to the extreme when he said they couldn't make a spouse testify against him. So why did Jack tell her? One possibility was to create a smoke screen. Jack sacrificed one secret to guard another. Could that secret be Terri Ackerman? Third, Jack was lying to her when he claimed he had no idea that his company had falsified the test results for their new sodium-sulfur battery, and Jack knew Katie could tell he was lying. He felt threatened by her. Jack's behavior was unstable and unpredictable.

Katie heard herself say, ". . . and if Terri is having an affair, maybe it started after she and Richard agreed to get divorced. They're basically separated but living in the same house. Richard sleeps in the basement while they work out the details of him moving out." Katie ran out of things to say. She wasn't even sure what she had said while thinking about Jack.

Sandra spooned more whipped cream into her mouth. "Why are you defending Terri? Because I'm not accusing her. I'm just concerned for her and I wanted to share that with you because you're her friend, too."

"I'm not defending Terri. There's nothing to defend. I'm just considering other factors that could explain her behavior."

Katie considered sharing her troubles with Sandra. About Jack disappearing and his problems at work. The work issues would be known soon enough if that *Wall Street Journal* reporter followed through with her story. Rebecca Wong. So pretty. So petite. And she was about to bring down Jack. Maybe bring down the entire Kuhlmann family.

And again Katie thought that might not be a bad thing. She liked the Country Club neighborhood. She liked the house. She liked nice things. Who doesn't? But the true cost of those things was not money. The true cost was a disinterested, disengaged Jack. From her and the kids. And that was not worth the price paid.

Katie felt she couldn't tell Sandra about Jack's odd behavior or his trouble at work. Country Club was such a close-knit collection of streets, the neighbors were so focused on the houses and lawns around them, that if she told one person, even her friend Sandra, Jack and Katie would become the talk of the neighborhood. Maybe even the pariah of the neighborhood. Kids could overhear parents gossiping. It could boomerang back to Elin and Kaleb and affect their friendships. What a mess that would be.

So Katie said nothing other than, "How do you think we can best help Terri?" even though Katie wasn't sure she wanted to help Terri. Not if Terri was sneaking off to see Jack.

"Honestly," said Sandra, "I think the best thing we can do is just keep our ears and eyes open. We can't approach her about the affair because that would seem judgmental. And it's not about judging her. It's about thinking maybe there's another layer to what's going on with her. But only so we can be there for her if she needs us."

Katie popped the last of her chocolate cube into her mouth and said, "I agree."

Katie finished her shopping just after five o'clock. She was hungry and wanted a drink and, more than anything, wanted to call Noah. But she restrained herself. She could handle the path she and Noah were on now. Skiing. A meal once in a while. A text here and there. He had told her about his impending divorce, which helped Katie feel not alone. He had given her solicited advice and introduced her to Makeena the P.I. But Katie was lonely in her marriage and keenly aware of it. Seeing Noah that night would make the path too slippery. It was a terrible idea. She decided she wouldn't even call him.

The kids wouldn't be home until tomorrow. Katie felt uncomfortable in the house with Jack. She wouldn't even suggest a date with him that night because for the first time, she did not want to be with him. In her head, that idea seemed obvious. It seemed logical. But not wanting to be with Jack made her heart hurt. Jack was her husband. She had created her life with him. She had created more lives with him. She and Jack and Elin and Kaleb were a family, and family was supposed to be a person's foundation. A safe place from which one could venture out and take risks to make their way in the world, knowing that base was always there for support. For comfort. Family was supposed to be a haven for unconditional love. That's what Katie strived to offer Elin and Kaleb. And also Jack, but he seemed to have no interest in providing that for Katie. The feeling uprooted and disoriented her.

She headed to Tilia in Linden Hills where she could sit at the bar by herself to think and eat dinner. There, she ordered a bowl of pappardelle with a starter salad and a glass of wine and thought her way through a second glass of wine and a slice of flourless chocolate cake. So much for being in training for the Birkie, but she needed time to think and the pasta and wine and chocolate helped.

As she ate the last bite of cake, she reduced her thoughts down to one: determine whether or not her marriage could be salvaged. To do that, she had to get to the bottom of what Jack was up to.

· CHAPTER 25 ·

Katie was about to head home when she received a text from Sandra:

Saving you a seat at Cuzzy's. Where are you?

Katie had forgotten about Cuzzy's. It was the book club's annual holiday tradition. They had long given up on a book club meeting in December. The holidays had everyone bouncing around pell-mell, and it seemed impossible to find one evening when they were all free. But the female half of the club still managed a December get-together, not to discuss books, but as a sort of Christmas party and brief retreat from the chaos of holiday obligations.

The tradition was to meet at Cuzzy's, a dive bar on Washington Avenue in the North Loop. Unlike most of the other buildings in the area, Cuzzy's had not been updated, retrofitted, remodeled. The building was a rectangle made of bricks. Flat walls. Flat roof. Glass brick windows. The only thing that wasn't flat was the hamburgers, which seemed constructed more for snakes that could detach their jaws than they were for human beings.

Katie walked in and found Sandra, Latisha Nicolaides, Miriam Friedman, Terri Ackerman, and Jane Hansen.

"Where the hell have you been?" said Miriam. Her gray curls subdued from the arid winter air or a hat or both. "This pitcher of Mistletoe Manhattans isn't going to drink itself."

"It doesn't have to, Miriam," said Latisha, "you're here." Latisha smiled, and her glacier-like eyes rivaled the tinsel and lights strung about the bar.

"I am particularly festive," said Miriam. "Can't help it. It's my nature."

Cheap stools and cheap tables, a pine-topped bar with pine paneling behind it. The kind of place the waitresses still wore something tight in hopes of increasing their tips. The ceiling and paneling were covered in dollar bills, each stuck there with a thumbtack. The clientele was a mix of blue-collar workers enjoying their Hamm's beer and wealthy, insulated comfort-seekers like Katie and her friends who drank Hamm's ironically. It was perfect for a holiday get-together.

"Sorry I'm late, everyone," said Katie. "Lost track of time." This was, of course, a lie. Katie had completely forgotten about December book club, as they called it. "Okay if I pour myself a Manhattan?"

"They're Mistletoe Manhattans," said Miriam. "And please, let me pour. It would be my honor."

Jane Hansen rolled her eyes. She was not the type to let herself go for an evening. You could see the muscles flex in her jaw. "None for me, thanks. Tomorrow morning we're off to Palm Springs and I don't like to fly dehydrated."

"We're thinking of buying in Palm Springs," said Latisha. "Owning in Florida is too stressful during hurricane season. We all should buy there. We could chip in on a private jet. It makes flying so much easier."

A private jet? thought Katie. She liked her Country Club friends but . . . *a private jet?*

"And pay California taxes?" said Miriam. "No thank you. We'll stick with Florida. Plus Sanibel Island is Minnesota South. Plenty of people to share a PJ with. And you can trust you'll be around good people."

Katie felt the Mistletoe Manhattan doing its job and couldn't help herself from asking, "What do you mean by *good people*?"

"You know," said Miriam, "ordinary folk like us. Salt of the earth. Palm Springs is full of Bentleys and Hollywood types and all that mid-century-modern bullshit. If the aesthetics of the 1950s were so great, we would have held on to them."

"Like you're holding onto the aesthetics of the 1850s," said Sandra.

"Hey. Our home is a traditional Colonial and we decorate accordingly. As a matter of fact, I just ordered a gas lamp for our front porch. It's stunning."

Katie said, "Natural gas? I thought you were concerned about global warming."

"I am. But one gas flame isn't going to melt Antarctica. You'll see ours and within six months you'll all have gas lamps." Miriam turned to Sandra. "What about you and Lucas? Florida, Palm Springs, or that old Minnesota standby, Scottsdale?"

"When Hannah graduates we're buying in Florida," said Sandra. "At least that's what Lucas says. Live there fifty-one percent of the time and goodbye Minnesota state tax."

Who are these people? thought Katie. *Have they always been like this?* Katie wondered if Jack's odd behavior had jolted her back into reality. She had so wanted to assimilate into Jack's life from the moment they started dating. To feather herself into Jack's normal so she could be a good wife, a good sister-in-law, a good daughter-in-law. The transition was not smooth. When they first started dating, Jack chided Katie for her bargain wardrobe, her choice of bag-it-yourself grocery stores, her rusted Ford Escort, her imperfect bottom teeth, that she'd never been outside of the country. But she endured the bumpy adaptation for Jack and for herself because she loved him and that was what spouses did for each other and besides, Jack's world was the American Dream, wasn't it?

Terri, who hadn't uttered a word since Katie arrived, said, "My travel days are over for a while. I don't want Richard's lawyer to claim I've spent joint funds frivolously."

"That's temporary," said Miriam. "So what is your ideal warm-weather location?"

"Mexico," said Terri. "Not the Riviera but the Pacific Coast. I love Cabo."

Cabo? thought Katie. That's where Jack said he wanted to winter and he hadn't even been there.

"Richard and I took the kids a few years ago. You can get a lot for your money down there, and it's refreshing being out of the country. You meet people from all over the world."

"People from all over the world aren't the best on the beach," said Miriam. "You got your topless women, your men wearing banana hammocks. I have a hard enough time patrolling my kids' internet use—I don't need to give them the real thing up front and bouncing around in person. What about you, Katie?"

Katie's head was still on Terri Ackerman and Cabo. "What?"

"Pay attention. Where are you and Jack going to migrate to when you're snowbirds?"

"I don't know. I like winter." Katie looked Terri Ackerman dead in the eye. "But Jack talks about buying a place in Cabo. And he hasn't even been there."

Katie kept her eyes on Terri until Terri looked away, then Katie glanced at Sandra to see if she'd noticed the awkward moment. Sandra raised her eyebrows in an *I told you so* kind of way.

Miriam poured from pitcher to glass. "Sandra," she said, "show the ladies your early Christmas present."

"Miriam. That's a secret."

"It is a secret," said Miriam, "because it's concealed." Miriam smiled and handed the Manhattan to Katie. "Get it, everyone? It's concealed. And being carried. My oh my, I wonder what it could be."

Terri Ackerman snapped back to attention and leaned forward. "No," she said to Sandra, "since when?"

Sandra looked resigned. "Lucas bought it for me. To help me with my anxiety. I wasn't going to say anything, but the town crier over there"—she nodded toward Miriam—"can't keep her mouth shut after she's had a few. And don't worry. I've taken lessons and have a permit."

Katie couldn't help but think, *Oh great. First Bagman in the guest suite and now Sandra living behind me. Me and my kids are surrounded*. It wasn't like Katie had never been around guns. They were plentiful when she'd moved down to Elba, Minnesota, to live with her grandparents. The town was full of hunters. Most residents had plenty of land and felt it was their responsibility to protect it and themselves. But Sandra Dahlstrom? Come on. With her sometimes blond, sometimes brown hair and designer clothing and aristocratic air? Carrying a gun in her Hermès purse?

Katie sipped her Manhattan and looked at Terri as the conversation moved on to the holidays and family get-togethers. That last topic seemed to send Terri Ackerman into a shell, and Katie thought this would be a painful holiday season for the long-legged Norwegian.

And yet, *Cabo*? It was just a place, a word, really, and maybe a coincidence, but Cabo seemed like the key that might unlock the mystery of Jack's distance and Terri's awkwardness around Katie. She couldn't take it anymore—this state of not knowing the truth felt unbearable.

Katie finished her drink and made an excuse about not feeling well. To her neighbors' disappointment and a lambasting from Miriam, Katie left and headed home to do what she could not put off any longer.

CHAPTER 26

Katie's plan was simple. Jack had repeatedly gone to the basement, disappeared from the house, then reappeared from the basement, making some excuse about being in the workshop or laundry room or mechanical room. Maybe he had removed the alarm sensor from one of the egress windows and crawled in and out of the window well. Whatever he was doing, Katie was determined to discover what it was.

She got home just before nine o'clock. Jack wasn't there, but his car was. Bagman's car was there, too. Katie went downstairs and checked the egress windows, which served as emergency exits and also let more natural light into the basement. Outside the egress windows were large window wells about six feet deep. They had little ladders built into them to help a person crawl out if they fell in from outside or crawled in from inside the house. Katie went back upstairs, put on her winter boots, and walked the perimeter of the house. There were no footprints in the snow near or around any of the egress window wells. There were no doors leading from the basement to outside. It appeared Jack had not entered or exited the house that way. But with Jack, appearances meant nothing as of late.

Katie returned to the house, went upstairs, grabbed the latest Ann Patchett novel from her nightstand, and descended into the basement. She made sure the alarm was set to chime, which she could hear from the control panel in the basement. There was a large, cedar-lined closet near Jack's bar. It was designed to store the family's hoard of winter coats and sweaters during the warm months, and it was half empty in December. Katie turned off the basement lights, slipped inside the closet, left the door slightly ajar, and retreated into the far recesses. If Jack was going to somehow appear in the basement, she would be there when it happened. She had grabbed a headlamp from their camping supplies, and started to read.

It was just after 10:30 when she heard the alarm chime. A moment later, voices. They were coming down the basement stairs, and they belonged to Jack and Bagman. Both men were unnaturally loud, which Katie interpreted as both men were drunk. She was surprised to hear the door to the basement close. Jack never shut the basement door. Katie turned off her headlamp.

"We'll crack open a new bottle," said Jack.

"You got ice down here?" said Bagman.

"Do I have ice down here? What do you take me for, a caveman? I have regular ice. And I have big ice. One cube barely fits in the glass."

"Yeah," said Bagman. "I like big ice. One of those. And pour the rye over the cube so it gets real cold."

Katie crawled up to the crack between the door and frame. She saw Jack standing behind the bar, pouring two lowballs of rye. Bagman sat on a barstool like a regular. Jack had not materialized in the basement like Katie had hoped he would. He came down the stairs like a mere mortal. She was trapped in the closet, and hoped they wouldn't just recount old college stories she'd heard a thousand times after all the trouble she'd gone through.

"Got to talk to you about something," said Adam.

"My listening skills are best when I'm behind the bar."

Bagman swirled the rye in his glass and said, "I'm in trouble, Jack."

Jack sipped his rye and said, "Yeah?"

"I need to leave the country. And I need to borrow some

money. I'll pay it back. I promise. I have plenty of cash. I just can't get to it now."

Katie felt a twinge in her gut. This was not the conversation she hoped Bagman would have with Jack.

Jack said, "Do you want to tell me what kind of trouble you're in?"

"Actually, I do. I don't have anyone to talk to about it. But it's probably best for you if you don't know. So I won't."

"Why don't you start," said Jack, "and I'll stop you if I don't want to hear any more."

Bagman considered Jack's suggestion for what felt like a long time to Katie as she sat on the floor of the cedar closet. The darkness seemed to crank up her olfactory prowess. The cedar smelled sharp and good.

Adam Bagman Ross said, "You knew me in college. I was a total fuckup. I didn't belong there. Street smarts, I got. Book smarts, not so much. But my family wanted me to get a normal job, a real job, you know, my own career so I didn't end up working in the family business."

"What's wrong with the family business? They do well, right? Commercial construction?"

"Yeah to all of that," said Bagman. "My great-grandfather moved from Brooklyn to Miami. He ran rum and cigars and sugar from Havana up to Florida. This was before Castro. Before the revolution. He started the construction business with the profits from cigars and rum and sugar. The construction business was and is legit, but some parts of my family's business are not legit. It all stemmed from my great-grandfather selling on the black market. Let's just say he expanded his product line, and even though he could have made a nice living in construction, something about the guy, I don't know, he liked being in the game."

"The game?" said Jack.

"The underworld."

"Oh."

Oh? thought Katie. *That's all you can say, Jack? Don't you understand what he's telling you? Don't you understand who he is? What he is? Living with us for six weeks? With our children?*

Bagman said, "Maybe my great-grandfather was bored. Maybe he was just greedy. I'm not sure. I never met the man. Just know he died when he fell off his boat. My guess is he didn't so much fall as got nudged. Or maybe tossed."

"Jesus. I had no idea," said Jack, topping off his and Bagman's drinks.

"I didn't, either. Until high school. His son, my grandfather, focused on construction. He didn't want anything to do with 'the game' part of the business, which my great-uncle ran after my great-grandfather washed up on a beach in Miami. But my father. He's different. He has that same bug my great-grandfather had. He's less interested in construction and more interested in the distribution of goods and services frowned upon by Uncle Sam."

"And you?" said Jack.

"I tried to work the construction business, but after my grandfather died, my cousin took over. He's a real by-the-book straight-and-narrow kind of guy, and he didn't appreciate my style. But my dad, he knows my strengths and weaknesses. When he saw me struggling to make a legit living, he gave up on me living a respectable life and offered me a position in the other side of the family business. He didn't want to at first. That's why he sent me to college. But when it became clear I wasn't a desk jockey, I wasn't a sales guy, I had a problem with authority, well . . . he found a spot for me."

Jack said, "And that's how you make your living?"

"Yeah."

"So you're not in the industrial heat shield business."

"No, I am not."

Katie could see Jack's face—he looked stunned. If she could have seen her own face, it, too, would have looked stunned. Their old friend Adam Ross lived in a world they'd only heard about.

Jack ran his fingers through his tousled hair. "How much money do you need?"

"It's just a loan. I'm good for it. Remember that. I mean, you know me, Jack. I'm a lot of things. But I ain't no deadbeat."

"How much?"

Bagman sipped his drink. His shoulders slumped forward. "Three hundred thousand."

"Holy shit."

"I need to grease some palms to get out of the country. And I got to be gone for a while. That's the amount I need to lay low until things cool off."

"And you won't tell me what things need to cool off?"

"Listen. Jack. I'm skipping some details for your own good, but I'll tell you this much: I'm a low-level guy. Mostly an errand boy for my father. But things got messy with the business. Let me clarify: messier than usual. Different organizations were trespassing on each other's territories and products. One of those products crossed the line for me. Human beings should not be bought and sold. That was the first strike. And things were heating up for a real bloodbath between organizations. That was strike two. Then my father pulls me aside and asks me to take point on the conflict. A no-win situation. Strike three. So I quit."

"You quit the family business?"

"Yeah. Except quitting that kind of business is different than quitting a legit business. Different in that they don't let you quit." Adam paused, picked up his glass and drank the last of his rye. "I'm on the run." Bagman poured himself more rye. "If they find me, they'll kill me. You're the only person on this earth I trust, Jack. Even though we've been out of touch since college. Some stuff doesn't fade, you know? You live with a guy for a couple years, you get to know him. That bond is real. The bond stays strong. I wouldn't have told you any of this if I didn't believe that's the absolute truth."

"So . . ." Jack sipped his rye. "You need to lay low for a while. Maybe a long while."

"Exactly. See, you're smart, Jack. You've always been smart. That's why you're the guy who got Katie. I got nowhere else to turn. The organization, they got people everywhere. I can't use an ATM. I can't use a credit card. My cash is running low. I use it to buy Visa gift cards so I can get gas without attracting attention. Cash is a red flag these days. I traded my Porsche for the Lexus at a huge loss so they don't know what I'm driving. You letting me stay here in this place that's so fucking under the radar groundhogs don't know it exists, you're saving my life. But I have to get farther away. I've already been here a month and a half even though I thought a month was the longest I should stay. My luck won't hold out forever."

Jack looked contemplative. Or at least he tried to. Bagman had put Jack in a position of power. A position from where one could exercise great wisdom and loyalty to an old friend. But Katie saw what Jack did not. Adam Bagman Ross had played Jack. He had just obligated Jack to help him. Because what could Jack say in response? No, I won't help you? But you can stay here as long as you want. You, the target of hired killers. Yes, please stay with me and my wife and my adorable children. Attract dangerous people into our precious little lives. Jack would realize that he had no choice, but not right away. He said, "Three hundred thousand dollars is a lot of money. I don't just have it laying around. I'd have to liquidate equities. All our investments are in mine and Katie's names, so I couldn't hide it from her."

Give him the money, Jack. Give him everything we have. Katie tried to steady her breathing. The closet felt like it was closing in on her. *He needs to leave our house.*

"You don't got another way to raise the money?" said Bagman. "And you'll get it back. Every penny. Plus interest. Here." Bagman took off his watch and set it on the bar. "Take this. It's an Audemars Piguet. It's worth over a hundred grand. Consider it collateral on my first loan payment."

Jack picked up the watch and looked it over.

Adam said, "Take the watch, and I have some unmounted stones, too. I can't fence 'em now—it's like putting a bull's-eye on my head. But you can hold 'em. If something were to happen to me—it won't—but let's say it did—all you got to do is let things die down and then you can unload the watch and stones. That won't happen. I promise. But just for peace of mind."

Jack said, "Let me look at a few options. See what I can come up with."

"Thanks, buddy. I knew I could count on you. And hey, now that you know my troubles, how are you doing?"

Jack sighed. "Honestly, I've been better. Things with Katie are bad. Things at work are even worse."

"Sorry, man," said Bagman.

Katie thought she heard something odd in Bagman's voice. Was it aloofness? Disinterest? There was something unsympathetic in Adam's response. He said, "Can things with Katie turn around?"

"I don't think so. Pretty sure she's seeing someone."

Katie could feel her heartbeat. Jack implying she was the problem made her want to jump out of the closet and defend herself. She stayed put to give Jack a chance to clarify himself. Jumping out of the closet wasn't an option anyway, not with what Bagman had told Jack. Bagman could never know that Katie knew his real line of work.

Bagman said, "I don't believe it. Not Katie. She wouldn't have an affair."

"Yeah? Check this out." Jack showed Bagman his phone,

swiping the screen with his thumb, and Katie was sure he was showing the pictures of her and Noah together.

"Nah. I won't believe it," said Bagman. "In my line of work, you got to be a good judge of character. In an instant you have to know who you can trust and who you can't. Katie is trustworthy. I'm sure of it. Those pictures . . . looks to me like they're just friends."

Katie could have hugged Adam Bagman Ross for defending her.

"Maybe they are just friends," said Jack. "But that's how these things start."

"Have you talked to her about it?"

"Yeah. Sure. She denies she's having an affair. He's supposedly a ski friend. And maybe it doesn't matter if he's a friend or more than a friend. Things haven't been good between us for over a year."

Bagman grabbed the bottle of rye. "There's something you're not telling me, Jackie-boy." He poured rye into his glass. "You got some extracurricular activity going on?"

Jack reached for the bottle. "No."

"Mmmm," said Bagman. "You're going to have to do better than that."

"I don't," said Jack.

Bagman laughed. "You are not a good liar, my friend. So let me ask this: Is your problem with Katie also your problem with work? Is that where you met the mistress who, according to you, does not exist?"

"No," said Jack just as Bagman finished the question. "My problems with Katie and work have nothing to do with each other."

"That," said Bagman, "I believe."

The image of Terri Ackerman flooded Katie's vision. Tall, fit, beautiful, smart. How could Richard let her go? Maybe he had no choice. Maybe it wasn't as mutual of a split as Terri had claimed. Maybe Sandra was right. Maybe Terri was leaving Richard for Jack.

Bagman said, "So if it's not a personal relationship, what's happening at work?"

Jack told Bagman about the falsified data from the sodium-sulfur battery and Rebecca Wong, the *Wall Street Journal* reporter who seemed intent on ruining his life.

Bagman said, "Why haven't they run the story yet?"

"I don't know."

"Jackie-boy. Pay attention. Think this through. I've seen this a few times in my line of work. A reporter gets the goods on someone. They want to write the story. But it doesn't happen. Why doesn't it happen? I'll tell you why. The powers that be don't want to risk falsely accusing someone. They want more evidence. More sources."

"What are you saying?" said Jack. "The article might not happen? Some higher-up will kill it?"

"It's possible."

Neither Jack nor Bagman spoke for a while. The silence felt interminable. All three heads in that room went in the same direction. If Rebecca Wong did not write an article exposing Electro-North 45 and Jack Kuhlmann of willfully falsifying data from the sodium-sulfur battery to raise the stock price, then the whole issue might go away. There seemed two ways that article could get buried. One, if Rebecca's publisher killed it. Or two, if Rebecca Wong could be persuaded not to write the article.

Jack said, "How desperate is your situation? How much time before you have to get out of the country?"

Adam Bagman Ross exhaled. "It's desperate. I'm good at covering my tracks. Mailed my cell phone west in case they have anyone at AT&T on their payroll. Haven't used a credit or debit card. But it ain't exactly a secret I went to school here. If they start nosing around in Minnesota, asking who my friends were, well, I don't want to put you and the family in danger."

· CHAPTER 27 ·

The men talked for another hour and retreated upstairs. Katie waited twenty minutes, used the basement bathroom, then crept up to the second level and entered her bedroom where she saw Jack passed out on his half of the bed. On top of the covers. Still clothed. A drunk's slumber.

Katie hated Jack in that moment. For ruining their family—she was sure at this point he had been cheating on her. Maybe not with Rebecca Wong but with someone. For jeopardizing their financial stability—if Electro-North 45 went down, it could take the Kuhlmanns with it. A less posh, simpler life felt like it might be a good thing. But not if Jack wiped them out. And what about Jack inviting Bagman into their home—a man who carried a gun and who, if he was telling the truth, had a price on his head? Katie felt tempted to get in her car, drive two hours north, pick up Elin and Kaleb from their uncle's cabin and disappear.

But she was tired. So tired. Katie left her bedroom, her and Jack's bedroom, walked down the hall and crawled into Kaleb's bed. How many times had she slept in that room? When Kaleb couldn't fall asleep without her. When Kaleb woke at two A.M. with a nightmare. When he was sick. Kaleb's room was one of the few untouched by the remodel, and its familiarity brought Katie back to a time she missed. Before the $2 million remodel/addition. Before Jack had grown cold and distant. Before Elin felt the stress of adulthood reaching for her. It seemed the only one who hadn't changed was Kaleb, still bright-eyed and happy-go-lucky. He, like his room, with its life-size cardboard cutouts of Chewbacca and C3PO, reached across the expanse of space and time.

When Katie woke, the gray light of early morning seeped into Kaleb's room, beckoning Katie to the window seat where she contemplated her day. She would check in with the kids. If they weren't driving back to the cities early, she'd get in the car and drive north to get them. Katie grabbed her phone but she had not charged it overnight and it was dead. She went down the hall to see if Jack was sleeping but he was gone. She grabbed the charger off her nightstand and headed downstairs for coffee.

While the coffee was brewing, Katie looked in the garage. Bagman's car was gone. She could only hope he wouldn't return, but nothing from the conversation last night between Bagman and Jack made her think that might be true. She returned to the kitchen and discovered that her phone had come back to life. Katie had a text from Jack: *Drove north. The kids want to spend another day or two at the cabin. Will drive them back tomorrow or the next day.*

Jack did not seem to care the kids had a few more days of school before winter break. He did not invite her to join them. She felt unwelcome. Alone. Katie had not felt so alone since she'd lost her family. Her first family. Her parents and brothers. This situation, thought Katie, was intolerable. When she was ten, she had no choice but to do what she was told. Pack up her few personal belongings. Say goodbye to her friends. Attend the impersonal funeral service. Move to southeast Minnesota to live with her grandparents. Ella and Rolf Ecklund were lovely people. Almost young enough to be her parents. But she suffered without her actual parents and brothers, suffered for eight long years before leaving for college.

Katie would not be a victim this time.

She dialed Jack. The call went to voicemail. She dialed him again. And again. And again. Until he picked up.

He answered the call. "Did you get my text?"

"Yes. That's why I'm calling. Elin and Kaleb have to come back for school."

"Come on, Katie. Half the kids leave early for vacation. It's okay if they miss a day or two."

Katie knew that was true. The last few days of school before break were spent watching movies and eating cookies. "Okay," she said, "But why didn't you invite me up there?"

"I didn't know I needed to. You're welcome to go up anytime."

"You made it quite clear you would return with the kids in a day or two," said Katie. "You and only you."

"Yeah. Well. I suppose it wouldn't be a terrible thing if you and I had a break from each other."

"A break? Seriously, Jack. We barely see each other now."

"Okay, yeah," said Jack. "That's true. We'll talk about it when I get home."

"And what about Bagman?" said Katie.

"What about him?"

Katie wanted to say, *How could you leave me alone with a criminal?* But she could never let Jack know what she'd overheard in the basement. She didn't trust him to keep that secret and she didn't know how Adam would react if he knew what she'd overheard. Besides, would Jack protect her if he were there? She was beginning to doubt it. Katie said, "You just left him here with me? How come you never spend time with him? He was your best friend."

There was a pause, and even from a hundred miles away, Katie could hear the gears turning in Jack's head. "Bagman is fine. He doesn't need anyone to babysit him."

Katie was tempted to ask Jack about Terri Ackerman but

feared he would just deny the affair. Katie had a better plan to get to the bottom of that.

"Katie," said Jack, "I have to stop for gas."

"Do you, Jack?"

"What do you mean by that?"

"I don't believe you. I don't believe anything you say anymore."

"Nothing I can do about that," said Jack. "We'll be back tomorrow or the next day. Call the kids. They'll let you know the plan. If you want to drive up and join us then drive up. I have to go."

Jack ended the call. Katie was about to call him back to say she was headed up to get the kids right now when Noah called.

"Have you seen the news?"

"No," said Katie. "Why?"

"Rebecca Wong, that reporter we saw with Jack the other night at the Hewing Hotel? She's dead."

· CHAPTER 28 ·

"Oh my God," said Katie. "What happened?"

"A car accident. The police are investigating. Apparently at about four in the morning she drove from downtown to Taylors Falls and her car went off the road and fell a few hundred feet."

"What was she doing way out there at four in the morning?"

"No idea. And the police didn't release her name, but someone from *The Wall Street Journal* tweeted that they'd lost one of their own. I have a friend who's a reporter there, so I sent a text and he confirmed it's Rebecca."

Katie did the math. Bagman told Jack he needed money to leave the country. Jack told Bagman he would be in trouble as soon as *The Wall Street Journal* published their story on Electro-North 45. Bagman was gone. Jack had changed his mind and driven north to his brother's cabin. Why? He said he couldn't go because he had too much work to do. Now Rebecca Wong was dead. And Bagman was gone—Bagman, who wasn't a salesman of industrial heat shields. No, he had worked for his criminal father and now he was on the run. Desperate for cash and desperate to get out of the country. That was his story to Jack, anyway. Had he and Jack just danced the dance of quid pro quo?

Katie said, "Noah, do you have any time this morning?"

"Sure. What's up?"

"I don't want to tell you over the phone. Meet you at Nicollet Island Inn at nine o'clock and we'll walk from there?"

"See you then."

Katie ended the call and went to the kitchen's built-in desk. She opened the top drawer on the right, sifted through paper clips, rubber bands, a loose roll of stamps, and found the spare key to the guest house over the garage. Adam's car was still gone, so she went into the backyard and climbed the steps up to the entrance. Bagman was not there, but he had not moved out. She was surprised to find the space clean and tidy. The kitchen was spotless. No dishes left in the sink. The refrigerator contained plenty of food, but was well-organized. The bed was made. Adam's clothes hung neatly in the closet or lay folded in the dresser.

Katie checked the nightstand drawers in search of Adam's gun, but both drawers were empty. She looked under the bed, in the garbage, high in the closet where they stored extra blankets and pillows. She found nothing.

She expected to feel relieved, but she had a nagging thought: if what Adam Bagman Ross had told Jack was true, he was a professional criminal. He wouldn't leave any evidence of his profession for his hosts to find. For his enemies. For the police. Cleanliness and tidiness were probably part of his job. He had to be organized and efficient. There was no room for sloppiness.

Katie wondered if he'd set up some sort of indicator to tell if anyone had entered the guest house while he was gone. She'd seen that done in movies. A hair tied between the door and doorjamb. The fibers of the entryway rug all brushed one direction so a footprint would show up if the rug were stepped on. But it was her house—if she needed to go in the guest space for something, she needed to go in. No great violation of privacy there.

When Katie had seen the blueprints for the addition/remodel, she asked Jack why the guest space had a separate entrance. His answer was that if the guest space didn't have a separate entrance, their guests would be living in their house, and what was that old saying about houseguests and fish after three days? Jack had seemed so interested in the spatial aspects of the remodel/addition. Katie hated to admit it—it was so stereotypically female—but she had focused more on the decorating.

Katie returned to the main house, got dressed for her walk with Noah, and headed downtown.

Nicollet Island sits in the middle of the Mississippi River between downtown Minneapolis and the Saint Anthony Main area, which in the early twentieth century was the hub of the country's grain milling industry. Most of the old buildings had been converted into condos, restaurants, and hotels. The small island's streets were still cobblestone, and horse-drawn carriages carried couples around the area so they could pretend they were in love in the time of cholera.

Katie met Noah outside the inn's main entrance. Noah looked half concerned and half hopeful, as if Katie might tell him her life had fallen apart and he would be the beneficiary. She took that as an invitation, and hugged Noah before saying a word to him.

Noah held Katie and said, "Are you okay?"

She said, "Let's walk."

Walking paths lined both sides of the Mississippi and a series of bridges connected them over the big river. Katie led Noah southeast toward the Stone Arch Bridge, which was now reserved for pedestrians and cyclists only. You'd think there'd be no cyclists in late December and you'd be wrong. The area was crowded with pedestrians, runners, and cyclists, each mummified in down, wool, and fleece.

Katie didn't trust Jack, but she trusted Noah and she couldn't hold Bagman's secret by herself. It was too heavy. So she told Noah everything she'd heard while hiding in the cedar closet. He let her tell the whole story without interrupting even though he already knew that what Katie overheard from inside the closet escalated Rebecca Wong's death from tragedy to horror show.

She said, "So after your phone call this morning, all I can think is I'm married to a man who may have hired someone to kill a reporter who was about to expose him and his company to criminal liability. What do I do with that? Do I go to the police? Do I call the editors at *The Wall Street Journal*? Do I drive north and get my kids and continue up into Canada? I don't know who I can talk to or who I can trust."

The sun was out, but white flakes began to fall, blowing over from a cloud miles away. Noah said, "I think we should ask Makeena to meet us for lunch."

Katie nodded. "Thank you."

An hour later they slid into a quiet booth toward the back of Wilde Cafe and relayed the whole mess to Makeena. She listened patiently then removed a pen and small notebook from her purse and said, "Is Bagman one word or two?"

"One. But that's just a nickname. His real name is Adam Ross."

Makeena's questions continued. What years did he attend the University of Minnesota? Any other known friends in Minnesota? What did he look like? How old was he? What kind of car was he driving?

A few minutes later, Makeena said, "Be right back." She slid out of the booth and walked away.

"Thank you," said Noah.

"For what?" said Katie.

"For calling me. For sharing this with me."

Katie thought for a moment then said, "I feel bad about it."

"Why?"

"Because of what we said the other day. What we admitted. About being attracted to each other. I don't want to take advantage of that. I mean, that's not why I'm here. I'm here because you're smart and know people who can help me. Ugh. That sounds even worse. Like I'm using you. I just don't want you to misread the situation."

Noah smiled. "Me misreading the situation would be to think you made up some crazy story about your old college friend being a mobster *after* I called to tell you Rebecca Wong died in a car accident. All that so you would have an excuse to see me. Which you never need. You can just call and say, Hey, want to walk around the Mall of America? And I'd say, I hate the Mall of America but I'd be happy to walk around with you."

Katie exhaled. "Please don't say things like that."

"Like what?"

"Like nice. Don't be nice to me. You'll crush me."

"I don't want to crush you."

"Good."

"But I will be nice to you," said Noah. "I don't know how else to be around you."

Makeena returned and slid into the booth next to Noah. "I just spoke to a contact at the FBI. Your old friend, Adam, is telling the truth about one thing—the Ross family is a crime organization in south Florida. Just as Adam told Jack. Great-grandfather, grandfather, and his father were and are who Adam says they are. But he's lying about his involvement in the family business."

"He doesn't work for his father?" said Katie.

"Worse than that," said Makeena. "According to the FBI, Adam Ross doesn't exist."

CHAPTER 29

Katie looked from Makeena to Noah and then back to Makeena. She was sure she had misheard what Makeena said, but the expressions on both Noah's and Makeena's faces indicated otherwise. She needed to hear the words again. "What did you say?"

"Adam Bagman Ross," said Makeena, "does not exist. At least not legally. No birth certificate. No Social Security number. No internet presence."

"But . . . ," said Katie. "I went to college with him. The University of Minnesota must have a transcript and registration records."

"The FBI is checking with them but my guess is they won't find anything."

Katie looked dumbstruck.

Noah said, "How is that possible?"

Makeena said, "He probably went to college with false documents. Fake high school transcript. Fake driver's license. Fake Social Security number if they required one. He may have used a fake name, as well. At least officially. Do you remember seeing his student ID?"

"No."

"A name doesn't have to be off by much to hide in an institution as large as the University of Minnesota. Did you have any classes with Adam?"

"No," said Katie. "He was in General College. Jack didn't

have any classes with him, either. But what about after college? Wouldn't he have to have a real Social Security number to work?"

"Not if he worked for his family," said Makeena. "And if they only paid him in cash and he never filed a tax return, then the IRS wouldn't know about him."

"But he has to have a birth certificate," said Noah. "If they know who his parents are, can't they check hospital records in Florida?"

"Yes," said Makeena, "and they are. But it's possible he never received a birth certificate."

Katie felt her guts churn. This was getting weirder by the minute. "How?" said Katie. "How could that happen?"

"This is a guess," said Makeena. "Some people birth a baby at home and never report it. It could be for a number of reasons. They distrust the government. They're undocumented and fear getting deported. Or maybe they're trying to hide the birth for socially sensitive reasons. Like Adam's mother is not his father's wife."

"You mean a mistress?" said Noah.

"Possibly. Or the woman was a prostitute. Or an underaged girl. Or another member of the family. Then again, maybe Adam Ross isn't a Ross. Maybe he's just using the name as a cover and he has no relation to the Ross family."

"But someone must know the man living in Katie's house," said Noah. "He must have friends in Florida. And he has a car— they can run the plates."

"They will when we give them the plate number. The thing is . . . my contact said that it's possible Adam could be a missing puzzle piece for the feds."

"What does that mean?" said Katie.

"Usually when criminal organizations kill someone, it's as much about sending a message as it is ending a person's life. They want high-profile killings to dissuade others from stealing from them or infringing on their territory. But the enemies of the Ross family tend to die another way. They often meet their end because of an accident."

Katie pictured Rebecca Wong outside her house asking for Jack. She looked at Noah and said, "Like a car accident?"

"Exactly like a car accident," said Makeena. "Or a fire. Or choking on a piece of steak while eating alone at home. Or falling into a ravine during a hike. A hunting accident. A robbery gone bad. Drowning in their pool . . . The FBI has long suspected the Ross family has had an invisible hand in these deaths. But they've never been able to pin it on anyone. Most shooters keep a low profile, but they're known mob associates. But because Adam technically doesn't exist, that adds a whole other layer of covertness."

"My God," said Noah. "At least now the FBI knows where he is. They can just go pick him up and bring him in."

"Based on what evidence?"

Noah shook his head. "You're right. And I suppose they don't want to question him because that will scare him underground. But they can put him under surveillance."

"I hope they do," said Makeena.

"Wait," said Katie. "That's it? That's all they'll do? Adam lives in *my house*. With *my kids*."

"You can ask him to leave," said Makeena. "But the FBI has asked that you don't. Adam has lived his entire life under a cloak of invisibility. He has had the luxury of law enforcement never suspecting him of anything because law enforcement didn't know he existed. If you ask him to leave, he'll know something's up. That could scare the hell out of him and he'll disappear. Probably forever."

· CHAPTER 30 ·

After lunch, Katie went home to get her gear. Adam's car was not in the garage and Jack's, according to Jack, was up north. She went inside, changed into her ski clothes, loaded her equipment into the Volvo, and started down the block when she saw Terri Ackerman chipping ice off her driveway.

The majority of Minnesotans shoveled and mowed whether they could afford to pay someone else to do it or not. It brought them down to earth, and Terri Ackerman chipping away at her driveway that was wide enough for three cars did exactly that. Her giraffe neck and legs and gray eyes framed by long blond hair yielded to the humility of ice chipping. Terri was a goddess no more. She wasn't someone to be feared. She was someone to be dealt with. Head-on. Katie pulled into the Ackermans' driveway and got out of her car.

Terri looked up and smiled. "Hi, Katie. Going skiing?"

Katie stepped toward Terri. Walked right up to the boundary of Terri's personal space and then some. "I need to ask you a question, Terri. It's important."

"Of course. What's up?"

Katie hesitated. Sighed. Shut her eyes. And just said it. "Are you having an affair with Jack?"

"What?"

Katie was so prepared for a yes or a no, she didn't understand the meaning of Terri's answer. So she repeated the question. "Are you having an affair with my husband?"

Katie felt like she was about to get in a car accident. She could not stop her car nor could the other driver stop theirs. There would be a collision and there was nothing anyone could do about it. Time slowed. Almost stopped. Katie's life was about to change.

"No, Katie," said Terri, "I'm not having an affair with Jack. I'm not having an affair with anyone."

Katie studied Terri's face. No anger. No defensiveness. No patronizing pity.

Terri reached out her mitten and took Katie's hand. "Are you okay?"

Katie shook her head.

"I'm sorry," said Terri. "Come in for a cup of tea?"

Katie nodded.

At the Ackerman kitchen table, Katie told Terri about Jack's distance and unkindness and disappearances. She did not mention Adam Bagman Ross, Rebecca Wong, Noah Byrne, Makeena Chandler, or Electro-North 45. But it felt good to tell someone other than Noah and Makeena about Jack.

Terri listened with patience and kind eyes and said, "I can't tell you whether or not Jack is having an affair, but it sure sounds like your relationship is broken. When Richard and I started having problems, I spoke to friends. Not right away. It took a while because I was so ashamed, but eventually I opened up to people. And I am telling you, Katie, most of them understood what I was talking about because they had similar issues in their marriage. Or they empathized because they'd been sick. Or their spouse had been sick. Or they'd lost a pregnancy four months in. Or had career trouble. Or money issues. I don't know why but most of us want to hide those troubles. We don't want to bother anyone with our problems. It's such a Minnesotan thing to do. Stoic Scandinavians whether we're Scandinavian or not."

Katie sipped her tea and kept her eyes on Terri. "We really are fucked up, aren't we?"

"A marriage ending is terrible," said Terri. "If that's the way it goes for you and Jack, it will be sad. It's such an isolating feeling. Your person isn't your person anymore. The world feels cold and lonely and raw. But, for me at least, my pain has attracted others' pain. Even though my marriage is dying, new connections are blossoming. I know that's not why you came over today. You came over because you thought I might be involved in causing your pain. Taking your husband.

"I promise you, Katie. I have nothing to do with whatever's going on with Jack. I barely know him. I'm an open book. Come over anytime. Check up on me. You'll see I'm telling the truth. And the other truth is this: I'm glad you came over today regardless of the reason because I've always liked you, Katie. Always. But we've only had neighborhood time. It'd be nice to spend some one-on-one time. Just hang out. We don't have to talk about relationships. Or kids. Maybe we can ski together. I had so much fun at the Birkie last year. I'm signed up again for this year. Are you?"

"Yes," said Katie. "Definitely." She sipped her tea. "Training for it is the only thing keeping me sane right now."

"Anytime you're going, please let me know."

Katie had yet to let down her guard. Terri was so forthcoming, so open, so warm, it caught Katie by surprise. She tried to evaluate Terri's truthfulness and heard Kaleb's favorite saying in her head. *Search your feelings, Mom.*

Terri said, "What you smiling about?"

"Just thinking of something Kaleb says to me." Katie searched her feelings. Everything she knew about Terri Ackerman told her Terri was telling the truth. They were not close friends, but they had been to book club together, birthday parties, kids' parties, and had shared living space at the Birkie. There was a girls' trip to Chicago a few years back. Katie had seen Terri around food and liquor and money and shopping and men. Plenty of men because she magnetized them. And in all those situations

Terri had never acted in a way that called her character into question. "I'm going skiing right now," said Katie. "Please join me if you'd like."

Terri held up both hands, palms up, as if she were comparing weights. "Go skiing. Chip ice off the driveway. Go skiing. Chip ice off the driveway." She smiled. "I'll get my gear."

"Good," said Katie. "I'm looking forward to the one-on-one time. Our neighborhood friends are lovely—they really are—but these lives we live. They're so insular. Sometimes I walk away from our conversations not liking myself very much."

Terri nodded. "I know what you mean. The next few months are going to be hard for me. But I'm looking forward to going back to work full time. To living my life again. Not trying to avoid it."

"You're singing my song, sister," said Katie. She held up her mug of tea and Terri clinked it with hers.

· CHAPTER 31 ·

While Katie waited for Terri to change into her ski clothes, she called Elin.

"Is Daddy there?"

"Yes. Do you want to talk to him?"

"No. I just wanted to know if he'd made it yet. Is everything okay?"

"Everything's okay here," said Elin, "but you sound kind of weird."

"I'm fine, honey. One more question. Is Bagman up at the cabin?"

"Adam?" said Elin. "The dude who lives above our garage?"

"Do you know a lot of people named Bagman?"

"Ha, Mom. I thought sarcasm wasn't becoming of a young lady."

"I'm not young. Is he there?"

"No. Why would he be here?"

"No reason. Just promise me you'll let me know if he shows up."

"I promise."

"Thank you. Can't wait to see you tomorrow. May I talk to your brother, please?"

When Katie pulled into her garage after skiing, she saw Bagman's Lexus parked in its spot and felt both relief and fear. Relief that he was far from her children. Fear that he was close to her.

She considered backing out of the driveway and spending the night at a hotel, but she had to do what Jack had not—protect her children.

Katie went inside and dialed her friend Debra, who worked in HR at General Mills. "Hi, Debra. This is Katie. Sorry to bother you so close to the holidays, but do you have time for a quick question about my 401K."

"Sure. Ask away."

"Am I allowed to borrow a large sum of money from the account?"

"Ah. Well, this I know off the top of my head," said Debra. "People ask it all the time. You can withdraw any amount of money without penalty, but only for up to sixty days. You must repay the full amount withdrawn before then, otherwise you'll be taxed in your current income bracket."

"But if I take the money and return it before sixty days, no penalty?"

"That is correct."

Ten minutes later, Katie took a deep breath to calm her nerves and climbed the steps behind the house and knocked on Bagman's door. He answered wearing an apron and a smile.

"Katie! Nice to see you. Come on in."

This, thought Katie, from a man who legally did not exist. She entered as if she were visiting Bagman's home, not her own. She said, "I was hoping you had a few minutes to talk."

"For you? I got nothing but time. Can I offer you something to drink? Beer, whiskey, gin, vodka, bubbly water, orange juice—that's what I'm marinating tonight's skirt steak in—the acid breaks down the toughness. That and a little soy. Well, a lot of soy. I should have been a chef. A chef with a TV show. I'd be rich and famous and beloved by women all over the land."

"Yes, you would," said Katie with a forced smile, thinking that Adam was one hell of a domesticated criminal. She guessed he'd learned to take care of himself when laying low. That in Adam's life, there were periods of time that were too dangerous for him to dine out. So he learned to cook. To make his space comfortable. "And no thank you on the beverage offer. I'm good."

Katie had planned for this moment. She had two objectives. The first was to convince Bagman to leave. The second was to conceal that she had overhead the conversation in the basement. If what Bagman had said was true, if he really did work for his criminal father, and if what Makeena said was true, that not even the FBI knew of him, then he must have maintained his virtual invisibility by holding his secret close. Yes, Bagman and Jack were old friends. The best of friends twenty-some years ago, but it seemed odd to Katie that Bagman revealed his true occupation to Jack. More than odd—worrisome. Did that make Jack expendable? Did he feel the threat, too? Is that why Jack drove north? If so, how sweet it was of him not to protect his wife.

Katie said, "I hope this doesn't make you uncomfortable, Adam. But the reason I came up here is Jack told me you asked him for a loan."

Adam Bagman Ross poured orange juice into a gallon-size Ziplock bag then reached for the soy sauce. He opened the bottle and peeled off the governor so the liquid would flow freely. He said, "What exactly did Jack tell you?" He poured the entire bottle of soy sauce into the bag and looked up at Katie with cold, puffy eyes. Baleful eyes.

Katie steeled herself and said, "Jack told me things hadn't been going well with work and you have some expenses coming up and he's considering lending you a large sum of money. He asked what I thought, and I said, $300,000 is a lot of money, but you're our oldest friend. We wouldn't have met if it weren't for you. And that counts for a lot. Far more than money."

Katie could see relief on Bagman's face. Jack, apparently, had not told her the real reason Bagman wanted the loan. And Katie, apparently, was sympathetic to Bagman's plight.

"Yeah," said Bagman, removing long folds of skirt steak from a white paper wrapper. "I've had some bad luck lately. I don't expect you two to help me with such a big chunk of change, but what the hell, you know? I thought I'd ask. You've already been so generous letting me stay here. Above and beyond, you know? I'm indebted to you as it is."

"Not at all. It's our pleasure, Adam. The space is just sitting here. We're thrilled you can use it."

Bagman dropped the folds of beef into the marinade and sealed the bag. "You've always been kind, Katie. Since I met you. I was such a loose cannon in college. My East Coast vibrato rubbed the prim and proper Midwesterners the wrong way. But you, Katie. You've always been good to me. People like you are a rarity in this world." Bagman placed the bag in the refrigerator, propping it between a six-pack of beer and carton of milk so it wouldn't topple over.

Katie said, "I want to help, Adam. I'll get you the $300,000 in a few days."

Adam Bagman Ross shut the refrigerator door and turned to Katie with an expression she interpreted as suspicion. "Gee, Katie. If I didn't know you better, I'd think you were trying to get rid of me."

"No," said Katie. "I love having you here." Katie felt the lie in her gut. Heard it in her voice. Tasted it on her tongue.

"Uh-huh," said Bagman, unconvinced. "And you and Jack discussed this?"

"No."

"Then—"

"Adam, I don't know if you've noticed this, but Jack isn't the same man I married. He's selfish. He's distant. He loves the kids, I'm sure of that, but he has not put his family first. And he's pretty much put me last. He is not a generous soul. I want you to have the money. I know you'll pay it back when you can. Like I said, you should have it in a few days. You can count on it. So if you need to make arrangements to do whatever you need to do, you should go ahead and start that process."

Bagman opened the refrigerator again, removed a bottle of beer from the six-pack, and set it on the granite counter. "And Jack is just going to be okay with this?"

"Jack doesn't know about it and he's not going to. Not all of our assets are jointly held. I've been very fortunate, Adam. If I can't help my friends, what good is it?"

Bagman found a church key and opened the beer. He took a sip and said, "I think I'm okay now, Katie, but thanks for the offer."

Katie nodded. She didn't want to risk speaking, giving something away in her voice. Bagman's declination could mean a number of things, but one was obvious. Jack didn't lend Bagman the money. Jack *paid* Bagman the money. And now Rebecca Wong was dead. Katie felt an urge to run out of the guest quarters, get in her car, and drive away. But that would tip off Adam that she knew more than she was letting on. And that could be dangerous. Very dangerous. Instead, she swallowed her fear, took a breath, and said, "I'm surprised. The way Jack told it, you're in a tough spot."

"I was," said Bagman, "but it looks like I'm going to close a huge deal with a power plant in southeast Minnesota. It's going to cover me and then some. But thank you, Katie. Seriously. It means a lot."

He lies well, thought Katie. Either he lied to Jack or he was lying to her. Either way, he did so effortlessly. Katie felt her heart race. "Of course," she said. "Hey, I think I will take one of those beers."

"That a girl," said Adam, who retrieved another bottle from the refrigerator, opened it, and said, "Want a glass?"

"Don't insult me. I remember where I came from. All this . . ." She waved her hand with a flourish, indicating the house, ". . . is Jack. I'm just an innocent bystander." Katie raised her beer and said, "Congratulations on your big sale. Does this mean you'll be heading back to Florida soon?"

"I don't think so," said Adam. "It's nice being back in Minnesota. And I've just scratched the surface of the market here. Hope it's okay if I stay while I'm looking for a place of my own."

Ask him to leave, thought Katie. *Insist he leave.* "Of course," said Katie, acquiescing to the FBI's request that Adam stay put. "You're welcome to stay as long as you'd like." The FBI is right, thought Katie. Better to keep Adam close and friendly. Kicking him out of the house would do nothing to protect her. If he was who he claimed to be, who Makeena suspected he was, moving out would hardly be an obstacle for Adam Bagman Ross.

"Thank you," said Adam. "I appreciate it." He took a swig of beer. "But one thing, Katie, if you ever need to come in here, will you please ask me first?" Adam smiled but his eyes darkened. *How did he know?* thought Katie. Bagman laughed. "You never know—I could be entertaining a lady friend."

"Sorry," said Katie. "Jack's mother called to say she might have left a sweater here last time she visited. She can be, what's the nice way of saying it? Persistent. You weren't home so I just thought I'd take a quick look. I'll check with you next time."

Bagman smiled but his eyes said, *You'd better.*

· CHAPTER 32 ·

Katie returned to the main house minutes before hearing the doorbell. She opened the front door and saw her mother-in-law standing there and a silver Jaguar in the driveway.

Gwen Kuhlmann had bottled blond hair puffed and swirled into a force field atop her head. She was always dressed and bejeweled as if going to dinner at the Edina Country Club, where she chaired the membership committee and tore up the golf course during Ladies' Club on Thursday afternoons. Her husband, Jack's father, had died four years ago.

Despite Gwen's loud comforts, Katie liked her mother-in-law. She wished Gwen had raised Jack with more guidance. More of an appreciation that Jack was one person among billions rather than the most important person in a world of billions. Jack Kuhlmann could do no wrong in his mother's eyes even when he objectively had done wrong, like the time Jack burned down the family cabin in high school because he'd snuck up there with a girl and left with a fire burning in the fireplace and no screen to stop flying sparks. "Boys will be boys," Gwen said of the incident. She said something similar when Jack tried to speed across a patch of open water on a snowmobile. He didn't make it. The snowmobile sank to the bottom of the lake, and Jack would have drowned if not fished out by some buddies who stood by videotaping the stunt. "Well," said Gwen, "that's a curious mind at work. All the great scientists have curious minds." But despite

Gwen's blind spot for her boys, Katie found Gwen kind and loving and incredibly generous.

Which explained the armload of packages Gwen had carried from the trunk of her Jaguar to the front door.

"Katie! I'm so glad you're home."

"Gwen, you've outdone yourself. Here. Let me help you." Katie took a few packages from Gwen.

"Thanks, sweetheart. There are more in the car. I got Jack that stereo and record player he wants. They're awfully heavy. Maybe you could help with those."

Ten minutes later, the Christmas tree was surrounded by professionally wrapped gifts that crowded out Katie's and the kids' home-wrapped gifts like an invasive species. Katie and Gwen sat in the living room with glasses of San Pellegrino blood orange, cans of which they kept on hand for her visits.

"I hope you don't mind me stopping by unannounced," said Gwen, who always stopped by unannounced. "I'm on my way to the club and thought I might as well bring the presents over since Thomas was so kind to load them into the car for me."

Katie had no idea who Thomas was but guessed he might be a doorman at Gwen's condominium.

"And," said Gwen, after leaving a thick smear of lipstick on her glass, "I was hoping you'd be home, Katie, because I'd like to ask you a favor."

"Of course."

"My broker called and said I had to take a distribution before the end of the year and I do whatever my broker suggests because, well, she's done very well by me. Don handled all the money when he was alive, and I've just stayed the course. Anyway, my investments did quite well—I don't know how with all the socialists in our government now—it's a large sum and I won't live forever and to tell you the absolute truth, Katie, I still feel like a kid. So I thought while I'm still young and spry, I want to take my grandkids on a trip. Elin and Kaleb and their cousins."

"That sounds great. Of course you can take Elin and Kaleb. They'll love it."

"I think so, too. The favor is I'd like to take them in two days."

"Over Christmas?" said Katie. She had intended her words to come out as pure curiosity but heard dread in her voice.

"Yes. I know Christmas is family time, and you and Jack have your tradition, and I respect that, but I really am feeling the best I have in years thanks to Hector and Nancy."

"Who are Hector and Nancy?"

"Oh, didn't I tell you? Hector is my new trainer and Nancy is my new nutritionist. They really have done wonders for me and I just have a feeling now's the time to take this trip."

"But over Christmas? Couldn't you go the week after?"

"I tried, but Susan said it was all booked up."

"Who's Susan?"

"My travel agent," said Gwen. "She tried everything but said there was nothing available the week after Christmas. Susan also said if I wanted to give the kids a trip they'll remember forever, I need to do it right. We're going to Disney World, not Disneyland, because I'm not a California type of person, plus there's Epcot and Universal with Harry Potter World in Florida, which Susan says is better than the one in Hollywood. And Susan found us the most marvelous hotels and, well, the really special part is that there was no way at this late date I could book us all on the same flight in first class. You know I can't fly coach, darling, I've tried. It's not like it was when travel was classy, the way they just cram all of humanity back there and expect you to survive on a plastic cup of water.

"So we're going to fly private. I know, I know, it sounds extravagant and it is but it's so much fun. You just drive right up to the plane on the tarmac and get in. It costs a fortune, but I can't take it with me and the kids and I will have the most lovely time and I'd invite you and Jack and Dougie and Hope but the children will gravitate toward their parents if you're there and I want them to gravitate toward me. I'll be seventy-five in February and well, you never know how much time you have."

Katie knew Elin and Kaleb would love that trip—would indeed remember it for the rest of their lives. But over Christmas? Was she supposed to spend the holiday without her kids? Was she supposed to sit around the tree, opening presents and drinking eggnog with a houseguest who didn't legally exist and a husband who was hiding things from her?

"Gee, Gwen," said Katie, "the trip sounds so extravagant."

"I know, Katie, I know how it looks. Don't forget, I'm just a girl from the Iron Range. I come from humble beginnings like you. Did you know I was only nineteen when Jack's father spotted me on a fishing trip?"

"I have heard that, yes."

"He took me from the only world I knew. Of course, he was fifteen years older, and I wasn't accomplished on my own like you are. By the time I'd realized what happened, I had two children and lived in a house that had more rooms than I knew what to do with. But now I'm over fifty years into my new life. I'm used to it, and if you're not used to it, darling, you'll be used to it soon. So I'm asking you to indulge me on this dream trip with my grandchildren. Please."

Katie pictured spending Christmas without Elin and Kaleb and just the thought of it felt impossible. Elin, at twelve, had tried to hide her excitement for the holiday. As if she were trying to deny the child still in her, more conscious of how she appeared than how she felt. But Katie knew the child would break through and Katie would not witness that if Elin were in Florida. And Kaleb. He'd already told Katie he wanted to wake up *super early* to open presents. She told him no alarms on Christmas morning and Kaleb said he didn't need an alarm. He was going to drink a huge glass of water just before bed so he'd wake up to pee and then he'd be up and could open presents. And the morning routine of coffee and cinnamon rolls before opening presents. And scrambled eggs with Canadian bacon and fried diced potatoes. Katie could easily skip that tradition with Jack, but not with Elin and Kaleb. "I don't know, Gwen. It's such late notice."

"I understand. And I'm so sorry. I called up to the cabin on the drive over here and Jack and Dougie and Hope think it's a great idea."

Katie's heart sank. She'd been to that cabin a hundred times. It was lovely, but it was not a place you went for privacy. One big kitchen-great room with a gigantic TV and pool table where everyone hung out all the time because the bedrooms were down a separate corridor and just big enough to sleep in. Like dorm rooms. The place was designed for family time, together time, which meant at five o'clock on a December afternoon, when it was dark and everyone was in from sledding and snowshoeing and snowmobiling, the kids were almost certainly in the big room when Gwen called.

Katie said, "The kids know already, don't they?"

"That was not my intention, darling. It really wasn't. But the moment I brought it up with Dougie he announced it to the room. The kids screamed with delight. *Screamed.* Kaleb said it was going to be the best Christmas ever. Something about seeing stars at Disney World."

"I think it's Star Wars," said Katie.

"Oh. That makes sense."

Katie felt something she couldn't pinpoint. Her heart and her head were far apart, and the dissonance disoriented her. Then she recognized what she was feeling—it was relief. Spending Christmas without her kids (and even worse—just with Jack) should feel disastrous and heartbreaking but instead she felt relief. Why? And then it hit her: because the kids would be far more safe in Florida than around their gaslighting father and a maybe-maybe not hitman.

"The thing is," said Gwen, "I know what it's like to be a mother. So I know how hard it would be to not have your kids with you over the holidays. It's easy for Dougie and Jack to let them go. They're still boys themselves, in a way. Even with their tremendous success. But I want your and Hope's blessings. I just wouldn't be able to enjoy myself otherwise."

Katie smiled, "Of course you have my blessing, Gwen. The trip is very generous of you. The kids will have a wonderful time and never forget it."

The plan, Katie learned, was that Jack and Dougie and Hope and all the kids would return from the cabin tomorrow, spend one more night at home, then Gwen would pick them up the next morning in a limousine because *a limo will be so much fun.* Katie smiled and nodded and wondered, *How did my life get so far off track?*

· CHAPTER 33 ·

1988

It is supposed to be the best New Year's Eve ever for Katie Ecklund. The best ever because she is ten years old and has never stayed up until midnight before. Last year she tried but conked out at 10:30. This year she has a plan. She stayed up to ten o'clock last night and slept in this morning. She even tried to take a nap this afternoon, but her twin brothers, Neil and Blake, who are five, made that impossible when they decided to play Nerf basketball in the bedroom that the three of them share.

Katie doesn't realize what it means at the time, but her parents, Tim and Christi, never leave their kids at home with a sitter on New Year's Eve. When she'll look back on it years later, it will seem extraordinary because her parents were so young. This year, Tim and Christi are only twenty-nine. That means they haven't gone out on New Year's Eve since they were nineteen.

"Amateur night," Katie's father calls it.

Katie sniffles. "What does that mean?

"It means if you need a special day to go out and celebrate, maybe you don't have enough to celebrate in your everyday life. I have you and Mom and the twins. I don't need a day on a calendar to give me a reason to celebrate."

"Besides," says her mother, "who in the world is better to

celebrate the New Year with than you and Neil and Blake? I'll tell you who. No one."

Katie nestles between them and stares at the Christmas tree. It's a cheap tree, the kind with not as many branches and too many barren spots, but Katie has no idea. Her mother and father turned it just so in the stand so it looks full and balanced. They decorated it with chains made of colorful construction paper and strings of popcorn and tinsel and shiny ornaments they purchased at Kmart. The lights are different colors—Katie will be told years later by Jack and his mother that only white lights will do, multi-colored lights are garish—but Katie likes the different colors.

She loves to shift the focus of her eyes so the whole tree goes blurry. The lights quasar into stars like the Star of Bethlehem, which she knows about from picture books and Christmas specials on TV. Katie's parents aren't religious. Tim and Christi Ecklund are Reagan-era hippies, but Katie has no clue about that, either.

There is a TV in the corner with rabbit ears on top tuned to *Dick Clark's New Year's Rockin' Eve*. Only half an hour until it's the New Year in New York. Katie understands that doesn't count in Minnesota but it sure feels like it does. All those people celebrating in Times Square. There is no thought of turning the channel.

Neil and Blake have fallen asleep on the living room floor. Tim carries them into the bedroom one at a time and then returns to his wife and daughter, giving Katie some rare alone time with her parents.

"Any more thoughts about your bedroom in the basement?" says Christi.

Katie turns her back to her mother, literally not figuratively, an unspoken request for Christi to braid Katie's hair. Katie sniffles and says, "I think I want my room to be a bright color so it's not too scary in the basement. And please don't hang up any

shirts to dry in the laundry area because if I get up to go to the
bathroom and have to walk by them, they'll scare me."

"I think we can take all shirts down before bedtime. French
braid or regular?"

"French, please," says Katie.

"On one wall," says Tim, "I'll build in shelves and a desk for
you. You can pick the color of that, too. It's going to look like a
kitchen counter."

"That'll be cool," says Katie.

"And we'll put nightlights outside your room and on the stairs
so it's never totally dark. I'll start on it as soon as we get back
from Canada."

"I can't wait to have my own room. Neil and Blake are turning our room into a basketball court."

"You sound stuffed up, sweetie. Do you have a cold?"

"No," says Katie. "Definitely not."

Tim and Christi look at each other. Christi feels Katie's forehead and says, "Oh, sweetie."

"I'm not sick."

Tim pulls a tissue from the box on the coffee table, hands it
to Katie and says, "You know what to do."

Katie puts the tissue over her nose and mouth and makes a
raspberry sound.

"Nuh-uh," says Tim. "Blow for real."

Katie blows and says, "I'm not sick. I feel fine."

Christi takes the tissue from her daughter, looks at it and says,
"It's dark green. You're warm. You have a sinus infection."

"But I'm fine."

"You know what the doctor said," says Tim. "You can't fly
with a sinus infection."

"But I've never been on a plane before. It's not fair. Please don't
go without me."

Tim and Christi share another look and Christi says, "I'm

sorry, sweetie. The tickets are nonrefundable. And we're going ice-fishing. You're not crazy about doing that anyway. You'd be miserable."

"But I want to fly on a plane to Canada."

"We'll get you on a plane ride soon," says Christi. "I promise."

"To where?" Katie is sulking now. She pushes Christi's hand away. She no longer wants a French braid.

"I don't know where," says Christi. "But someplace fun. Maybe Chicago."

"What's in Chicago?"

"The Art Institute. The Museum of Science and Industry. Lake Michigan. We'll make it a special Mom and Katie trip. Or Dad and Katie trip. No Neil and Blake. What do you think of that?"

"I don't want to go to Papa and Grammy's tomorrow. It's so boring in Elba."

Tim says, "What if we got you that microscope?"

"You said we can't afford it. That's why I didn't get it for Christmas."

"But," says Tim, "when Papa and Grammy got us the fishing trip for Christmas, they included some spending money for each of us. Since you're not going to Canada, we could use your spending money to buy a microscope. We can buy it tomorrow. Then when you're in Elba you can explore the farm and find things to look at under the microscope."

Katie thinks about that. "I guess that'd be okay."

"And the Whitewater River doesn't freeze," says Christi, "because the water comes out of the ground. I bet if you collected some river water in a jar and put a few drops under the microscope you'll see living things in it."

"Yeah . . . But, please. Can't I just go with you on the plane?"

"The pressure could really damage your ears," says Christi. "And once you're in the plane, there's nothing we can do about it.

A plane can only land as fast as it can land. I'm so sorry, honey. It's a risk we can't take."

"This sucks," says Katie.

"Yeah, it does," says Tim. "But tomorrow, first thing, we'll pick up some antibiotics then get a microscope. Grammy and Papa will drive up to get you. You'll have fun. I promise. Oh, look, it's almost New Year's in New York. That means we have just over an hour. Want to set up a fort and sleep in it?"

"Neil and Blake will be mad if they wake up and we're all sleeping in a fort and they didn't get to."

"How about we build the fort," says Tim. "It'll be the biggest one ever. We'll use every blanket we have and take up the whole living room. We'll celebrate New Year's together and then, after midnight, I'll carry Neil and Blake into the fort. They'll wake up inside it tomorrow and be thrilled."

Katie nods. "I'll get my stuff."

Two days later, Katie sits in the guest room at her grandparents' farmhouse examining some dirt she excavated from under an overturned rock. She sees tiny beetles and wood lice and identifies them with a book that came with the microscope. She's flipping through that book in search of a long worm-like creature when she hears her grandmother wail then scream, "No, no, no, no!"

Katie looks out the bedroom window. A police car is parked in front of the farmhouse. She has no idea what that might mean.

She cries for three days straight. Cries until she has nothing left inside. The fishing lodge sent a van to the airport in Winnipeg. On the way between the airport and lodge, the van hit a patch of black ice, skidded across the highway's centerline and crashed head-on into a logging truck. None of the nine passengers in the van, nor its driver, survived.

Katie Ecklund will live with her paternal grandparents in Elba, Minnesota, from age ten to eighteen. Elba is a speck of a town in Winona County east of Rochester. Winona County is unlike the rest of the state. Long ago, the glaciers drifted south, flattening most of Minnesota, gouging the land here and there to dig a crater for one of its ten thousand plus lakes. But not in Winona County, the one corner of Minnesota where the glaciers never ventured. Rivers and spring creeks carved the land into valleys bordered by limestone bluffs, leaving hills covered in maples, oaks, cottonwoods, and spruce. The land on top is flat and farmed, but water doesn't hold there. It runs downstream where it joins the spring creeks and rivers, running alongside towns like Elba, eventually making its way to the Mississippi River near La Crescent.

Her grandparents are in their early fifties when Katie lives with them. They reside on a hobby farm, but both make their living teaching high school. Academically, Katie rockets ahead of the other kids her age. She devours books, mathematical concepts, anything they put in front of her. Knowledge is an anesthetic for Katie. As long as she keeps learning she can stave off pain. It never goes away completely, and creeps back up and blindsides her sometimes. Knocks her down for a whole week. But the pain eases as she grows older.

Her grandparents also teach Katie to cross-country ski. They are avid skiers, hikers, and campers, and take Katie on trips to Colorado and Montana. But mostly, Katie develops her skiing skills and fitness in Elba, ascending from the river-cut gouges to the farmland on top.

Katie Ecklund dedicates her life to living for her parents, Neil, and Blake. If they can't live, she will live for them. She is the best student and Nordic skier at her high school. Her understated personality and humility make her well-liked, but she socializes little—not because she doesn't want friends but because their families remind Katie of what she's lost. She becomes a National Merit Scholar and accepts a full ride to Carleton College. Katie has other offers, but the idea of leaving Minnesota feels like she'd be abandoning her memories. At Carleton, she continues to excel academically and athletically.

She transfers to the University of Minnesota after her second year to attend a major research institution and to ski Division I. She wants friends in college more than she had wanted them in high school, but her social skills have atrophied. She spends more time alone than she wants to. That changes in November of her first year at the University of Minnesota. While attending a hockey game, a boy approaches Katie. He carries a cardboard tray that holds three cups of beer. It is Adam Bagman Ross, and he points out his friend, Jack.

· CHAPTER 34 ·

Gwen left with her heart full of joy and her eyes twinkling with the expectation of flying her grandkids to Florida. Her car was empty of presents, while Katie's living room was full of them.

Katie knew that as a child, if she'd seen what her life would become, the house she lived in, the spectacle of material wealth, the opulence in which she lived, she would have said something like *lucky*. And she was lucky. Beyond fortunate. She had a life most people dreamed of. Not only dreamed of, but struggled for, fled their homelands for. Katie had everything, well, almost everything. She did not have a good marriage. Not anymore.

The marriage used to be good, thought Katie. Or had it only felt good because life was moving forward the way she had assumed it was supposed to? Katie had found Jack. Together, they built a life. Created a family. Helped each other so each could focus on their careers. They bought a house. And then another house. And then remodeled and added on to the second house. It was only when everything seemed in place—the kids, the house, the cars, the careers, the vacations—that the marriage waned.

Or had the marriage just revealed its true nature without the distraction of pursuit? Maybe it had never been good, thought Katie. Maybe she had deluded herself. Would Katie trade the big house on Browndale for a good marriage? Absolutely. Would she trade the nice cars? No doubt. The trips she'd taken to Italy and the Galápagos Islands? In a second.

She would trade those things for a good marriage, not because marriage is everything, but because living in a bad marriage is living a lie. She would trade all she had to live an honest life. To Katie, marriage was important. She had grown up around happy marriages. Whole marriages. True partnerships. First with her parents and then with her grandparents. Nests of support and emotional safety. What she had now with Jack felt unstable, unsafe, intolerable. It was a lie and she could feel that lie in her body and wondered if it was the kind of dishonesty that could make a person mentally or even physically ill.

She wondered if Jack had ever loved her. Was her twenty-year-old self capable of knowing if the handsome boy who said he loved her actually did love her? Was Katie, at twenty, able to discern romantic love?

Katie gathered the shopping bags Gwen had used to bring the presents over and took them into the garage to put them in the recycling. She was surprised to see she'd left her garage door open. *Where is my head?* she wondered. She was about to push the button to close it when she saw something bright and red on the driveway, like a bandana. She walked toward it and saw it wasn't a bandana. A male cardinal lay motionless, its neck cocked at an odd angle. It was completely red other than the black mask around its eyes and under its beak, which was also red.

Cardinals were one of the few birds not to migrate south in winter. They lived in the boughs of pine trees and frequented bird feeders. The male's bright red feathers looked Christmassy against the green pines. The cardinals' presence was, to Katie, a jewel in the crown of winter.

"Shit," said Katie. She went inside, found a plastic grocery bag, and returned. Katie placed her hand in the bag and picked up the dead bird. It was still warm.

"Hey, Katie. What are you doing?"

Katie looked up and saw Sandra Dahlstrom walking by. "Just picking up a dead bird."

"What happened?"

"I don't know. I found it on the driveway. The poor thing must have flown into a window."

"Shouldn't Jack be picking it up? Isn't that what husbands are for?"

"I can manage. Thanks."

Sandra said, "Are you okay?"

"Yeah. It's just a dead bird."

"You sure?" said Sandra. "You seem . . . down."

"Not a good day," said Katie, "but I'll be okay. Thanks."

"Call me if you want to talk."

Katie thought of inviting Sandra in but decided she wanted alone time. She said, "I will. Thanks."

Sandra continued on her walk. Katie tied the bag's handles, entombing the cardinal, its red body visible through the translucent white plastic. She took it to the garbage, opened the lid and stopped herself from dropping it in. She didn't want to leave it on top. If Kaleb or Elin saw it they'd be devastated. She picked up a bag of kitchen garbage to bury the cardinal underneath.

That's when she saw it.

The duct-taped bag that Katie had seen stashed behind the driver's seat in Bagman's Lexus. His car was in its stall. Katie placed the bird into the garbage, looked back to make sure no one was watching, then removed the duct-taped bag and threw it in her car.

"Katie."

Katie whipped around to see Bagman standing in the driveway.

CHAPTER 35

"Adam . . . ," said Katie. She had no idea if he'd seen her pull the duct-taped bag from the garbage.

Adam said nothing. He just stared at her with dull eyes and no smile. "Did I interrupt something?"

"No," said Katie. "Of course not. What would you be interrupting?"

Adam took a deep breath and said, "I'm headed out. And sorry. Didn't mean to scare you."

"You didn't."

"Something did. If you don't believe me, look in a mirror."

"Oh. Yeah, well, I just found a dead bird in the driveway. That's what I was doing. Throwing it in the garbage."

"Uh-huh. Hey, do you know where Jack is?"

Katie knew exactly where Jack was. Two hours north at his brother's cabin. With Elin and Kaleb. "Probably at the office. He said he has fires to put out at work."

"I bet he does." Bagman looked tired. The Minnesota winter did not help his appearance. His Florida tan had faded to something pallid. The bags under his eyes seemed to have grown. And it looked like he'd gained more weight. Then, as if controlled by a switch, Adam smiled and his eyes sparkled. Maybe that was Adam's real talent, thought Katie. Maybe that's how he gained people's confidence. He had always been an easy person to be around, even when he was a mostly drunk disaster all those years ago.

"For what it's worth, Katie, your husband is a weak man. A small man."

Though it probably wasn't Bagman's intention, Katie felt seen. Heard. Appreciated. But she said, "I'm surprised to hear you say that. You two used to be best friends."

Adam opened his car door and sat in the driver's seat. "We were. Who's to say why people become friends? For me and Jack, we lived on the same floor in the dorm freshman year. We both hated our roommates and gravitated toward each other. I'll be honest. I was no hero back then. There were a lot of perks to being friends with Jack Kuhlmann. He was a rich kid who grew up on Lake Minnetonka and had a cabin up north. He attracted girls so they were always around. I mean, I grew up with money, too. But it was different. Less classy. It felt good when Jack welcomed me into his world."

Adam pushed the button on his visor, and the garage door behind his car lifted with a whisper.

"So why do you think he's a small man?" said Katie.

"One of the reasons I stayed out of touch so long is because, as I got older, I realized Jack liked hanging out with me because he could dominate me. He saw me as some putz from Florida. I didn't talk right. I didn't dress right. I didn't know anything about Minnesota. I was there because the University of Minnesota had the General College back then—it was the only school I got into. Jack had total control in the friendship. I needed him and he knew it. Sometimes he was an asshole to me. Really mean. And I just took it because who else did I have? No one."

Katie said, "I'm sorry. That must have felt horrible."

"You know what it feels like, Katie. Jack did the same to you. You're ten times smarter than Jack and me put together. But when you met Jack, you were broken. And he knew he could step in and be your savior. I mean, I didn't understand it at the time. I didn't realize it until years later. Jack's an exploiter. He feeds on those who are weaker. He's not as smart as his father was. Or his brother is. He also doesn't have their work ethic. So that's how he compensates. Jack's one of those assholes who gets born rich and because of it thinks he deserves to be rich. No appreciation. No respect. And you and I were both victims of it."

Katie wanted to dismiss what Adam was saying but couldn't. It was true. All of it. But who wants to think such things about their partner in life? The father of their children? No one. Katie overlooked the ugly truth about Jack. Overlooked it for nearly twenty-five years even though she knew in her heart Jack was just as Adam described him. Selfish. Arrogant. Exploitive. Now would she ever be able to see Jack any other way?

Then a thought came to Katie uninvited. This was the first time Adam had expressed anything negative about Jack. But it wasn't just negative. It felt like hate—long steeped hate—and Katie couldn't help but wonder if Adam had come to kill Jack. Her mind skipped along a dark path: Jack doing who knows what to finance his failing business. Jack in over his head with the wrong people. Adam Bagman Ross arrives as an old friend and house guest. All that cooking in the guest suite. Was it all just a long preamble to an accident? A fire on the stove? A short in the electrical system? Was Bagman just biding his time until the right moment presented itself?

Adam started his car, shut the door and rolled down his window. He slowly backed out of the garage, and Katie walked alongside him. As Kaleb often suggested, she searched her feelings and knew what Adam said was true—he hated Jack. And Adam believed Katie had reason to hate Jack, too. Adam just put into words what Katie had known all along.

When the car was out of the garage, Adam stopped and said, "Jack thinks he has the upper hand with you because his inherited wealth and his big job gave you this house. This life. He doesn't realize that you don't care about this. He doesn't understand that all you care about is family. It's the thing that makes you tick. Which is totally understandable. And admirable. Now that you have Elin and Kaleb, you don't really need him anymore, do you?"

"You make me sound like a spider."

"I'm not saying that. I'm saying I see you with your kids and I see *love*. I see *family*. They are your antidote to your personal tragedy. Not Jack. He's made himself obsolete."

A cold wind blew. Was Adam justifying killing Jack? Is that what this conversation was about? Katie fingered her necklace and although she already knew the answer she said, "So you think Jack didn't love me in college? He just loved playing *rescue Katie* so I'd feel obligated to him?"

Bagman shrugged. "That's one guy's opinion." He smiled. Again, like he flipped a switch. "One guy who has never been married and never had a relationship last longer than six months. I tell ya, I have the emotional intelligence of a grapefruit. So take that into consideration when I flap my lips about people. Hey, what is so special about your snowflake necklace? You've worn it since I met you."

Katie smiled. "It's not a snowflake."

"Looks like a snowflake. Or a coronavirus."

"Not that, either."

"You're not going to tell me what it is?"

"We all get to keep a few secrets."

"Fair enough," said Bagman. "Well, I'm off to meet some people. See you later." Adam rolled up his window, disappeared behind the tinted glass, and backed out of the driveway.

Katie walked into the garage and closed the two opened garage doors. She opened her car and removed the plastic bag sealed in duct tape. She ripped it open and found a man's dress shirt soaked with blood. At least she thought it was blood. The plastic had kept it from drying. Katie pinched one section of the stain. It felt sticky. She held up the shirt and shook it out. It was large. Big enough to fit Adam Ross. Katie's stomach felt like it was trying to escape through her mouth.

CHAPTER 36

Katie returned the shirt to the ripped-open plastic bag, went inside and resealed all of it in a new kitchen garbage bag.

Bagman's assessment of Jack and why Jack had befriended him and courted Katie rang so true the bell was still vibrating. And yet, that insight had come from Adam, a mobster at best and a possible hitman. How could Katie trust him? How could she trust a man who kept a bloody shirt in the back of his car then tried to bury it in the family garbage bin. She couldn't. She knew she couldn't. But what Adam had said shook something loose in Katie. Maybe that something was all the bullshit in the name of Jack Kuhlmann. She wanted the truth.

Katie felt a primal urge to get out of that house. Tomorrow the kids would return. She couldn't stand being there another minute until they did. She called Noah.

"I know it's last minute, but are you by any chance free for a drink?"

"I'm supposed to meet a friend for a drink but I'll cancel that. Where would you like to go?"

"A friend?"

"It was going to be a first date," said Noah. "I wasn't excited about it. Just thought I should get out on a Saturday night."

"Go on the date," said Katie. "I'll do some shopping and if you don't fall in love at first sight, we'll meet later."

"And if I do fall in love at first sight?"

"Then I'll be happy for you."

"You're a kind person, Katie Kuhlmann."

Katie grabbed Adam's bagged bloody shirt and left. She loathed to return to the Mall of America with its crowds just before Christmas but both kids had grown since the summer and she worried their current warm-weather clothing wouldn't fit for their trip to Florida. It was hard to find bathing suits in December and the Mall of America had a specialty store. She also shopped at the Columbia store for shorts and T-shirts and sandals. Early Christmas presents for their trip to Florida.

The clerk rung it all up and said, "I'm sorry. Your credit card has been declined. Happens a lot this time of year."

"Odd. There's no balance on that card."

"It might have been declined just because you're shopping here," said the clerk. "When thieves steal credit cards, a lot of them come straight to the Mall of America. I think the credit card companies are super sensitive about anything purchased in this mall."

"Try this one," said Katie, handing the clerk a different card.

The clerk ran Katie's new card. "All good. Went through no problem."

The clerk bagged the kids' clothing. Then Katie stepped out of the store and called the declining credit card company. She waited in the phone queue while shopping at two more stores until a representative came on the line.

"Mrs. Kuhlmann, the reason the purchase was declined is because the card is over its limit."

"Then there must be some sort of fraud—we pay off this card every month."

"It is the holiday season. Maybe someone in your family made a large purchase."

"A $25,000 purchase?"

"I can check if you'd like."

Katie considered whether or not she wanted to know if Jack

had run up the credit card or if it was fraud. When they purchased gifts for each other, they used individual credit cards. Not that all money wasn't joint money—it was—but using their individual cards, accounts they'd carried since before marrying, preserved the surprise of gifts. So why would Jack buy her something extravagant with a joint card? He wouldn't. Joint cards were for family expenses. Things for the kids. Groceries. Trips. The card being maxed out had to be fraud.

"Yes," said Katie, "I'd like to know what's maxed out our card."

"One moment, please . . ."

Katie shopped at one more store before the representative came back on the line.

"Actually, Mrs. Kuhlmann, it wasn't a purchase. Jack Kuhlmann took a cash advance for the available balance of the card."

"When?" said Katie. It didn't come out sounding like a question. It came out like a dog's bark.

"This morning," said the representative. "Is there anything else I can help you with?"

Katie went to one more store. Nordstrom. There she purchased an overnight bag and some items to fill it. She would not go back to the house until Elin and Kaleb were there.

Holiday traffic clogged the freeway, which had slowed to an endless snake of red taillights. The Mall of America was close to the airport, so the buildings nearby were also topped with red lights, and though the scene was nothing more than heavy traffic, commerce, and safety precautions for air travel, the slow pace and lights and fields of snow around the tarmac felt festive. Katie loved this time of year, when winter and the holidays wrestled away all power, and she had to yield to their forces. It freed her of responsibility, just in small moments, and that freedom felt like relief.

Katie let her mind wander. The last days she spent with her parents and brothers were between Christmas and New Year's.

And yet she still loved this time of year. Perhaps that's *why* she loved this time of year. The lights. The music. The glitter and wrapping paper. She associated those things with her most vivid memories of them.

She was not paying attention to the vehicles around her. She paid attention to the flow of traffic and drove safely, but not to the individual vehicles. There wasn't much to see other than head-lights, taillights, and the blinkers of those changing lanes. Katie did not see the van that pulled next to her. She didn't see that it was faded to a dull green and splotched with patches of rust.

The Lumineers played on the car stereo. Katie turned up the volume on "Angela" and, between the booming chorus and the Volvo's soundproofing, Katie didn't hear the first pop. She didn't hear the second pop, either, nor the third. It wasn't until she heard the first boom that she looked to her right and saw the van burst into flames. The other cars and trucks moved away, but Katie found herself pinned near the van. Then the booms and bangs erupted like a heavy metal drum solo. Traffic scattered. Katie gunned her station wagon into an opening and was thirty feet away when the van exploded. She felt the back end of the car lift off the ground before returning with a crash, the shocks bottoming out and the rear window shattering into a million pieces and falling in the telltale pebbles of tempered glass.

· CHAPTER 37 ·

1989

Tim, Christi, Neil, and Blake Ecklund fly in cargo from Winnipeg to Minneapolis-St. Paul airport a few days after being pronounced dead on arrival at a rural Manitoba hospital. Katie's grandfather, Rolf Ecklund, meets the bodies at the airport. He grew up in Elba, Minnesota, the tiny town just north of Whitewater State Park, the town in which he still resides. Elba is a tight-knit community, and learning of the deaths, the fire department volunteered to transport the bodies from MSP to Elba, a two-hour drive southeast.

It has been three days since ten-year-old Katie lost her parents and brothers. Her sinus infection has ebbed, beaten down by antibiotics and grief. Katie's grandparents, both high school teachers, have surrounded her with counselors and therapists. They do not ease her pain—that's impossible—but give her broken heart a chance to function the way a well-set broken bone can function.

Katie's grandparents do not stop with counselors and therapists. Rolf teaches history, and often brings speakers into his classroom to supplement the textbooks and memoirs with living history. Among them: a Holocaust survivor, a Vietnamese woman who came to Minnesota as a young girl in 1975 after losing her entire family in the war, and a wife and mother of a man and two sons who were lynched in Texas in the 1960s. Rolf contacts all three, and all three travel to Elba at their own expense to sit and talk with ten-year-old Katie.

Ella and Rolf Ecklund give Katie an arsenal of coping tools, except for one. On the day before the funeral, when Rolf and Ella are busy preparing for a gathering at the house, accepting deliveries of food and flowers, meeting with the funeral director and the cemetery people, Katie comes down from her bedroom and approaches her grandparents, who sit at the kitchen table going over documents.

"I want to see them," says Katie.

Rolf looks up and says, "What, honey?"

"I want to see Mom and Dad and Neil and Blake."

Katie and her grandparents decided the bodies should be buried in Elba since Katie will be living there until she moves away. That way, she can visit them whenever she wants.

"What do you mean, sweetheart, by see them?" says Ella.

"I want to see their faces and bodies. I want to see them to say goodbye."

There is a knock on the kitchen door. The junior pastor of the Lutheran church enters to discuss the eulogies because the senior pastor is away leading a bible study cruise in the Mexican Riviera. The junior pastor is in her late twenties, blond with soft features and kind eyes.

"We'll be with you in a moment, Marilee," says Ella. "Do you mind waiting in the living room?"

"Not at all," says Marilee, who offers Katie a warm, sad smile before continuing into the living room.

Ella turns back to her granddaughter. "Katie, dear. We think it's best if we don't view their bodies."

"Why?"

"Because, honey," says Rolf, "their bodies are not your mom and dad and brothers. They're just bodies. Like shells. Their souls have left. The people we love so much are not in there anymore, and we don't want to remember their empty shells. We want to remember their smiles and laughter and voices."

"But then how do I say goodbye?" says Katie.

"Well," says Ella, "I am choosing not to say goodbye. Because they are no longer living in their bodies, but they are living in here." Ella places her hand over her heart. "And in here." She touches her forehead. "And I want them to stay alive in me as long as I am alive. That way I don't have to say goodbye. I can carry them with me wherever I go."

Katie thinks about this then says, "So I can't see them?"

"We think it's better if you don't," says Rolf. "You can understand that, can't you?"

Katie cannot understand that, but she nods anyway. She goes up to her room, sits down with her microscope and looks at a slide of water she scooped from the Whitewater River. There are living things in it, small organisms, but there are dead things, too. Katie thinks that even though they're dead, that doesn't mean they aren't real. Or count any less than the living things—they, too, lived once.

Her grandparents have been so good to her. Katie doesn't understand why they won't let her see her family one last time. But she is only ten years old. What can she do? She starts to make a list of reasons why she should get to see them. She'll present it to them before the gathering. *1) They're my parents and my brothers so it should be up to me. 2) I'll never forget them being alive so seeing them not alive won't make my memories go away. 3) . . .*

Katie hears a gentle knock on her door. She hides her list in a desk drawer and says, "Come in." She expects to see Grammy or Papa, but her guest is neither.

"Hi, Katie. I'm Pastor Marilee from the church. Do you have a moment?"

"I guess," says Katie, who has talked to so many people already.

She doesn't love the conversations, but always feels better after. Maybe Pastor Marilee, whom she's never met before, has dead parents or siblings. It seems everyone has something like that to share with her.

Pastor Marilee enters and shakes Katie's hand. "I was wondering if you're up for a walk. Just you and me."

"Are you going to talk about God?"

Pastor Marilee smiles. "Do you want me to talk about God?"

Katie shrugs. "You can if you want."

"I might want to do that. But I want to talk to you about something else just as important."

"Why do we have to do it on a walk?" says Katie.

"I find that when you're walking with a person but not looking at them all the time because you're looking at the buildings and trees and people in town, sometimes it's easier to talk. That's how I've had some of my best conversations. Have you ever experienced that?"

Katie thinks. She's had good conversations while walking. And also while riding in the car. But she doesn't want to think about cars. A car is what killed her family. She says, "If it's okay with Papa and Grammy, then sure, I'll go."

Ella and Rolf think it's an excellent idea, and a few minutes later, Katie and Pastor Marilee, both wearing coats, hats, mittens, and winter boots, head out the back door for their journey through the small town.

Marilee tells Katie she grew up in Rochester about an hour away. And that she went to college at Bethel University in Saint Paul.

"I go to Saint Paul sometimes," says Katie. "Once on a field trip to see the state capitol. Once to the Ordway Theater to see a play. I think I've been there some other times, too, but I can't remember. Is that what you want to talk about? Saint Paul? Because that's about all I know."

"No, Katie. I have a confession to make to you."

Katie thinks she knows what that means, but isn't sure.

Pastor Marilee picks up on that because she says, "A confession is when you tell the truth about something. Usually something you did or thought and maybe you weren't supposed to."

"Like you did something bad?"

"Sometimes, yes. Or sometimes you did something that some people think is bad, but you don't."

"And you want to tell me about it?" says Katie, who all of a sudden sounds interested.

"I do. If that's okay with you."

"Sure," says Katie, who now has a spring in her step.

"The thing I want to confess to you is that when I came over today, and your grandmother asked me to wait in the living room—"

"Yeah?"

"Well, I kind of eavesdropped on your conversation."

"Eavesdropped?"

"Spied. I listened to what you talked about."

"Oh."

They arrive at a small city park. Katie walks toward the swings. She sits on one, and Pastor Marilee sits on the swing next to her. "And I'm wondering if it's okay if we discuss what I heard."

Katie likes Pastor Marilee. She asks Katie's permission a lot and isn't bossy like most adults she knows. "Sure," says Katie. "We can talk about that."

"One of the reasons I wanted to go for a walk and talk is because I didn't want to tell you this in your grandparents' house. They are lovely people. Smart and kind and generous. We're lucky to have them in Elba. And although it might not seem like it right now, you're lucky to have them, too."

Katie nods.

"But, I don't agree with them about you seeing your parents' and brothers' bodies."

Katie wipes a tear off her cheek and says, "You don't?"

"No. I mean, it's true, their souls aren't in their bodies anymore. But their bodies represent their souls, and I think you're right about wanting to say goodbye. I think it would help you. In a lot of cultures and religions, after a person dies, their body stays at home for a day or two. That way the family can spend time with it to say goodbye."

Katie nods and says, "I want to say goodbye."

"And I want to make that happen for you."

"You do?"

Pastor Marilee turns her swing toward Katie, the chains crossing overhead. "Your parents and brothers are in the church basement right now. Sometimes the funeral home brings them the day before the funeral—we have a special room down there. And if you'd like, we can go there right now and see them."

Katie considers Pastor Marilee's offer. Does she really want to see her parents and brothers dead? Will it be too scary? Will they be all smashed up from the accident? It will be hard, no doubt. Katie can't understand why, but she has to see the bodies. She just has to. She turns her swing toward Pastor Marilee and says, "I want to see them. If you'll go with me."

The room in the church basement has cinder-block walls painted white and a ceiling made of wooden boards. The light comes from misfit lamps that look like they belong nowhere else but the room with the dead bodies. Some have shades. Some have naked bulbs. The floor is made of linoleum squares, a gold and maroon checkerboard.

It's cool down there, like being inside a refrigerator. And dead quiet.

Four caskets, two large, two small, rest on stout tables made of raw oak. Katie feels her heart pound. She begins to tremble and cry.

Pastor Marilee puts a hand on top of one of the small caskets and says, "Maybe this is enough, Katie, just to see the caskets. You can say goodbye to them with the lids closed."

Katie lets her tears fall and shakes her head. "I want to see them."

"Do you want to hold my hand?"

"No thank you."

Pastor Marilee walks to the big casket on the end. "Are you ready?"

Katie nods.

Pastor Marilee lifts the lid. Tim Ecklund lies still, wearing jeans and a flannel shirt, his skin gray like granite, his face bruised with splotches of dark purple. His hands, also granite, rest at his sides. Katie steps toward the casket. Her father is impossibly still. Her grandparents were right—Tim Ecklund is no longer in his body. But Pastor Marilee was right, too. The body is a representation, and seeing it helps Katie. Her fear fades. She says, "Goodbye, Daddy. Thanks for being the best. The best ever." She reaches forward, drawing her hand near her father's face, and grazes his cheek with the tip of her index finger. Touching his cold, paper-like skin is all Katie needs to confirm he isn't in there. She nods toward Pastor Marilee, who closes the lid.

They repeat the process with her mother and brothers, each wrenching a new level of sorrow out of Katie, but each also confirming that they are gone. It feels extra hard for Katie to see her brothers because they were so full of life and also because she's seen them sleeping a thousand times. It looks like they should be sleeping in their small, wooden boxes. But it isn't sleep. It isn't anything.

Katie and Pastor Marilee walk back to the house exchanging

few words. Katie feels distant, as if some part of her has gone off in search of her family's souls. She will learn, in time, she cannot do that—she'll have to wait for them to come to her. And they do in moments when Katie doesn't expect them. She hears her mother's voice, her father's laughter, the shrieks and screams of Neil and Blake. Her grandmother was right when she said Tim, Christi, Neil, and Blake will reside inside Katie and be very much alive.

When Katie and Pastor Marilee arrive back at the house, Katie says, "Are you doing the funeral tomorrow?"

"Yes."

"That's good."

Pastor Marilee smiles. "I'm glad you think so."

Katie lies in bed that night thinking about her walk with Pastor Marilee and their time in the church basement. Even at ten years old, she gleans a lesson that will serve her for the rest of her life. When she feels strongly about something, like she did about seeing her parents' and brothers' bodies, she has to pay attention to that feeling. She has to trust that voice in her head.

· CHAPTER 38 ·

The van that had pulled up next to Katie on the freeway exploded in a span of seconds, and it wasn't until Katie put some space between her and the van that fear seized her muscles and organs, as if she'd been dropped into ice water and the cold immobilized her.

She managed to look back and saw the van engulfed in flames like a roasting marshmallow left to burn. She felt its heat through her vacant rear window frame, wondered if anyone was still inside but couldn't see beyond the smoke. Katie considered pulling over—the police would be looking for witnesses. But she continued forward on the freeway, the wind roaring outside her missing window as she accelerated away. A glance in the rearview mirror told her no other cars were on fire, or at least none she could see.

The Volvo's screen indicated Katie had a text from Noah. She touched the screen and the robotic voice read: *It was far from love at first sight. Where to for a drink?*

She was about to respond when the thought entered her mind: Was the exploding van meant for her? Katie hesitated, looked at her overnight bag on the passenger seat floor, and said, "The Freehouse on Washington in an hour." Katie didn't care who saw her with Noah Byrne. Next she called Makeena, asked if she could drop something off, and did so. Makeena took the bagged, bloody shirt, and said she'd get it to her contact at the FBI.

Katie and Noah met at the restaurant full of twenty- and

thirty-somethings and massive stainless steel fermenter vessels. She told him about her conversation with Adam, the exploding van, the bloody shirt and speculated on whose blood it might be and why Adam buried it in the trash. They laughed about Noah's terrible date.

"It's amazing," said Noah, "that a person no longer talks to their parents, their siblings, or their children, and she somehow doesn't realize she's the problem."

They were halfway into their second cocktails when, out of the blue, Katie said, "I'm done with Jack. It's over." She looked for Noah's response. He gave nothing away except in his eyes, which shined like polished stones. "I'll tell him as soon as the kids get on that plane to Florida."

Noah's eyes dropped.

"What?"

Noah looked up and said, "It may not be that simple."

"Sure, it is," said Katie. "He can't stop me from leaving. He's not the Taliban." Katie half smiled at her joke, an attempt to counter Noah's uncharacteristic melancholy.

"I don't mean it's not that simple legally," said Noah. "Of course you can leave. I just wonder . . ." Noah looked down at his drink.

"You just wonder what?"

"Maybe that van blowing up next to you on the freeway wasn't an accident."

"What do you mean?" But Katie knew what Noah meant. She'd had the same thought.

"I'm not implying someone was trying to hurt you. From the way you describe what happened, it sounds like the blast wasn't big enough to cause concussive damage. It didn't take out any other cars. If any kind of shrapnel had been used, people would have died. But Jack or Jack and Adam might be trying to scare you. To knock you off your game."

"Why would they want to do that?"

"My guess is Jack regrets telling you about the falsified data at Electro-North 45. He probably chose the lesser of two evils because telling you took the heat off his strange disappearances in the house and him going cold on you. Plus he had to explain Rebecca Wong. But now, with Rebecca Wong dead, the Electro-North 45 story might go away. And if the story goes away, the SEC may never learn about the bogus battery claims. So maybe Jack now sees you as a liability."

"Why? I won't get involved in whatever Jack has been up to. His business is his business. I want nothing to do with it."

"Unfortunately, you have everything to do with it. At least you will if you divorce him."

"What do you mean *if* I divorce Jack. It's *when* I divorce him. And what does that have to do with it?"

"*When* you divorce Jack, the lawyers and court will open up the books. All the books. Personal finances and business. That could expose something he doesn't want exposed. Jack wants quiet now. He wants everything to appear ho-hum, business as usual. Whatever's going on at Electro-North 45, whatever caused him to take a large cash advance from a credit card when you have, I assume, ample personal assets, he'll want to keep under wraps. I haven't taken a cash advance from a credit card in twenty years, but if I remember right, they start compounding the interest the moment you take the money, not at the end of the month like a credit card purchase. Do you have any idea why Jack would do that?"

"None."

"Have you checked your other accounts? Credit cards? Savings? Brokerage?"

Katie shook her head. "Stupid of me not to."

"Give yourself a break. The son of a bitch has turned your life upside down. I've been there. Common sense isn't as common as it should be when your life is in chaos. And I'm just thinking out loud here . . ." Noah looked away again.

Katie was learning that was what Noah did when he didn't want to say something difficult. He was looking for the best words. The kindest words. And she appreciated the effort. "You're just thinking Jack will try to intimidate me into staying with him?"

"From what you've told me about him, he sounds like the type."

"And he thought exploding a van next to me would somehow make me go running back to him?"

"People don't make the best decisions when they're acting out of fear," said Noah. "Maybe Jack knows that, if not consciously then subconsciously. Sounds like he bullied Bagman in college and maybe he's bullying you, too. Disappearing on the kids the way he has then acting as if it's somehow their fault, that's another form of bullying. It's autocrat 101."

"That won't work with me," said Katie. "The more he behaves like that, the more he'll push me away."

"You know that and I know that, but Jack obviously doesn't. You've given him ample opportunity to repair and rekindle your relationship. He's balked every time. My guess is he only has one gear. Win through intimidation. Domination. Lying. Cheating. If the van doesn't scare you, I'm worried about what he'll try next."

Katie fingered her snowflake-like pendant. She knew Noah was right. Jack was, at best, an asshole when he wasn't desperate. Who knows how low he could sink if he felt cornered?

"I think . . ." said Noah, "I think I'm going to pull Makeena off her current case. Just for a few days. See what she can come up with on Jack and Bagman. If that's okay with you."

"I thought you couldn't do that."

"Yeah, well, I've changed my mind. Perks of being the boss."

Katie nodded. Her phone lit up. A text from Elin. *Back to-morrow before lunch. Can't wait to see you!* Katie smiled.

"Good news?" said Noah.

"Elin returned my text. The kids will be home before lunch tomorrow. No word from Kaleb. He sees texts as one-way communications. Me to him. Every couple of months I threaten to take his phone away if he doesn't respond to calls and texts, then he does for a few days, and then he goes right back to not responding. It's not willful on his part. It's just the way his boy brain works. Or doesn't work."

"They say boys mature later than girls." Noah smiled. "I think girls get there at about twelve and boys at about forty."

"I think maybe a little later than forty."

The server approached. "Another round?"

Noah said, "Yes. I'm not driving."

Katie said, "Same."

The server walked away, and Noah said, "You're Ubering back to Edina?"

Katie drained the last of her old-fashioned and said, "I'm not going back to Edina tonight. I don't want to be in that big house without the kids. I'm staying at the Hewing."

· CHAPTER 39 ·

Noah had walked from his apartment to the restaurant, an easy mile over the Mississippi then north. The Hewing Hotel was on his way back home so he walked Katie down Washington Avenue, three cocktails in each of them, their bodies jostling off each other like two paramecia under a microscope. A half inch of snow had airbrushed the warehouse district white, and the restaurants and shops glowed orange-yellow like welcoming beacons.

Snow continued to fall, and when they arrived at the Hewing Hotel, Katie reached up and brushed the flakes off Noah's shoulders. "Cordial at the bar?"

Noah didn't answer right away. He looked away but only for a moment. Then he turned back to Katie and said, "Think that's a good idea?"

"The cordial at the bar? Definitely. After that I have no idea. Come on." Katie took Noah's arm, and the doorman opened the door.

It was the same hotel where Jack had met with Rebecca Wong the night Katie and Noah followed him from work, but neither Katie nor Noah mentioned that. A lie by omission on both of their parts, the kind of thing not said that sustains an evening. As far as Katie was concerned, this was her last night as a married woman. She owed Jack nothing. Not loyalty. Not fidelity. Not honesty. Adam Bagman Ross had rung the bell and now she couldn't not hear it.

But after two glasses of port, Katie felt she owed something to herself. Integrity. Decency. A walk on the high road. Her problems with Jack weren't about sex, though his rejection of her hurt—her problems with Jack ran much deeper. Sex wouldn't make anything better. There would be plenty of time for sex after she told Jack the marriage was over.

Those thoughts filtered through Katie's brain, woven in and around silences between sentences. When the bartender asked if they wanted another round, they each said no. Katie asked for the check, then turned to Noah.

"Want to hear a really bad idea?"

"You mean another bad idea?"

"Yes," said Katie, "much worse than inviting you in here."

"Regale me."

"I want you to come up to the room, but we'll keep our clothes on."

"Which one of those two things is the bad idea?"

Katie smiled. God, she longed for a man with a sense of humor. "You coming up to the room is the bad idea. Maybe. Us keeping our clothes on is an excellent idea."

"That's the worst excellent idea I've ever heard. Who would want naked intimacy?"

"To be honest, I would."

"But not with me."

"Oh, definitely with you. But not tonight. In the future."

Noah reached for his glass of port but saw that it was empty. "How far in the future? Jetpacks and flying cars?"

"Hardly. The day after tomorrow, when the kids have left, I'll tell Jack it's over. After I do that, it's the future. The divorce could take forever. I'm not waiting for a legal document. That would give Jack even more power than he has now."

"So me coming up to your room and keeping my clothes on," said Noah, "is that a firm rule or a conversation starter?"

"A firm rule. I completely understand if you don't want to. I declined your invitation to come up to your apartment once. I will not hold it against you in the future."

"The future," said Noah, "that starts the day after tomorrow."

"Yes. After I tell Jack he and I are done."

"Did you get a room with two queen beds or one king?" said Noah. "Because you must have foreseen the possibility of this situation when you checked in."

"One king," said Katie. She smiled. "And yes. I did foresee this possibility. I just didn't foresee that you'd foresee that I'd foresee it. I don't know if I like being around a man who's as smart as I am."

"Keep me around, Katie Kuhlmann, and I will challenge you."

"I might keep you around. And from this point forward, my name is Katie Ecklund."

· CHAPTER 40 ·

Katie and Noah entered the hotel room.

Katie said, "It's almost ten. I want to see if there's anything on the news about that van blowing up." She found the remote and turned on the television. "So I know where to send the bill for replacing my rear window."

"I'm still not used to the news being on at ten o'clock. Everything's an hour earlier in the Midwest. Why is that?"

"We want to get to bed earlier. You know, so we can not have sex."

"You're kind of drunk."

"You're kind of right."

Katie switched the channel on the television. The room was a salute to yesteryear. Wooden furniture, bullet-headed lamps, an analog alarm clock, a winged armchair upholstered in leather and brass nailheads, a simple iron headboard up against a wall of raw brick. Katie kicked off her shoes and plopped on the bed.

Noah said, "Want me to take the chair?"

"Up to you," said Katie. "As long as you can control yourself."

"I can. At least physically. My problem with you is here." He pointed to his heart.

Katie sighed. "Quit saying things like that. You'll melt my resolve."

"I don't want to do that. I really don't."

"I believe you. Now shut up and watch TV."

It was the lead story.

Strange happenings on 494 West near the Mall of America. A little after seven P.M., a cargo van with Wisconsin plates burst into flames. It was filled with fireworks, which are legal in Wisconsin. Standard firecrackers, bottle rockets, and some powerful M-80s, which are the equivalent to a quarter stick of dynamite. Some nearby vehicles suffered minor damage, and fortunately, no one was hurt.

The news showed cell phone video of the van in flames. Katie found Noah's hand and squeezed it.

Police say the van was reported stolen two days ago in Baldwin, Wisconsin. The strangest part of the incident, no driver was found in or near the van. Nor has anyone come forward. Police are currently reviewing cell phone video taken by those nearby and traffic cams in an effort to learn who was driving the van and where that person might have gone. They are asking for the public's help. If you were near 494 at the time of the incident and saw something of note, please contact Bloomington Police or the Minnesota State Patrol.

Noah said, "Are you going to contact them?"

"I didn't see anyone in or near the van."

The news anchor moved on to the next story. Katie rolled onto her side, her back to Noah. She reached behind her, found his hand, pulled his arm around her, and clutched his hand under her chin. They lay like that for a few minutes, through a commercial break, each of their heads fuzzy with drink, each grateful for the moment and silently questioning the rule to keep their clothes on. Katie's mind wandered back to the van. What if it had been a bomb, not fireworks? She'd be dead. We are all so vulnerable every time we leave the house. All it takes is one bad actor to step outside the lines. To think the unthinkable. To do the unthinkable.

They talked a bit more as the news gave way to *The Late Show* and *The Late Show* gave way to *The Late Late Show*. They took breaks to brush their teeth and wash up. They fell asleep mid-conversation, clothed on top of the blanket. They slept without touching, without checking in by offering a hand or placing one on the other's shoulder. They slept like children at a slumber party, isolated in their individual cocoons but thrilled to be with each other.

"Late last night Adam Bagman Ross drove up to the Black Bear Casino south of Duluth. He spent the night there with a woman who I'm pretty sure was an escort. Either that or she should have hang-dried her dress instead of putting it in the dryer. Thing was shrink-wrapped on her. Adam picked her up in the cities before heading north."

Noah had put his phone on speaker. Katie lay in bed next to him listening to Makeena Chandler's voice.

"Thanks, Makeena," said Noah. "I feel better knowing he's out of town."

"Why are you talking so quiet? It's eight A.M. Late one with a lady? She sleeping next to you or something?"

"Just did a little body-guarding last night."

"I bet you did," said Makeena, her laugh pouring out of Noah's phone.

Noah squeezed Katie's shoulder and said, "Let me know if he heads back toward the cities."

"Will do, boss," said Makeena. "One more thing. Just the way Bagman carries himself up here, the way he tips bartenders and servers and fraternizes at the poker table, the man looks comfortable, like a casino is his natural habitat, you know what I'm saying? It's far from Vegas, but still."

Noah ended the call and Katie said, "Makeena must have had a late night."

"It's okay. She's used to it. Part of the job. And it's far better that Adam is there than here. Especially with the kids coming home today."

"Agreed."

She looked down at her rumpled clothing and said, "Well, we made it through the night. Good for us."

"We are heroes."

Katie said, "You snored a little."

"I blame it on the whiskey and wine."

"It was comforting," said Katie. "It reminded me you were here."

"You say that now . . . ," said Noah.

Katie smiled. "And I will say it in the future."

"The future? According to my calendar, that's tomorrow."

"Really? My calendar has it the day after tonight."

Noah sighed. "I can't do this banter thing without coffee."

"Come on," said Katie. "I'm buying."

CHAPTER 41

Katie called the auto window replacement company, drove home, and showered. Shortly after a man and his van replaced the Volvo's rear window, Jack arrived with Elin and Kaleb. Katie hugged her children and ignored her husband. Without discussing it first with Jack, she told them they were celebrating Christmas that night since Elin and Kaleb would be in Florida on actual Christmas. They'd start with Christmas dinner then unwrap presents and pack for the kids' trip.

Jack avoided eye contact with Katie. She didn't know if he was aware that Katie had not come home last night or that she had learned about the cash advance. She guessed he knew about both and thought he could just not look at her and the problems would go away.

The family of four ate lunch in the nook, Katie's nook that she had asked for and Jack had granted. The one thing in the whole remodel/addition. And as much as Katie had loved the nook when the house was complete, she now saw it as her betrayer. The nook had promised her shelter for the family but it didn't deliver. How could it when the nook was up against Jack Kuhlmann?

After lunch, Kaleb retreated to the den to fire up the PlayStation, and Jack scurried into his home office to catch up on work. Katie and Elin headed to the supermarket, despite Elin complaining that they were perpetuating traditional gender roles by planning a meal and doing the shopping.

"You're right," said Katie. "You're a hundred percent right. But do you want Christmas dinner cooked by your father and Kaleb?"

"Uh, that would be horrible," said Elin. "So we'll do it. As usual. But let's make them clean up."

"Deal."

They were a few blocks away from the supermarket when Elin said, "What's going on with you and Dad? Are you fighting?"

"Why do you ask?"

"Because whenever you called up to the cabin, you never asked to talk to him. And when we got home, you kind of pretended he wasn't there. And he did the same to you."

Katie believed in telling kids the truth, as much as their little spirits could handle, anyway. She was lucky to have the grandparents who raised her after her parents and brothers died. Both teachers. Both emotionally intelligent. They never sugarcoated the tragedy. Never said things like *they are all in a better place* or *everything happens for a reason*. They told her it was a tragic accident. Happenstance. Black ice. Invisible. Deadly. If the logging truck hadn't been on the other side of the road, Katie's family would have walked away from the mishap. But it was there, and their lives ended and Katie's changed forever.

Her grandparents told Katie these things with kindness in their voices and love in their hearts. They, too, were devastated, losing their only child, their daughter-in-law, and two grandchildren. They weren't looking for answers the way ten-year-old Katie was, and they'd had more experience coping with grief, but their loss was also unthinkable. Still, they understood it was infinitely worse for young Katie, so their lack of sugarcoating was balanced with an abundance of love, kindness, and patience.

Katie didn't realize it until she was older, but her grandparents' straightforwardness kept her sane. The accident was horrible. Nothing shy of that. She understood that with her total being, and if they would have tried to tell her otherwise, the dissonance would have broken her.

That's why she was so furious with Jack for disappearing on the kids. For telling them, basically, that he was right in front of their eyes—they just couldn't see him. He gaslit them, and Katie knew how damaging that could be. When her family died, others did it to her. Friends, parents of friends, relatives other than her grandparents. She felt the cruel dissonance between *when God closes a door He opens a window* and *my family is dead.*

"The truth is, honey," said Katie, "Dad and I are having some problems. In our relationship. This happens with adults just like it can happen with kids. Dad and I need to do more talking, but I want to be honest with you—"

Elin interrupted. "Are you getting divorced like the Ackermans?"

Katie said, "How do you know about the Ackermans?"

"Everyone knows about the Ackermans."

"Really?"

"Yes. Josh Ackerman told practically everyone on our bus. He said his dad is going to move to a super cool apartment downtown with a gym and a pool and heated parking underneath and he'll get to stay there lots of times."

"Is Josh sad?"

"He doesn't seem sad. Maybe he is at home but he's not on the bus."

Katie took a deep breath and said, "How would you feel if Dad and I got divorced?"

"It'd be pretty sad," said Elin. "But I don't know. Maybe it would be better. You guys kind of seem like you shouldn't be together. At least not anymore. I can't remember when I was little. But now . . . Some moms and dads, like Uncle Dougie and Aunt Hope, they seem like boyfriend and girlfriend. They kiss each other in front of everyone like they're not embarrassed or anything. They seem like they just want to be together. You and Dad don't."

"I'm sorry you have to see us like that."

"It's okay. But if you get divorced, Kaleb would probably cry like a baby because he practically is one. But maybe not. Dad's been kind of not around anyway. I suppose if I had to go see him at some apartment and have my own room there and I could decorate it more like an older kid, that would be okay."

"You sound like you've thought about this," said Katie.

"Yeah. Well. I have like three friends whose parents got divorced. So yeah. I wondered what it would be like. You probably never thought about it because you were only ten when your parents died. That really blows. I didn't know how much it blows when I was little but I know it now. I'm really sorry, Mom."

"Thank you, sweetheart. That's a very nice thing to say."

"I wish I would have known them. I barely remember Dad's dad and Grandma Gwen is nice but kind of weird. I mean, it's great she's taking us to Florida on a private plane and everything, but I bet your mom and dad would have been more like grandparents who bake cookies with you and tell you stories and stuff like that."

Katie pulled into the supermarket parking lot and wiped her eyes. "They definitely would have been those kind of grandparents."

"Oh well," said Elin, "guess I'll have to settle for a first-class trip to Florida." She smiled at her mother, trying to cheer her up. A twelve-year-old carrying the responsibility again.

Katie returned the smile, wanting to take that responsibility away from her daughter. She said, "Hey, let's keep this between us. We'll all talk about it when you get back from Florida, but for now, please don't say anything to your father or grandmother or cousins and especially not to Kaleb. He's younger and will have a harder time with it, which is okay, but I want him to enjoy his trip to Florida."

"It's not because he's younger. It's because he's Kaleb."

"Promise?"

"Can we make candied yams with melted marshmallows on top even though we just had them for Thanksgiving?"

"Sure."

"Then I promise."

CHAPTER 42

Katie and Elin made a whole turkey breast and two thighs and one leg so Kaleb could pretend he was Robin Hood, mashed potatoes, stuffing, a green salad, braised carrots, and candied yams with marshmallows melted on top. Dinner conversation centered on Florida, the limo, the private plane. Kaleb hoped he'd have enough money to buy a Stormtrooper helmet at Disney World and a Ron Weasley wand at Harry Potter World. Elin wanted a Ravenclaw sweater and hoped to drink butter beer.

Jack and Katie barely spoke to each other, nor did they look at each other. For them, dinner was the long burn of a slow fuse.

Afterward, they opened presents. Katie and Jack had purchased some presents for the kids separately. Jack bought them Visa gift cards for their trip. Katie bought them clothing for the warm weather and portable battery chargers for their phones. They ate dessert after presents and then commenced packing for Florida. Jack disappeared during packing because of course he did.

When they were done, Katie challenged fate to repeat itself or correct itself. She said, "How about we make a fort in the living room tonight and sleep in it?"

"Yes!" said Kaleb.

"Would Dad sleep in it, too?" said Elin.

"That's up to him," said Katie, though she was pretty sure Jack would not join them. He'd bow out with an excuse about working late or his back needing a real bed. That's what she hoped, anyway. There was no way she was going to share a bed with Jack. Sleeping in a fort with the kids would be the least awkward way of accomplishing that.

Jack did not sleep in the fort despite Kaleb's protests of "Come on, Dad!" and "What are you, chicken?" Jack said he had an early meeting tomorrow before everyone at work left for the holidays. He said good night to the kids and turned away. Elin and Kaleb, in unison, booed him. He did not come back. He did not even turn around.

They built the roof out of blankets suspended between chairs, tables, and the couch. They unrolled sleeping bags inside, and used electric candles and lanterns for light. Katie set up her sleeping bag between Elin and Kaleb. She had brought half a dozen books, including *Harry Potter and the Sorcerer's Stone* in case the kids wanted to get themselves pumped up for Harry Potter World in Orlando.

But it was Kaleb who sidestepped the books when he said, "I want to hear a Neil and Blake story."

"Yeah," said Elin, "we haven't heard a Neil and Blake story in like forever."

Katie said, "All right. There's one I've been saving. Waiting until you were old enough. I think you are now."

"This is going to be awesome," said Kaleb.

"Expectation is the root of disappointment," said Elin.

Katie laughed. "Where did you hear that?"

"In gym class. Dylan Jordahl practically had a temper tantrum because he struck out in softball, and Ms. Gegner said he was mad because he expected to do better but he never practiced so he shouldn't expect to do better but he did expect to and that's when she said expectation is the root of disappointment."

"Well," said Katie, "Ms. Gegner is wise."

"Enough already," said Kaleb, "let's hear the story."

"Okay," said Katie as both kids snuggled closer to her. "When I was a girl, we lived near some woods. Not a forest or anything, but a little patch of woods that ran behind the YMCA. And one day, when I was watching Neil and Blake, which I did sometimes even though I was only ten and they were five, they wanted to go exploring in those woods."

"Bad idea," said Elin.

"Well, yes. It was a bad idea. But I didn't know it at the time. I was only ten. My mom was at work and my dad was at law school. Babysitters were expensive, and remember, when I was a girl, we had very little money."

"And you had to walk to school even in blizzards," said Kaleb.

"I did have to walk to school in blizzards because I lived just close enough that the bus wouldn't pick me up. And we only had one car, which my mother took to work."

"Did your dad walk to law school?" said Kaleb.

"No, but he walked to the bus stop. He took the city bus down to the university. Anyway, the reason Neil and Blake wanted to go in the woods was because they had just got new sneakers. Neil got red ones and Blake got blue ones, and ever since they got them the boys swore they could run faster and jump higher. But what they really wanted to do was test them in the woods, climbing trees and hopping over logs. So I said sure, why not, and walked them up to the woods. It was only a few blocks away.

"The second we got there they took off and ran ahead of me. When I caught up to them, what do you think I saw?"

"I don't know," said Kaleb. "What did you see?"

"You're not supposed to know," said Elin. "It's a rhetorical question."

"A what question?"

"Never mind. What did you see, Mom?"

"Neil and Blake," said Katie, "both of them, up to their waists in mud. Apparently they had tried to jump over a patch of mud but didn't make it."

"Oh, yech," said Elin.

"Yeah yech. I told them to get out and they said they couldn't. They were stuck. Whenever they tried to lift out a leg, the mud sucked it back down."

"What did you do?" said Kaleb.

"Well, I wanted to run back to the neighbors for help. But I was afraid the mud would suck them all the way down and I'd never see them again. So I did something I saw on TV once when a character got stuck in quicksand. I found a big branch, stood close to the mud but not in it, and extended the branch toward the twins. First Blake grabbed on, and I pulled him out of the mud. And then Neil grabbed on, and I pulled him out."

"They must have been disgusting," said Elin.

"I wouldn't say disgusting," said Katie, "but totally covered in mud. My first thought was I was going to get in so much trouble because Neil and Blake's new shoes were ruined. I mean, mud was all over everything. I couldn't even see their shoes. And just when I was wondering how we were going to get those shoes clean, Blake said, 'My shoes! They're gone!' And Neil said, 'My shoes are gone, too!'"

"What happened to them?" said Kaleb.

"The mud had so much suction," said Katie, "it sucked the shoes right off their feet. And I thought, Oh no, the only thing worse than muddy shoes was no shoes. And I thought we should gather up the biggest branches we could carry and set them across the mud and I'd crawl out there, reach down and pull out the shoes. So we went to get branches, but Neil and Blake had to be careful where they stepped because they had no shoes, and by the time we returned with the branches, the holes in the mud where Neil and Blake had sunk were gone. The mud filled itself in, and the shoes were lost forever."

"Cool," said Elin. She smiled and nodded.

"Did you get in trouble?" said Kaleb.

"Kind of," said Katie. "My parents were disappointed I took Neil and Blake to the woods and let them run off. But they said it was partly their fault, too, because I was only ten, and that's too young to be babysitting five-year-old twins. And it was also their fault because they bought Neil and Blake's shoes a size and a half too big because they were growing so fast, so the mud had an easier time sucking the shoes off than it would have if Neil and Blake's shoes had fit properly."

"What was your punishment?" said Kaleb.

"We had a little vegetable garden in the backyard, and I had to weed it for the rest of the summer."

"I don't get it," said Elin.

"What don't you get, honey?"

"Why you couldn't tell us that story until now. It's a little kid story. There's nothing scary about it or anything."

"You're right," said Katie, "it's the next part that I didn't feel comfortable telling you until now."

"This is going to be good," said Kaleb.

"Shh," said Elin. "She can't tell us if you're talking."

Katie said, "I was ten years old. Neil and Blake were five. And from about the time they could walk, I thought my brothers were such a pain. Always getting into my stuff. Drawing on the walls. Running around making noise. Waking up in the middle of the night and screaming because one of them had wet the bed. And remember, I shared a room with them, so I had no privacy other than the bathroom. They drove me crazy."

"I would go crazy if I didn't have my own room," said Elin.

"You think that. But maybe not. Because when they were stuck in the mud, they were only waist deep, but I didn't know how far down it went. I thought maybe they'd get sucked under and die."

"But they didn't, right?" said Kaleb. "They died in a car accident."

"Yes," said Katie, "they died six months later. But I thought they might die then. And it scared me to death because even though they drove me crazy sometimes, even most of the time, I realized how much I loved them. They were the most important people in the world to me along with my parents."

"That's so sad," said Elin, "because they did die pretty soon after that. Is that what you couldn't tell us when we were younger?"

"No. Here's what I couldn't tell you earlier. After Neil and Blake died, and after I moved down to Elba to live with my grandparents, and enough time had passed that I could think clearly, I promised myself that if I ever had kids, I would name them after Neil and Blake. So, after I'd been dating Dad about six months, when it looked like it was getting serious, I told him about my promise to myself to name kids after Neil and Blake. I don't know why I told him. I guess I was looking for his support for the idea."

"But we're not named after Neil and Blake," said Elin.

"Well, when I told Dad, he thought the idea was morbid."

"What's morbid mean?" said Kaleb.

"It means unpleasant because it's about death. He said he didn't want any of his kids to be named after dead kids."

"And you listened to him?" said Elin, incredulous.

"I was in love with your Dad and wanted him to like me and so yes, I listened to him. When I first became pregnant with you, Elin, I brought it up with Dad again. I wanted to name you Neil. Even though Neil is usually a boy's name but lots of names are for anyone like Eliot or Riley or Chris. But Dad said no. We'd have to find another name we both agreed on. I was extremely disappointed. Devastated even, because I'd made a promise to myself and to the memories of Neil and Blake."

"So Dad got his way?" said Kaleb.

"Looks like it, doesn't it?" said Katie with a big smile on her face.

"Wait a minute," said Elin. "Oh. My. God. I can't believe it!"

"Can't believe what?" said Kaleb.

"Mom just switched the letters around. She tricked Dad."

"What?" said Kaleb.

Elin grabbed a gel pen and her sketch pad. "N-E-I-L," she said. "Switch the letters around and you get E-L-I-N. Neil turns into Elin." She showed Kaleb on her sketch pad.

"Cool!" said Kaleb.

"She did it with you, too. Blake is B-L-A-K-E. Switch 'em around and you get K-A-L-E-B."

Kaleb slapped his forehead. "Genius, Mom. You totally tricked Dad. Can I tell him?"

"Not yet. But pretty soon."

"Oh, man. He's going to feel so stupid. You totally got him."

"*Stupid* might not be the right word," said Elin. "*Pissed* is more like it. How could Dad not see that our names are anagrams of Neil and Blake? I figured it out in ten seconds."

"Not quite," said Katie. "You figured it out ten seconds after I told you there was something to figure out. But you've been able to read since you were five. That's seven years you didn't figure it out."

"But that's not fair," said Elin, "because I didn't know you could be so sneaky."

Katie put her arms around her children and said, "One chapter of *Harry Potter*?"

The kids agreed. Katie picked up a nearby lantern and brought it closer. She opened the book and began to read. She had not read out loud to Elin in three years and not to Kaleb in over one year, and she was comforted by the sound of her voice, her children's breathing, and how it was all softened inside by the fort made of blankets. And she was comforted by the idea that their fort was like a time machine. When they were inside it, she felt they could have been anywhere. In the house before the remodel/addition. Back when Katie felt Jack loved her. Loved their family. When her children were more dependent on her. And she on them. It was the best night Katie had experienced in years.

At the end of the first chapter, the kids asked for another, and then another. Neither Katie nor Elin nor Kaleb wanted the evening to end. Katie knew she was tempting history to repeat itself. Neil and Blake slept in a fort with her on their last night together. Now Elin and Kaleb were doing the same. Some people, she knew, would be terrified of the parallels. But Katie invited them. She had worked hard her entire life but, since the age of ten, she felt like a victim. Her parents and brothers were taken away from her. She was shipped off to live with her grandparents. She allowed Jack to pull her from the world she knew and hold her in his world.

It was as if she were traveling back in time in an effort to avoid a tragedy. That night in that fort made of blankets with Elin and Kaleb, rather than Neil and Blake, she would set things right. Katie read until she heard slow, steady breathing. She closed the book, turned off the lantern, and lay down, wriggling her shoulders to make a space for herself. And then Elin and Kaleb, like the mud from Katie's story, filled the empty space and pressed against her.

· CHAPTER 43 ·

A dozen neighbors came out to witness the event of Elin and Kaleb getting picked up in a limousine. The kids had told their friends and, apparently, it was a spectacle too spectacular to miss. Even Sandra, Lucas, and their daughter, Hannah, a gangly-limbed fourteen-year-old with highlighted hair and salon-tanned skin, walked halfway around the block to see it.

Sandra said, "You're making the rest of us parents look bad."

"It's not me," said Katie, "it's my mother-in-law."

Lucas said, "Then you're making Hannah's grandparents look bad." Lucas laughed at his joke, and Sandra looked like she'd just bitten into a bad apple.

Katie cried when the long car pulled away. She couldn't help herself, watching the people she loved most drive away from her and her ability to protect them. Jack turned and went back into the house without saying a word to her, and Katie lingered outside talking to Sandra and Lucas, Lucas insisting on repeating the story of their family tradition of driving three hours north every year to harvest a Christmas tree from their property on Leach Lake. He seemed far more excited about it than Hannah or Sandra.

Hannah said, "We'd save gas if we just got one from the Boy Scouts in Linden Hills like everyone else we know."

"But that's not our tradition," said Lucas.

"Yeah," said Hannah, "well, our tradition sucks."

Katie expected Sandra to reprimand Hannah, but instead

Sandra snickered and nodded, as if to say, *That's my girl.* Lucas's eyes and mouth shrank.

Katie found Jack in his office staring at his force field of computer monitors filled with numbers, numbers, and more numbers. She leaned against the doorjamb and folded her arms.

"Jack," she said.

"Now's not a great time."

"Look at me, Jack. Please."

Jack did not look at his wife. She waited thirty seconds, but he clicked away on his keyboard as if she did not exist.

"We're done, Jack," said Katie. "This marriage is over." She waited for his response, wondering if Noah would be proved right—that Jack would resist divorce because of what he'd told Katie about Electro-North 45's falsely hyped battery, and that divorce would expose Jack and his books to accountants and lawyers and the court.

Jack looked up from his screens but his head was still in the place it had been. He needed a few more moments to return to the present. When he got there he said, "What?"

"Our marriage is over. I won't live like this anymore."

Jack stared at Katie for what felt like a full minute. Eyes fixed on her. Expressionless. Then he smiled and said, "Katie, come on. We're not going to end our marriage."

Noah was right, thought Katie as she returned the smile. "It's not up to you. A marriage lasts when two people want it to. When one no longer does, it's over."

"Okay. Let's talk about this. I know I've been out of sorts lately."

"You've been a fucking asshole. To me and our kids."

"Is this about your boyfriend?"

"I don't have a boyfriend, Jack. Yesterday I went to the mall to buy Florida clothes for the kids and my credit card was declined. Our credit card was declined. Apparently, you took a cash advance and maxed out the card. Maxed out a card we pay off every month. You want to explain that?"

"Maybe," said Jack, "I bought you a very nice Christmas gift."

"With cash?"

Jack's smile faded. He took a breath, let it out, and said, "I needed the money for a legal retainer and I didn't want there to be a paper trail. You know I could be in trouble with the SEC. I've hired lawyers. Good lawyers. They're not cheap."

Katie felt her smile wilt. "You sure you didn't use the cash to pay Bagman?"

"What are you talking about?" said Jack. He folded his arms and leaned back in his office chair.

"Apparently Adam no longer needs $300,000," said Katie. "He told me he closed a big deal. But you and I both know Adam doesn't sell industrial heat shields. He does God knows what for a living and apparently makes quite a lot of money doing it. Would you know anything about that?"

"I don't know what you're asking me," said Jack.

"Did Adam's windfall come from you?"

Jack smiled as if the conversation were a game. "No, Katie. I haven't given a cent to Bagman. I swear."

"Your word means nothing, Jack. Absolutely nothing."

Jack ran a hand through his hair as if he were trying to make himself presentable. "You can't divorce me, Katie. Not now."

"Why not?" said Katie as if it were a question on a pop quiz. "Tell me, Jack. I'm dying to know."

"It's just a really bad time," said Jack.

"Yeah," said Katie. "It's a really bad time. For you. Everything is about you. Everything is always about you. But not anymore. When the kids get back from Florida, we'll tell them. If you're not man enough, I'll tell them alone."

"I'm not moving out of this house," said Jack. "Ever."

"Fine. You can buy me out."

"I can't afford to buy you out. I don't have that kind of cash. I don't have any cash. That's why I had to take the advance on the credit card."

"We have money, Jack. A lot of money. Plus you have a 401K. I have a 401K. We have a brokerage account. We have been extraordinarily fortunate. Obscenely fortunate. What do you mean you don't have money?"

Jack stood. He pointed a finger at Katie. She could see his teeth as if he were a dog warning her to back off. "I am trying to fix things. And you are not going to fuck me up by divorcing me."

Katie said, "Don't you dare point your finger at me."

Jack lowered his finger.

"What did you do with all our money, Jack? Did you pay Adam to kill Rebecca Wong?"

Jack stared at Katie with an expression of nausea and contempt. "How do you know Rebecca Wong is dead?"

"It was in the news."

"I don't think it was. I didn't read it anywhere."

"I saw it on Instagram. Someone from the *Journal* posted about it."

Jack looked dubious. He took a deep breath and said, "I had nothing to do with her death. The idea alone is batshit crazy. I would never do something like that. Ever. No matter how bad things got."

"You never would have done a lot of things, Jack. You would never have distanced yourself from me. Stopped touching me. Started lying to your kids. Cheated at work. Cheated investors. Cheated on me."

Jack's eyes gave him away. He was cheating on her. Katie could see it. She didn't know with whom, but she saw it all over his face.

"I just need a little time," said Jack. "Let me turn things around.

With work. With us. I'm going through a rough patch, Katie. Come on. Give me a break."

Katie stared hard at her husband. His eyes softened from hard to hopeful. He had given her this look since the day they met. When he called off a romantic weekend to go up to the cabin with the guys. When he said he'd be home at six o'clock and walked in at nine o'clock. When he couldn't attend Elin's championship soccer game because *something came up* and he had to fly to New York that day. It had worked, that look. Worked every time. Until now.

"We're done, Jack. Find yourself a family law attorney."

Jack refocused on his computer for a moment, typed something, then turned back to her. "It seems you've made up your mind."

"No, Jack, you've made up my mind." Katie's phone buzzed in her hand. She immediately thought of the kids—they wouldn't have taken off yet. One of them might need something or, more likely, Elin had texted her a picture of the private plane. Whatever it was, she decided it could wait thirty seconds. She had something to say. Something Jack needed to hear. She pulled her shoulder off the doorjamb, stood up straight and said, "I am so embarrassed that I married you."

Katie turned and walked out of the room.

She went to the kitchen, sat in the breakfast nook, and cried for a few minutes until her phone buzzed again. Katie looked at the screen. The text was from Makeena.

Bagman headed back to the cities. Seems to be in a hurry. Following south on I-35.

CHAPTER 44

Katie knew that the cash advance Jack had taken from their credit card and Rebecca Wong's death could be connected to Adam Bagman Ross. Plus she might have pushed Jack's panic button by telling him she was divorcing him. As Noah said, that would open Jack's books to the accountants, lawyers, and the court. So Katie went to the safest place she knew, the food science lab at General Mills. Hardly anyone was there—most of her colleagues had taken off for the holidays—but Katie still had to go through two levels of security to enter the place where the new flavor of monster cereals was guarded like nuclear launch codes. She worked to pass the time between texts from Elin and Makeena.

Elin: *Just landed.*

Half an hour later . . .

Makeena: *Subject branched onto 35W.*

Forty minutes later . . .

Elin: *At the hotel.*

One hour later . . .

Makeena: *Appears headed to the house. Where are you?*

Ten minutes later . . .

Elin: *At Disney World. Kaleb already bought a light saber at the big store right when you walk in.*

Katie told Makeena she was safe at work and told Elin that Kaleb could spend his money however he chose. Then her phone rang. Sandra (don't call me S-and-ra, it's S-ah-ndra) Dahlstrom showed up on the caller ID. Katie answered the call.

"I knocked on your door. Where are you?" said Sandra.

"At work."

"The day before Christmas Eve?"

"I just wanted to catch up on a few things," said Katie. She could hear the lie in her voice but didn't care.

"I have some bad news."

"Are you okay?"

"I'm fine," said Sandra, "but I just saw Jack drive by with Terri Ackerman. I'm sorry to be the one to tell you."

Katie was sure Sandra was mistaken. She must have seen some other blonde in Jack's car. Katie had spoken to Terri, and Terri denied the affair. Katie believed her. But even if Sandra wasn't mistaken, it no longer mattered. "It's fine," said Katie.

"What do you mean it's fine?"

"I don't care if Jack's with Terri other than I like Terri. She deserves better than Jack. She'll figure it out soon enough, I'm sure."

"Wait," said Sandra, "you don't care if Jack's having an affair?"

"Nope. I'm done with Jack Kuhlmann. Our marriage is over."

"Did he tell you that?"

"No. I told him that."

"You told Jack your marriage is over?! When did you tell him that? How long has this been going on?"

"I told him this morning. After the kids left for Florida."

"And what did he say?"

"He said, 'No.'"

"No?"

Makeena: *Are you in a safe location?*

"Jack doesn't want me to leave him," said Katie, "but that's only because he's a coward. He tried to tell me I can't leave. I told him that wasn't true. It's over. He won't move out. I suppose I'll have to, but I don't mind, really. That house is about him. He's the one who supervised the whole project. To tell you the truth, I'll be glad to move out of it. As long as the kids go with me, but I don't think he'll put up much of a fight on that. He's been so absent lately."

Sandra said, "I'm just . . . I'm just shocked. Absolutely floored. You didn't tell me you were having troubles."

"Are you really that surprised?"

"Honestly, yes. And now you're just going to walk away from the house?"

Elin: *Mom it's Kaleb. I'm texting on Elin's phone because I dropped mine in the toilet.*

Katie considered explaining the whole mess to Sandra. That she hadn't opened up about her marriage because it could have exposed Jack's problems with Rebecca Wong and his fraudulent sodium-sulfur battery. She still felt that way. She didn't want to spread those rumors. Jack's troubles would come out soon enough.

Katie said, "Sandra, I didn't tell anyone because I was hoping we could work things out without the entire neighborhood knowing our marriage was falling apart. I thought the gossip might somehow get back to the kids. But now that it's clear that the marriage is beyond hope it's not worth trying to save. At least for me it isn't."

"That asshole," said Sandra.

"Agreed," said Katie.

"You want to meet for a drink? You want to talk?"

Makeena: *Please confirm your location.*

"Not right now," said Katie, "but thank you."

"Call me if you change your mind. And I'm sorry, Katie. I'm really sorry."

"I'm not," said Katie, and she ended the call, looked at her phone and saw the texts from Makeena and Kaleb.

Katie: *At the office. Very safe.*

Katie: *Put it in the sun. It's waterproof enough and will be fine. And wash your hands!*

She had wanted to call Noah the moment she left the house to tell him her marriage was over. But that would have felt like she was leaving Jack to be with Noah, and that wasn't the case. Noah was handsome and smart and wonderful. As far as Katie could tell, he was also emotionally available. Jack was handsome enough and somewhat smart but an emotional dunce and unfit when it came to intimacy. Still, if Jack loved her, if he loved their family, she would have stayed with him. She would have sacrificed the possibility of having a satisfying romantic relationship to sustain her marriage and keep her family intact. It would have been a different kind of love than what she imagined was possible with someone else, but it would have been love and it would have been deserved love.

But Jack did not love her. He wanted his marriage to continue for the wrong reasons. For all the protesting he did when Katie said she was done, he never said that he loved her or that he wanted to save his family. Not once.

The phone rang. Katie answered on the first ring.

"He's not going to the house," said Makeena. "He's in Excelsior, standing on the lake where the public dock is in summer. It's odd."

Katie said, "Any idea what he's doing out there?"

"None. I'll keep you posted. Just stay where you are."

Katie thanked Makeena and ended the call. She'd received a few texts from Gwen while on the phone. Pictures of Elin in line for Space Mountain. Kaleb on the Jungle Cruise. Gwen sitting with her grandchildren on It's a Small World. Kaleb with an arm around Donald Duck. She texted back:

Thank you. Keep them coming!

A few seconds later her phone rang again. She looked down, expecting to see Makeena on the caller ID, but it was a number she didn't recognize. The area code was local, so Katie guessed it wasn't a telemarketer. She answered the call.

"May I please speak with Katie Kuhlmann?"

"This is she."

"This is FBI Special Agent Charlotte Nevins. I'm parked outside your house. Will you be home soon?"

CHAPTER 45

Katie considered asking what this was about, but she had a pretty good idea so she said, "I'll be there in twenty minutes."

She called Noah on the drive home and told him everything.

"I'm proud of you," he said. "What you did was incredibly difficult. I wish I'd been as brave."

"Thank you. But you didn't have a real friend to talk to when you were going through it. I did. And I appreciate it."

Noah paused. Katie wondered if her words had made an impact. Then finally: "Of course. Listen. I know you need time to process all this. I'm here if you need me, but I'll understand if you want to be alone for a while. Even a long while."

Katie loved Noah for saying that. She didn't know how to respond. She wanted to go over to his apartment and hug him. Hold him. But all she said was, "I'll call you after I talk to the FBI."

"Please do," said Noah. "You'll be safe as long as they're there. But the minute they leave, so do you. Sorry if I sound bossy but you can't stay at the house alone."

"I won't. Thank you," said Katie, thinking that was a stupid thing to say. So she added, "You've been a wonderful friend, Noah. I couldn't have gone through this without you."

Noah let that hang for a few seconds then said, "It's my honor."

Katie's eyes glossed over. "That's nice. Talk to you soon." She ended the call.

She pulled into her driveway next to a black SUV, opened the garage door, and drove inside. Jack's car was there. Adam Bagman Ross's was not. She met a tall woman in the driveway. She had dark skin and close-cropped hair and wore a navy pantsuit and white shirt.

Special Agent Charlotte Nevins introduced herself. Katie, ever aware of the nosiness in her neighborhood, invited Charlotte inside.

"Is this about my husband?" said Katie.

"Why? Is there something you want to tell me about your husband?" said Agent Nevins.

Katie smiled. "Does that trick ever work?"

Agent Nevins returned the smile. "Sometimes. It's always worth a shot. And yes, this visit is about Jack Kuhlmann. The FBI would like to talk to him. We're conducting a parallel investigation with the SEC regarding possible securities fraud."

"That doesn't sound good," said Katie, her tone upbeat.

"No, it's not good. And you don't seem surprised."

"I'm divorcing Jack. For unrelated reasons."

"Oh," said Agent Nevins. "Did Jack tell you anything about being investigated?"

"Are you here to talk to me or Jack?" said Katie.

"You. We've spoken to Jack. He told us to meet him here at this time for an interview but apparently he's not here. At least he's not answering the door, even though I see his car is parked in the garage."

"You know what kind of car he drives?"

"We're the FBI, Mrs. Kuhlmann. We know a lot more than that."

"Then you probably know more about him than I do. I don't

know where Jack is. He might be in this house somewhere—I can look."

"I'd appreciate it."

"And to save you some time," said Katie, "all I know is there are some problems with Electro-North 45's electric vehicle battery. I don't know how that happened. I don't know if Jack knew there were problems. I don't know what he did, if anything, to correct those problems."

"You said *some* problems with the new battery?"

"Yes."

"Try one problem," said Special Agent Nevins. "The battery doesn't work as advertised. The battery never worked. Jack knew it from the beginning and went out and sold investors like that battery was the second coming."

Katie said, "Would you like to wait in the kitchen or come with me?"

"I'll wait here, thank you."

Katie searched the house. Jack was not there. She even looked under a few beds and in the backs of closets. He could be hiding—she hid in the basement cedar closet while eavesdropping on Jack and Bagman—but it looked like he'd disappeared. Again. She checked the mechanical room and the laundry room and there was no sign of Jack. He had cleaned up the blankets from the fort Katie had built with the kids and thrown them into the dirty clothes cage, (a passive-aggressive move, thought Katie), but other than that, she saw no evidence that Jack was in the basement.

When she returned upstairs, Special Agent Charlotte Nevins sat in the breakfast nook looking at her phone. Katie said, "I didn't find him."

"Odd that he's not here and his car is. Think he walked to 50th and France to grab a bite to eat?"

"It's possible." She considered telling Agent Nevins about Jack's disappearances but decided not to. That would invite more questions she couldn't answer.

Agent Nevins set her business card on the table. "When he shows up, have him call me."

CHAPTER 46

It was six o'clock, and Jack had not returned to the house. Katie had just stuck a frozen chicken pot pie in the toaster oven when Makeena called.

"Someone picked up Adam on a snowmobile."

"A snowmobile on the frozen lake?" said Katie.

"Yes."

"That's odd."

"Sure as hell is. I'm keeping an eye on his car, but it's possible he'll never come back to it. I have no idea where he is or what he's doing. I've been given the slip before, but never by a snowmobile. I'll stay here for a while. If he doesn't show up soon, I'll pop a tracker under his car and head back into town. I really don't want to pop a tracker under his car—he seems like the kind of guy who would check for one. If he finds it he'll know he's being followed, but we don't have much choice."

Katie said, "Do you think I should check into a hotel?"

"Yes," said Makeena. "And erring on the side of caution here, but have Noah check into the hotel. Better his name be on the register than yours."

"What difference does that make?"

"People like me sometimes buy people inside the credit card companies. So I assume Adam Ross must, too. Not so hard to find someone when you know the last place they used their credit card."

Katie called Noah and they decided to meet for dinner. She removed her frozen pot pie from the toaster oven—it was still rock hard—bagged it and returned it to the freezer. She picked up Noah twenty minutes later and drove to the Longfellow neighborhood. They ate at Merlins Rest, an Irish pub with good meat pies and even better Irish whiskey. It was the kind of place that had live music and regulars, some pressed against the bar and others who gathered as whole families around pushed-together tables, their young children wandering around the restaurant like they owned the place.

"We'll check you into a different hotel tonight," said Noah. "The last thing you want to do is be predictable."

Katie pushed her fork through her corned beef hash and said, "Don't you think if Adam intended to kill me, he would have done it by now?"

"Maybe not," said Noah. He sipped from a lowball of Redbreast. "If he wants it to look like an accident, that reduces his opportunities. But with the kids out of town, a house fire sure would be convenient. Do you have a Christmas tree?"

"We have two."

"Natural?"

Katie nodded.

"A fire would be easy. If Jack's working with him, maybe they poured something into the water to help dry out the tree, make it more flammable. And not to get graphic, but a charred body makes it a lot harder for the medical examiner to determine cause of death."

"Wow," said Katie. "Now that I've told Jack it's over, you're pouring on the charm."

Noah managed a smile.

"How do you know all this? I thought you were a civil rights attorney."

"I worked in the D.A.'s office first job out of law school."

Noah took another sip of Redbreast. "And just to be clear, I am trying to get you into a hotel room tonight. But just you. My first concern is your safety. There will be plenty of nights after tonight."

"We keep saying that. Do you think it's true?"

Noah raised his glass to Katie. Katie met it with her glass. A faint clink in the loud din then Katie said, "I changed my mind."

"You don't want plenty of nights after tonight?" said Noah.

"I don't want to spend the night at a hotel," said Katie.

"Katie, you can't risk—"

"I want to spend it at your apartment."

Noah opened his mouth to speak but stopped. He gathered his thoughts and said, "I'd love you to spend the night . . ."

"But?"

"But I can't guarantee your safety. A hotel might be safer. There are more people around."

Katie set down her whiskey glass. "Makeena said it would be safer for the hotel room to be in your name. But Jack knows your name because I told him. I'm thinking it would be safest to go back to the Hewing Hotel and I'll get a room in my name, run my credit card so there's a record, then spend the night at your place."

Noah smiled. "How clandestine. And I thought you were but a humble food scientist at General Mills."

"Do not underestimate the cunning one needs to navigate corporate America."

Katie reached across the table, picked up Noah's lowball of Redbreast, and said, "I brought an overnight bag." Katie sipped the whiskey. "That's good." She returned it.

Noah reached across the table and took Katie's lowball of Jameson 15. "I need to tell you something." He sipped Katie's drink then returned it to her.

"That sounds ominous."

The screens on Katie's and Noah's phones lit up simultaneously. A text to both of them from Makeena. *No change. Calling it a night. Tracker in place. Will let you know if there's movement.*

Noah said, "Makeena's lost Bagman. Now you really can't go home."

Katie did not smile. "You were about to tell me something?"

"Yes. I hope you'll forgive me. There's something I haven't been honest about."

"Am I going to need another drink? Is this about Makeena?"

"No. It's not about Makeena."

"You're not really separated from Tana?"

"Of course I am. It's nothing like that." Noah caught the attention of the server and said, "Another round, please."

"So I will need another drink? How bad is this confession of yours?"

"Not *need*. Have to enjoy."

"I don't like the feeling in my stomach right now," said Katie.

"I'm sorry I built it up like it's a big deal. It's not."

"Uh-huh . . ."

"That first time we ran into each other skiing. It wasn't an accident. I knew you were going to be there. My hope was I'd run into you."

Katie needed a minute to let that sink in. How could Noah have known she was going skiing? As soon as she said, "But how did you know I'd be there?" she knew the answer.

Noah said, "Sandra Dahlstrom."

Katie said, "I don't understand," even though she thought she might understand. She thought she might understand *everything*.

"I ran into Sandra shortly after I moved here. She was with her husband at a restaurant. I was sitting at the bar, eating alone. She recognized me and said hello. She asked me for my business card so she could get in touch. A few days later she called and asked if I wanted to meet you and her at Wirth to ski. I said yes. The day we were supposed to meet, she called and said she couldn't make it. And she told me you were going through a hard time at home."

"Oh God," said Katie.

"And that maybe it'd be better if I *supposedly* ran into you skiing so it would be a surprise for you. Sandra said you really needed something good to happen in your life and she begged me not to tell you it was a setup."

"Holy shit, Noah."

"I'm so sorry I didn't tell you earlier. Sandra made me promise—"

"Don't you know what this means?" said Katie. Her voice sounded harsh. Raw.

"I'm sorry," said Noah. "I thought you might be disappointed. Hurt a little maybe. But not angry. Does it matter how we reconnected? It's been great, hasn't it?"

Katie took a deep breath. Her head swirled and it wasn't from the whiskey. She felt like she needed to grip the sides of the tables to steady herself.

"Katie? What's going on?"

Katie shut her eyes, took a few deep breaths and looked back up. "What's going on, Noah. What's *been* going on . . . Is that Jack and Sandra Dahlstrom are having an affair."

CHAPTER 47

"What?" said Noah. He leaned forward, his brow scrunched.

"How could I have been so stupid?" said Katie. "It was right in front of me."

"Jack and Sandra?"

"Yes. She set us up. But she didn't do it because I was having problems at home. She wasn't trying to help me. Sandra set us up to aid her own cause because she's having an affair with Jack, and Jack probably won't divorce me fast enough. Remember when you listed the reasons Jack might not want to end the marriage?"

Noah nodded.

"It would open up his books at home and at work. It would invite all sorts of scrutiny by lawyers and accountants. Jack not divorcing me is probably driving Sandra nuts. Then she runs into you. She knows we got along well at the Birkie because she witnessed it. She sets us up. We take the bait, sit in the chalet after, and those two women Instagramming their food sat next to us. They must have been Sandra's spies, Noah. Jack didn't send them. Sandra did. I knew I'd seen them somewhere before. They were at Sandra's daughter's middle school graduation party over a year ago. It all makes sense now." Katie sipped from her new glass of whiskey and shook her head. "That's why Sandra reacted the way she did when I told her I was divorcing Jack. She was genuinely surprised because he's been lying to her. He's been telling her he hasn't left me because I would make his life a living hell if he divorces me. So she was shocked to hear me say I didn't care if he was having an affair."

"I'm sorry," said Noah. "I should have told you right away."

"Yeah, Noah. You should have. It would have been the decent thing to do."

Noah winced. "Would you have been as interested in me if Sandra had said the two of you were going to meet for skiing and then she backed out?" said Noah. "Meeting me wouldn't have been a surprise, then. It wouldn't have seemed as magical."

"Yes. I would have been as interested in you. I don't need magic. Just the opposite—I need something real. I would have been equally delighted to know Sandra ran into you and made a plan for us to ski. This isn't about how I feel about you or us. This is about Sandra diverting my attention.

"If she had made a plan for the three of us to ski and backed out *and* I was suspicious of Jack having an affair, I would have put it together that he was having an affair with Sandra. Instead she tried to distract me by implying Jack was having an affair with Terri Ackerman."

"I fucked up, Katie. Bad."

"Any other lies by omission you want to tell me about? Or maybe just flat-out lies? I trusted you, Noah. I fucking trusted you."

Katie looked away. She was inside herself now. Not sure what to do. She had planned to spend the night with Noah Byrne. Packed a bag for it and everything. She felt so far away from him now. So far away and he was sitting across a tiny table for two.

And then the thought came. Jack's lack of interest in Katie. His lack of interest in sex. His frequent tiredness. His odd disappearances. It could all be explained by Sandra Dahlstrom. He was sneaking off to see her. To be with her. His mysterious hiding spot finally made sense—he was somehow sneaking off to the house directly behind them. Jack would leave without his car, his keys, and his phone. He'd slip in and out of the house without triggering the alarm. The question was how. How did he do that? Maybe he had some kind of fob that allowed him to pass through doors and windows without triggering the alarm. Something that bypassed the chime that sounded if a door or window was opened. That was possible.

More than possible. Jack oversaw the remodel/addition at the skeletal level. Katie paid no attention to that part. The foundation. The framing. The electrical. The HVAC system. The roof. The windows. The alarm system.

Noah interrupted the ideas ping-ponging around in Katie's head. He said, "What did Sandra say when you told her you ran into me?"

Katie looked at Noah. "I've never told her."

"Why not?"

"Because I wanted to keep you to myself. Separate from the rest of my life. Even my friends. Just for a while. You were my secret relief valve."

"Secret?" said Noah. Disappointment in his voice. Worse than disappointment. Sadness.

"Not like I'm ashamed to be friends with you. It was just so nice to have a friend outside of my bubble."

"*Was* so nice?"

Katie exhaled. She could smell the whiskey on her own breath. "I don't know. I don't know anything right now other than the FBI is sniffing around my husband, a hitman is living in my house, and my marriage is over. Oh, and also: I was betrayed by my two best friends."

"Ouch," said Noah. "Did you ever think I was doing the same thing as you?"

"What are you talking about?"

"Keeping you outside my bubble. One of the reasons I never

told you that Sandra set us up is because that would have brought Sandra into our orbit. It would have sullied our friendship."

"I don't understand what you're saying," said Katie.

"We know there's nothing unethical about our friendship. We haven't taken this relationship to the next level. I know what you're going through at home because I've gone through it myself. I have not taken advantage of the situation. Instead, I've tried to be a supportive friend, someone you can lean on until the right path reveals itself, *even* if the right path is continuing with Jack."

Katie's head swirled. Noah had been a good friend, but he should have told her about Sandra's setup. She felt burned by Jack's lies. Duped. But it was the last thing she'd expected from Noah. Katie said, "I know you're making a case for yourself. I'm not in the best place to hear it right now. I think maybe I'll just go home."

"Please don't, Katie. I won't—"

"I am not your responsibility, Noah. I'm going home, packing up my things then leaving for a few days. I don't know where to. But I need some time to myself to think all this through. Everything's happened so fast. My entire life has fallen apart. I'll let you know when I'm ready to connect again."

Noah finished the last of his whiskey. He rotated the glass on the wooden table, its ring of condensation allowing it to turn seemingly without friction. "Please take a moment to think this through. I was wrong not to tell you Sandra set up our meeting. But the reason I didn't was because I thought I was acting in your best interest. Again, I was wrong. One hundred percent wrong. And I am deeply sorry for my mistake. But it didn't come from a selfish place. My intention was good."

"No one intends to get into a car accident," said Katie. "But an accident can usually be prevented if people are paying attention. If they give half a damn about the consequences of their actions."

Katie opened her purse, fished out a fifty-dollar bill from her wallet, and set it on the table. "I have to go."

Katie stood from the table, gave Noah one last look, and walked away.

· CHAPTER 48 ·

Katie pulled into her garage and saw Jack's BMW parked in its stall and an empty space where Sandra had parked. She reached for the car's door handle but stopped. Did she want to be here? Even for a few minutes to pack up more things so she could leave town until the kids returned from Florida? Did she want to go into this house? *His* house? It sure felt like Jack's house. Did she want to be in a place where she couldn't help but see Sandra's house out the back windows? She could back out of the garage and go to Macy's and Target to get what she needed. But where would Katie go? Down to Rochester to visit her grandmother? Her grandmother who no longer recognized her. That wouldn't make her feel any better. *Damn Noah*, thought Katie. She was sure she would have spent the night at Noah's. With Noah. She'd packed for it. But she had a visceral reaction to his lie by omission. It triggered something in her. Walking away from Noah and out of the Irish pub felt like it was not a choice. His lie launched her out of there.

And then the thought hit Katie: Was Noah Byrne even interested in her? He was a civil rights lawyer. Maybe he was also a class action lawyer. Civil suits are civil suits. Did Noah befriend Katie to get information about Jack? How many individuals were out there who owned stock in Electro-North 45? Hundreds of thousands? Each one of them had a case against Jack for fraud. Is that the real reason Noah Byrne moved to Minneapolis? To bring a massive class action suit against Electro-North 45 after extracting information about the company from Katie? All under the guise of friendship and the lure of romance?

Is that why Noah planted the seed that divorcing Jack wouldn't be so easy? Was it an attempt by him to glean information from Katie and keep her at arm's length? She felt confused. Could Noah be that deceitful? Could her bullshit detector be that out of whack? Well, it certainly was with Jack.

My God, thought Katie. *I was raised by people who I could trust. That did not prepare me for the real world.* Katie took a deep breath and opened her car door.

She went into the kitchen. Three cupboard doors were open. It was not her doing. One of the cupboard doors belonged to a cupboard full of cereal. She didn't eat cereal. The kids did. Jack did. The kids were in Florida. Jack was not. And Jack had a habit of not closing cupboard doors.

She examined the open cupboards. One contained cereal, another contained canned goods. Beans, soup, tomatoes in various forms. Katie eyeballed the inventory. She had bought a half a dozen cans of chicken and wild rice soup last time she shopped. There were two left. She hadn't opened any yet. Other cans seemed to have disappeared, as well. She went to the third open door—this was the cabinet containing vacuum-sealed liquids for the kids' lunches. Milk, oat milk, and chocolate versions of the same. The cartons did not need refrigeration. Whole cases were gone.

For what felt like the hundredth time, Katie searched the house for Jack. His car was in the garage but he was not in the house. How did he hide from her? From the kids? Katie recalled her discussion with Makeena about hiding cameras. Makeena said the problem with cameras is they could be detected if someone was looking for them. Just turn out the lights and shine a flashlight around the room—if there's a camera, the lens will reflect back at you.

That's what Katie did. Room by room. Turned out the lights. Shined a flashlight around. Found a camera in a smoke alarm at the top of the second story. Odd. Katie stopped and listened for Jack but heard nothing. She searched some more and found a second camera in an air-conditioning vent in the primary bedroom ceiling. *In her and Jack's bedroom*. Katie shivered. Again she stopped to listen. No Jack. She continued her search. She found seventeen cameras, some hidden in the small air-conditioning vents in the ceiling. Some were hidden behind speaker grilles. Some were hidden in ceiling fans. Why would Jack have installed so many cameras? Why would he feel a need to spy on his family in their own home? Their one sanctuary. The answer brought Katie back to where she had started. Jack wasn't spying on his family. He was sneaking in and out of the house at opportune times, guided and informed by the cameras.

Katie felt nauseous. Jack had been watching her in her own home. Watching their kids. She went to the kitchen junk drawer and removed a pad of Post-it Notes. She'd get a ladder out of the basement storage room, cover each camera with a Post-it and put an end to Jack's spying. She was halfway down the basement stairs when she had a better idea. *If I cover the camera, Jack will know I'm onto the cameras. If I leave the house and somehow sneak in without Jack seeing me, he'll think he's in the clear.*

Leaving the house was easy. All she had to do was walk out. But how would she sneak back in? Kaleb. He made it possible. Kaleb had had a life-sized cutout of Chewbacca. The cardboard figure stood seven feet tall. Katie went into Kaleb's room and moved Chewbacca between the hidden camera in Kaleb's smoke detector and a window she could access from the lower part of the roof. She then unlocked Kaleb's window, went downstairs, and exited through the garage. She got in her car, drove the few blocks to downtown Edina, parked in a ramp, then began the short trek back to the house.

It was December 23rd. 10:05 P.M. Warm light filled large windows. Katie walked on sidewalks shoveled clean of snow and ice. Tomorrow night, on Christmas Eve, these sidewalks would be lined with luminaries, white paper lunch bags, each with a few inches of sand to weigh them down. Each with a lighted candle within. Every house in the neighborhood put them out, a tradition that began long before the Kuhlmanns moved into Country Club. The effect was magical.

It was also evidence of the neighborhood's uniformity. No dandelions. Perfect lawns in summer. Perfect sidewalks in winter. Luminaries lining block after block without a gap of nonparticipation.

The conformity was self-policed. Everyone in this neighborhood wanted to fit in. It's why people moved into the neighborhood. All eyes were watching. A vigilant eye was expected. Encouraged, even. So how could two back-to-back neighbors carry on an affair without detection? Katie felt she was about to find out.

She did not approach her house directly. Katie walked up the driveway next door, climbed the fence into her backyard and ascended the stairs leading up to the apartment over the garage. She swung one leg over the railing and launched herself onto an overhang in the roofline that circumnavigated the house between the first and second stories. The overhang was steeper than she'd guessed, and she wouldn't have been able to traverse it if not for her grippy-soled boots on the rough texture of the asphalt shingles. Still, she had to turn her back to the house, lean into the siding and crab walk sideways, her toes sliding forward and jamming into the ends of her boots.

Katie made it halfway toward Kaleb's window then stopped.

She felt paralyzed. What if Adam came back to the house? How hard would it be to make it look like Katie fell off the roof? And did Jack have cameras outside the house? She knew there was one in their doorbell and a security light over the garage, but what about in the back of the house? Was he watching her now? Had she made a terrible mistake to put herself in this most vulnerable of positions, balancing on eighteen inches of overhang while clinging to the house's cedar shake siding? And even if Jack wasn't watching her, Sandra could be. Easily. Katie looked up and saw every window on the back of Sandra's house. Katie felt like a fool. The only good thing was it was just as easy to continue to Kaleb's room as it was to go back where she'd started, so that's what she did.

When Katie reached Kaleb's room, she took her time turning around and holding tightly to the window's heavy trim. She opened the window and climbed in, making sure not to topple Chewbacca, who blocked the camera's view. She closed the window and took equal care sitting down in the space behind the cardboard cutout where she'd stashed a bottle of water and a peanut butter and jelly sandwich and a protein bar on a paper towel. She'd unwrapped the bar earlier. She didn't know how long she might have to wait or whether or not the cameras could pick up sound, and if she was hungry, she couldn't risk opening a mylar wrapper.

Katie had silenced her phone and had taken it off vibrate. She had missed calls from Makeena and Noah, but neither had texted her. She was just settling in for what might be a long wait when she heard something.

· CHAPTER 49 ·

The house was so heavily insulated, both in the exterior and interior walls, that Katie could barely detect noises in the kitchen. But with no TVs on, no appliances running, no kids shouting at each other, she could pick up faint sounds. Cupboards closing. The silverware drawer being slammed shut. She wasn't imagining it. Jack was not watching now. He was raiding the kitchen, and she was going to catch him in the act. Katie stood and walked out from behind Chewbacca. The insulation allowed her to slip out of Kaleb's room and into the second-floor corridor, as did the whole-house humidifier and carpet runner kept the wooden floors creak-free.

She was halfway down the stairs when she heard the unmistakable sound of urine hitting water. He was in the powder room peeing with the door open. If he came upstairs after he finished, he'd catch Katie on the stairs. But she wasn't doing anything wrong. She was in her house. It was he who would have to explain what he was doing and where he'd been. But he didn't come upstairs. He flushed the toilet and walked out of the powder room, down the front hall and back into the kitchen. It was Jack. She was sure of that. She could hear his footsteps, his familiar gait. It's something you learn about a person after living with them for twenty years.

Katie waited until she heard the rustling of paper grocery bags. And then, nothing. She continued down the stairs, through the front hall, and into the kitchen. Jack wasn't there. But the basement door was open. She peeked down and saw nothing. She descended the carpeted stairs and peeked into Jack's rec room. No Jack. She continued into the mechanical room. He was not there. She went into the storage room. Nothing but stored items. Katie could not help throwing up her arms and sighing. Then she heard a sound come from the laundry room.

She almost ran. Her footsteps on carpet over padding over concrete were silent. She entered the laundry room and thought she saw the wooden cage of dirty clothes move toward the wall. But that couldn't have happened. If the cage moved toward the wall, it meant it had been away from the wall. Katie crept toward it. She grabbed two of the wooden slats and pulled. Gently at first. Then harder. The cage did not budge.

The dirty clothes cage was built a few feet off the floor, supported by four legs, so the laundry-doer didn't have to bend over too far. Katie got down on her knees and slid her body underneath the platform. She saw nothing unusual. She pressed each of the wooden legs but they seemed anchored into the ground. She felt ridiculous.

Katie rolled onto her back and looked up at the underside of the laundry cage. Unlike its slatted sides and top, the floor of the cage was solid wood. Solid wood except for a small, opaque rectangle of glass. It measured about one by two inches. Katie had seen one like it before at General Mills. It was a sensor similar to the one she placed her finger on to enter the food science lab. She touched the glass with her right index finger. She expected nothing would happen and nothing did. She rolled back over to her stomach and inspected the poured concrete wall under the laundry cage. It looked perfectly normal. She placed her palm on it—it felt like concrete. So did the floor.

And yet Katie could have sworn that, as she entered the room, she'd seen the cage an inch or two away from the wall and then move back into place. A secret portal to wherever Jack was. A portal triggered by a sensor that did not respond to Katie's fingerprint. She used her phone to photograph all of it. The fingerprint sensor, the wall, the legs, the floor. Her phone lit up with a text.

It was from Elin. Photographs of the midnight fireworks show at Disney World. Katie sent hearts and kisses and a big, fat *I LOVE YOU BOTH AND MISS YOU SO MUCH!* Elin responded with a single heart.

There were texts from Noah and Makeena, too. She'd neither heard nor felt them when they came in because she'd taken her phone off vibrate. She read the first one from Noah. *If you are home, leave immediately!*

· CHAPTER 50 ·

Katie read the earlier texts.

From Makeena: *Adam's car is moving.*

Ten minutes later: *Adam headed back to the city.*

Then: *Adam headed back to your house.*

And from Noah just after Makeena's last text: *Bagman is parked .8 miles away in downtown Edina. If you are home, LEAVE.*

Then: *Why aren't you responding? Where are you?*

Katie crawled out from under the laundry cage. She inspected it more closely. If there was an opening behind it, the cracks in the concrete would be hidden by the frame of the laundry cage. The concrete wall behind the cage must move with the cage— it's the only way Jack could conceal the hidden entrance.

She used her phone's flashlight to search for more hidden cameras. She found none in the unfinished half of the basement. Typical Jack, she thought. Taking shortcuts out of hubris. Katie walked to the small workshop on the other end of the laundry room. It's where they kept tools for simple tasks around the house and the occasional project with the kids. Birdhouses. Popsicle stick architecture. String art on a board of nails. There she found a length of twine and tied it to a small screwdriver. She carried a step stool over to the cage and tied the open end of the twine to a joist in the open ceiling. She adjusted the length of the twine and placed the screwdriver on top of the wooded cage and against the concrete wall.

Katie went upstairs. It was 11:20 P.M. She went to the garage.

Adam Bagman Ross's car was not there. She checked her phone. No new texts from Makeena or Noah.

Katie exited the garage through the side service door and stepped outside. It was twenty-five degrees but, even without a jacket, she couldn't feel the cold. She walked to the front of the house and looked north down Browndale Avenue. No sign of Adam. She looked south and didn't see him in that direction, either.

She then walked halfway around the block and stopped in front of Sandra Dahlstrom's house, a white Colonial with a single electric candle in each window. White string lights wove in and out of the spruce trees on the home's front corners. More lights meandered through coifed junipers and the iron railings running along both sides of the front steps. Katie grew up in a house one-sixth of the size. A family of five in under nine hundred square feet. Sandra, her husband, and her daughter had all that space. But it wasn't enough. Not for Sandra. She wanted Jack, as well.

Katie searched her feelings. Did she care? She had lost respect for Jack as a husband, a father, as a businessman, and she'd lost respect for him as a man. She had guessed Jack was having an affair. When Noah admitted that Sandra had orchestrated Katie and Noah meeting on the cross-country ski trail, Katie realized Jack's co-conspirator was Sandra. Now standing outside the Dahlstrom house, Katie didn't have much more to figure out. To realize. Her brain had done its job and now it was her heart's turn. It wasn't sadness she felt. There was some, but that had already existed. She felt something stronger in that moment. She felt betrayed.

It looked as if every light in Sandra's house was on. Not brightly, but dimmed to an inviting glow. She wondered if the family was awake. Should she knock on the door at this hour of the night and confront Sandra about her affair with Jack? She didn't want to make a scene in front of Hannah—Sandra's daughter had done nothing to deserve that. Nor had Lucas, for that matter.

How had Katie's life ended up in this place? She felt responsible, as if she hadn't been paying attention. But she had been. She felt every bump. Jack's distance. His disinterest in her and the kids. His disappearances. It's just too easy for human beings to adapt to change, to absorb a shift in reality and refile it as something normal. Was this Katie's normal now? A secret safe room under her house? It was absurd. Crazy.

Katie's phone lit up the snow in front of her. Another text from Noah. *Please text me back or call me right away. It is URGENT.*

CHAPTER 51

Katie didn't want to talk to Noah. And she wasn't sure she believed him. Was it urgent? Or was he just losing in the race to bring a class action suit against Electro-North 45? Her gut swirled. It's what happened when her heart and head were out of sync. She put the phone in her pocket and started back toward the house when she heard:

"Hey neighbor."

Katie turned around. Lucas Dahlstrom walked toward her wearing a down puffer and a wool cap, hands in his pockets. "Hi, Lucas. I was just admiring your house. The lights are beautiful."

"Finally got them up. Better late than never, right? Hey, have you seen Sandra?"

"No," said Katie, trying to hide the rancor in her voice.

"She went on another one of her dang walks. Been gone for hours. I'm really starting to get worried."

Katie understood something some part of her had already known. Whatever space Jack disappeared into behind the laundry cage, Sandra was in there, too. The only thing she didn't understand is how Jack sneaked her in and out of there.

"Sounds like Sandra's on a long one," said Katie.

"I just worry about her," said Lucas. "I know sometimes she likes to walk to Lake Harriet then go around that and Bde Maka Ska and sometimes she even adds on Lake of the Isles. That's a twelve-mile walk. Most of it's in Minneapolis and, I'm sorry to say it, but the city is just not as safe as it once was."

"Did you try calling her?"

"She left her phone at home. Drives me crazy. She does it all the time. I remind her to take it, but sometimes she just forgets anyway."

Of course she left her phone, thought Katie. Just like Jack did. If they took their phones into their secret love cave and someone tracked them, their secret love cave wouldn't be secret anymore.

Katie felt herself washing away. Pulled out to sea by the absurdity of the entitlement exercised by her husband and friend. Correction: the person she thought was her friend. The two acted as if there were no other people in the world. Not their spouses. Not their children. No one.

Lucas said, "Well, Hannah's sound asleep so I guess I'll get in the car and take a drive. Maybe I'll spot her. At least it's winter and the leaves are down so I have a chance of seeing her from the road."

He looked pathetic. Lucas had let Sandra walk all over him for so long he couldn't seem to muster any anger toward Sandra. He was subject to her whim. She acted. He reacted. *How weak he must be,* thought Katie. Lucas didn't have the spine to stand up to Sandra, to stand up for himself. What a miserable way to go through life. How could he stand it?

Katie considered her response. She could play dumb. She could out Jack and Sandra's affair and she might have if she had hard evidence. Or she could light a fuse. Give herself the satisfaction of one tiny pushback and maybe inspire one in Lucas Dahlstrom, the most passive man she'd ever met. Just the idea of it was gratifying. She said, "Hope you find Sandra."

"Thanks," said Lucas. "Me, too."

"And if you see Jack out there, please send him home."

Lucas laughed but stopped when he registered Katie's expression. "You're serious?"

"Yes," said Katie. "I can't find him anywhere and he's not answering his phone. I guess he's just treating the kids' vacation to Florida like a mini-vacation for himself. I'm sure he'll show up sooner or later." Katie smiled.

Lucas nodded and forced a smile of his own. He hadn't put it together. There was a simple equation right in front of his face but it hurt to look at it. The sum was, however, undeniable, and the cogs in Lucas's accountant brain would crank and clang until he saw it.

Katie continued her walk around the block and saw Noah's 4Runner idling in her driveway.

CHAPTER 52

Katie wasn't ready to see Noah. She wasn't in the space to deal with pleas for forgiveness or, worse, duplicitous lawyer talk. But she was certain he saw her approaching down a walk banked with light-reflecting snow. There was no way to avoid him. Katie approached the truck, and the driver's window rolled down.

Noah looked disheveled. Worn. He said, "Thank God you're all right. Why haven't you answered your phone?"

Before Katie could reply, a figure leaned forward in the passenger seat. Makeena said, "Or responded to texts?" She glanced at her phone. "Adam is still parked downtown. He could be here in two minutes."

"I have to go inside and check on something," said Katie.

"No," said Noah. "You need to come with us."

"I *have* to. You're welcome to come with me."

Katie led Noah and Makeena into her home. They entered through the garage and locked the door behind them.

"Set the alarm," said Makeena.

Katie did. When she turned around, Makeena touched the outside of her jacket, and Katie knew that Makeena, like Bagman, was carrying a gun.

It felt like a smashing of the last boundary between Katie, Jack, and Noah. She barely made eye contact with Noah. She knew that logically, his transgression, his lie by omission, was not colossal. She could even make the argument that there was something sweet about it. By not telling Katie that Sandra had set them up, he gifted her a fairy tale of sorts. But she had felt so wronged. By Jack. By Sandra. By her soon-to-be-ex mother-in-law, Gwen. And even, she had to admit, by Elin and Kaleb, who chose Florida and a limousine and a private plane over spending Christmas with her. She didn't blame them. She didn't hold a grudge against her children, but she blamed the hell out of Jack and Sandra, and in Katie's raw state, it was hard for her to differentiate between the wrongs that had been done to her. That gave Noah little hope for redemption.

They moved into the kitchen as Makeena said, "The reason we drove over, other than you ignoring our calls and texts, is because of that bloody shirt you gave me. The FBI ran a DNA analysis and it came back a match."

"A match for who?" said Katie. "Adam?"

"A match for blood belonging to an individual who was present at several crime scenes. All mob hits where forensic investigators tied blood splatter to the victim, but also found blood of another individual. The FBI had never paired that DNA to a known person, but if the blood on the shirt you gave me is Adam Ross's blood, then he's their missing person of interest."

Katie said, "So you think Adam is who he told Jack he is."

"Yes," said Makeena. "And the FBI is most interested in talking to him."

"Why haven't they brought him in then?" said Katie. "You know where he is."

"I have no idea why they haven't brought him in. All I know is my FBI contact told me to regard him as armed and dangerous. Get the hell away, she said. Stay the hell away."

"Are they watching the house now?" said Katie.

"They don't need to," said Noah, speaking for the first time since they entered the house. "Makeena gave them the info to track the device she stuck under his car. Our main point is, you need to leave right away."

"I can't leave," said Katie.

"Why not?"

Katie didn't want to explain it. She didn't expect Noah and Makeena to understand. And she didn't have the energy to help them understand. She sighed and said, "I need to catch him."

"What?"

Katie explained that *him* was Jack and how she searched the house for hidden cameras and found seventeen. Then she left the house and snuck back in under cover of Chewbacca. When she heard Jack downstairs, she followed him into the basement where he disappeared as the laundry cage moved into place against the concrete wall. Then she found the fingerprint sensor. Jack was in a safe room behind that basement wall. And based on her conversation with Lucas Dahlstrom, Katie guessed Sandra was, too.

Neither Makeena nor Noah said anything for ten seconds then Makeena said, "Do you actually think it's possible Jack had a safe room or tunnel built without you knowing about it?"

Katie nodded. "We built the addition in the winter. Apparently that's the best time to build because of the low humidity. The only problem is the ground is frozen, which makes it near impossible to dig the foundation. So in the fall, before it freezes, they put giant blankets on the ground. I know it sounds ridiculous, a blanket keeping the ground warm, like the earth is a person or something, but it's true. Maybe that blanket wasn't covering just the ground. Maybe Jack had another basement room dug out."

Noah said, "Katie, I understand why you want to catch Jack going in or out of his secret lair or whatever it is. It'll confirm you're not crazy. But you are Elin and Kaleb's mother. Your safety is more important at the moment. And if Jack saw you checking out the laundry cage with his camera, or worse, if he's listening to us now, your life is even more in danger."

Katie started to speak when they heard a loud pounding on the front door. Makeena drew her gun and stood up from the table.

· CHAPTER 53 ·

Makeena motioned for Katie and Noah to stay put then exited the kitchen and entered the hallway. She moved through the foyer and toward the front "Who is it?"

There was no response. Makeena waited thirty seconds then said, "Who's there?" She crept forward, her pistol aimed at the door. "Stay back." Christmas lights lit up the front yard so she had no problem looking out through the side light window where she saw no one, and then the peephole in the front door, which wasn't really a peephole but a tiny door within the door like something a speakeasy would have.

"I don't see anyone," said Makeena. "I'm going to open the door. Is the alarm set to home or away?"

"Home," said Katie. "If you open the door, it'll go off instantly."

"Shit," said Makeena. "Turn it off. But stay near the panic button."

Katie disarmed the alarm.

Makeena said, "You two stay back. I'm wearing Kevlar."

Noah stepped between Katie and the front door. Makeena turned the lock, crouched, and pulled. She opened it an inch then backed up using the heavy oak door as a shield, her gun pointed at the opening. No one came inside. She waited a moment, then swung around, gun pointed at the front yard.

"You promise this neighborhood is full of nosy busybodies?" said Makeena.

"I guarantee it," said Katie.

Makeena flicked the front porch light on and off several times then left it on. She waited half a minute, then stuck her head out. First left and then right. She saw no one. Then she looked down at the doormat and said, "Damn."

Katie and Noah stepped forward.

"Is that the tracker?" said Katie.

Makeena turned toward Noah and held out her hand. "Give me your keys." Noah started to question why but Makeena cut him off. "I'm going to follow Adam until the FBI can catch up."

"But the tracker's right here."

Makeena kept her hand out. "I always use two trackers. One that's easy to find and one that's hard to find. Bagman found the easy one."

Noah pulled keys from his jeans pocket and handed them to Makeena, who ran to his 4Runner, leaving Katie and Noah standing in the winter night, thousands of holiday lights twinkling around them. They said nothing for a moment as their breath condensed in the cold and clouded the air between them.

It was Noah who broke the silence. "Let's get out of here."

Katie considered Noah's idea and shook her head. "I have to see Jack inside that safe room."

"But we can't get in," said Noah.

"I might be able to get in now." Katie explained how she'd tied a screwdriver to a length of twine, and tied the other end to a ceiling joist. She set the screwdriver against the concrete wall so that when Jack opened the door from the safe room, the screwdriver would fall just far enough to block the door from completely closing when he tried to shut it. If Jack had re-entered the house from the safe room anytime since Katie had left the house, there was a chance the laundry cage hadn't closed flush against the wall when he went back in.

"I bet," said Katie, "Jack hadn't prepared his safe room for a long stay. He can be so lazy with things like that—he thinks everything will always work out because his parents protected him from real consequences when he was growing up. So the safe room is understocked with food and clothing and supplies. When Rebecca Wong died, Jack probably relaxed. But now he knows the FBI wants to talk to him. He told them he'd be at the house this morning, but when they came, he didn't answer the door. Now he's officially 'on the run' but he hasn't run far. He's hiding in his own house. He just needs supplies. I've noticed food missing from the kitchen. He's probably taken several bottles of rye, too."

Noah reached for Katie but she backed away.

"Jack probably wasn't in a rush to stock his safe room because after winter break, the kids will return to school, and I'll go to work five days a week, and he'd have ample opportunity to sneak back into the house. I'm saying this because I think he's sneaking back in whenever he can to stock up, and I bet if we go inside right now he'll have to run back into his safe room, and because he's in a hurry, he might not notice that the secret door doesn't close all the way behind him.

"Then maybe I can pry it open and go in. I need to see him in there. I need to know my life with him is over."

Noah saw the determination on Katie's face but fought it anyway. "Your life with Jack is over, Katie. You've already told him that."

"No. I said our marriage was over. My life being over means never seeing him again. Protecting my children from him. There's a big difference."

"You don't need to go in there right now," said Noah. "Maybe not ever." Noah started to reach for her but withdrew his hand. "Please. You don't have to stay with me. You can go to a hotel. Or to a friend's house. Wherever you want. Just please leave here."

"That's exactly what I'm trying to do," said Katie. "I just have to do it my way."

Katie started toward the open door.

Noah said, "Then I'm coming with you."

Katie kept walking. "I won't try to stop you. But this is about me. Not us."

They entered the house. Noah trailed Katie through the front hall and into the kitchen. He grabbed an eight-inch chef's knife from the knife block, held it down by his thigh, and followed Katie down the basement stairs.

Her device had worked. The blade of the screwdriver fell just far enough to lodge between the safe room's hidden door and the wall. Without saying a word, Katie turned off the overhead light. In the dark, she and Noah could see a crack of light defining the safe room entrance. She turned the overhead on and faced Noah.

Katie whispered, "There's a crowbar on the work bench. I think I can pry—" Katie saw the knife in Noah's hand.

"I don't know what Jack will do if we go in there," said Noah, his voice hushed. "He might have a weapon. He might try to fight his way out."

Katie sighed. Noah was right. The safe room was a rat's haven. Exposing it would corner the rat. She went into the workroom, returned with a crowbar, and wedged it into the crack. Katie pushed on the crowbar, and the entire laundry cage came toward them along with the concrete wall behind it. It moved only a fraction of an inch, at first, then more. She handed the crowbar to Noah and used her hands to pull. The contraption was heavy but glided over the concrete floor as if there were ball bearings underneath the legs.

She took the crowbar from Noah, thought about putting it back but decided to hold on to it. Noah was right. Maybe Jack was armed. She had never known him to use a firearm other than while on his corporate team-building pheasant hunting trips, and she didn't believe he'd have a handgun. Yet there was so much she wouldn't have believed about Jack if you'd asked her two months ago.

Katie pointed up at the light. Noah nodded and turned it off. A wedge of light spilled into the laundry room from behind the laundry cage. She had opened the door to the safe room, or whatever it was, just enough for her and Noah to fit through. When she peeked inside, Katie saw a corridor made of poured concrete. The walls, the floor, even the ceiling were all concrete. A single light bulb hung inside a protective cage.

They slipped through the open door and started down the corridor.

CHAPTER 54

They walked like hunters stalking prey over dry leaves. Katie heard voices as they neared the end of the corridor, which turned to the right toward the east if she had her bearings straight.

Katie could feel Noah behind her but did not look back. She saw what appeared to be a fire door between the corridor and the room, but it was open. The room was lined with shelves, mostly empty, which as she'd guessed, explained Jack's frequent return to the house. She stepped forward, entered the room, and looked to her right.

Jack and Sandra sat on a queen-sized bed, holding hands, their bodies turned toward each other, their conversation muted. Katie saw what she needed to see. She said nothing. Jack and Sandra were too focused on each other to sense her presence in the concrete bunker. The overhead light cast her shadow behind her, and either Katie had stopped breathing or it just felt like she had.

The room had a desk with the same computer and monitor setup Jack had in his upstairs office. More metal shelving lined an entire wall. It held several cases of water and some food. There were two sliding barn doors, both closed, and Katie assumed one led to a bathroom and perhaps the other was a closet. She looked to her left and saw another corridor exiting the room.

Katie remembered something Sandra had said at the impromptu get-together she'd hosted for Terri Ackerman (which in hindsight, probably wasn't impromptu) after Terri had had a bad day. Sandra had joked Terri would get through her divorce with wine, and her wine cellar was Terri's wine cellar, and that Sandra and Lucas had so much wine in their cellar, they might have to expand into the bomb shelter. She said they really did have a bomb shelter and could you believe people in the '50s actually built bomb shelters?

Was it possible? thought Katie. Was it possible that Sandra's bomb shelter connected to Jack's safe room? Underground? In two hidden chambers that merged into one? Is that how they carried on their invisible affair?

Katie turned back to Jack and Sandra. Something struck her as odd between her husband and best friend. It was Jack's posture. Slumped shoulders. Head bowed, looking up at his lover despite being taller than she. Sandra sat straight-backed, a smile on her face and in her eyes.

"This will work, Jack," she said. "Everything will be fine. I promise you. Trust me. Please trust me. We're so close."

"I'm sorry I lied to you. I'm so sorry."

"It's okay. I understand. As long as you're telling me the truth now. Are you telling me the truth, Jack?" She placed a hand under Jack's chin and raised it so he would look her in the eye.

As Jack did just that, Katie was sure he'd become aware of her presence. Why he said nothing or even looked at her, she had no idea. It was Sandra who looked first, tipped off by the fear in Jack's eyes.

Sandra focused on Katie's stone-like expression, then her gaze drifted down to the crowbar. It took a few seconds—time seemed to have slowed—then Sandra registered Noah. She saw the knife and stuck her hand into her purse and pulled out a pistol. It was small, and light shined off its chrome finish.

CHAPTER 55

Katie couldn't look away from Sandra's gun, the luster of its chrome barrel juxtaposed against the dull, gray concrete.

"Katie," said Sandra. "What are you doing?"

Katie wasn't sure how to answer that question. Sandra asked it as if Katie had done something wrong. A few seconds of silence ticked away, and then Katie said, "Nothing. I'm doing nothing."

"Don't come any closer."

"I won't," said Katie. "I've seen all I need to see."

"Why did you need to see anything? You told me you don't care if Jack is having an affair."

"I don't. Not anymore. Is that what he's been lying to you about? That I wouldn't let him leave me?"

Sandra did not answer Katie's question. She sighed then said, "You don't seem surprised that Jack and I are together."

Jack said nothing. Jack had yet to say anything.

Katie shook her head. "I'm not surprised. I realized it the moment Noah told me you had set us up to meet on the ski trail. Plus you trying to distract me with Terri Ackerman . . . You obviously don't know Terri well. One conversation with her and I knew she had no interest in Jack." Katie smiled and waved. "How are you doing, Jack? Getting enough to eat down here?"

Jack hesitated then said, "Things like this happen. People fall out of love. People fall in love. I didn't do it on purpose."

"Things like this don't just happen," said Katie. "This underground safe room or whatever it is just didn't happen. Why'd you have it built, Jack? Did you know they would come for you? Did you know this room would connect with the Dahlstroms' bomb shelter?"

Jack ignored Katie, eyed Noah and said, "Is that your boyfriend?"

"I am her friend," said Noah. "Come on, Katie. Let's go."

"Did Jack tell you why he didn't want to divorce me?" said Katie. Sandra didn't answer so Katie continued. "Let me guess. He said I'd take half of everything. Everything he had worked for." Katie saw a flicker in Sandra's eyes. "But it's worse than that. So much worse."

Jack looked at Katie. He was pleading with her. Begging her not to say more.

Katie said, "I think Jack's been about as honest with you, Sandra, as he has been with me."

"I need you to drop the crowbar," said Sandra, "and Noah, you need to drop the knife."

"So you two are just going to run away together?" said Katie. "Leave your kids? Maybe never see them again?"

"What are you talking about?" said Sandra. "Why would we run away?"

Katie said, "Ask Jack why he'd run away, Sandra. By the way, goodbye, Jack. I'm going upstairs to call your friends at the FBI. They've been looking for you. That's your warning if you want a head start."

Sandra glanced at Jack. "What is she talking about? The FBI?"

"I figured," said Katie. "You have no clue. And Jack, do you know who sent you the picture of Noah and me at the chalet the day we first ran into each other? Do you know how we first ran into each other? Turns out it wasn't dumb luck. It was all arranged by your girlfriend."

Jack couldn't hide his surprise.

"You two really got the person you deserve," said Katie. "Enjoy your lives together."

"Katie," said Noah. "Let's go."

Katie nodded. "Yeah. Okay." Katie started to turn then stopped. "Is there anything else you want to know, Jack? Ask now before I leave. Because I am never coming back to this house. I'll send someone for my things. And for the kids' things because they're not coming back, either. You wanted this house—you got it. Your fortress. It's all yours. You can *both* have it. Anything you're wondering about? Ask away. Because I have nothing left to ask you."

Jack said nothing. He looked so weak. So pathetic.

"Well, I know you two have a lot to talk about so—"

BANG! A report rang off the concrete walls. Katie Ecklund lost her sense of space and time.

CHAPTER 56

Instinct. Self-preservation. Katie shielded her face with her arm. She felt a hand on her shoulder. Another *BANG*! Her ears rang. The air was acrid in her nose and mouth. Her sinuses. Whatever burned when she inhaled compelled her to keep her eyes shut. The hand on her shoulder pulled. She had to take a step back to keep her balance.

"You knew! You fucking knew and didn't tell me!"

Katie opened her eyes. They stung. They watered. She squinted through the haze.

Lucas Dahlstrom stood holding a pistol so large it mocked other pistols, smoke rising from the end of its barrel. Katie glanced at the bed. Jack was crumpled forward on the floor, a hole in his back the size of a baseball. Sandra sat back against the wall, a quarter-sized hole in her forehead and the concrete wall behind her awash in blood.

Katie felt blood pushing through her veins. She swiveled her head back toward Lucas. Even through the smoke, his eyes looked like blue flames. Unleashed. Wild. "Why didn't you tell me?!" Spittle flew from his mouth. "How could you not tell me?!" He raised the gun toward Katie.

"She didn't know anything! We just found this place!" Noah Byrne stepped between Katie and Lucas.

"Who the hell are you?"

"My name is Noah. You've met me before. At a restaurant downtown."

"Don't you lie to me, too!"

"I'm not lying. Sandra saw me at the bar and came up to me. Do you remember? You were with her. She used me to divert Katie's attention. She tried to make Jack think that Katie and I are having an affair."

"Are you?"

"No."

"That's true." Katie heard herself speak. She didn't recognize her own voice. "Lucas. I swear. I just found out about Jack and Sandra."

"Then why did you say what you said tonight?! That thing about not knowing where Jack was when I was about to drive to find Sandra?! Because you knew then. That's how I figured it out. Why didn't you tell me?!"

"I didn't know then," said Katie. "Not for sure. I just discovered this bunker. Jack had a hidden entrance built. I just saw Jack and Sandra together for the first time." Katie knew the answer to her next question but asked it anyway. "How did you get down here?"

"Our bomb shelter," said Lucas. "We keep the door locked so Hannah doesn't wander in there. I noticed footprints on the carpet near the door. I've noticed them for months. Sandra claims she stores wine in there sometimes." Lucas looked at the bed. "Oh, God. Sandra. Oh, God." He kept the gun pointed at Katie but looked at the dead lovers, their blood merging from separate pools into one.

Katie was afraid that if Lucas didn't shoot her on purpose, he would shoot her accidentally. He had snapped. He was a madman in a cardigan sweater and no-iron slacks.

Noah must have felt that, too, because he said, "Please, Lucas. Put down the gun. You don't want to hurt innocent people. Sandra and Jack deceived Katie just like they deceived you. You're both victims."

Lucas rotated his head back toward Katie and Noah, whose words seemed, if anything, to further enrage him. Katie realized she still held the crowbar. She glanced down at Noah. He held the knife but had slipped his hand behind his hip, trying to shield it from Lucas Dahlstrom's view. If they could keep him talking, she thought, maybe, somehow, he'd put down the gun. Either that or he'd distract himself to the point where they could use one of their two weapons against him.

Katie couldn't help but look over at Jack and Sandra. The violence. A single shot to Jack's chest. Another to Sandra's head, her sometimes blond, sometimes brown hair now dark with blood. The stillness of their lifeless bodies. Katie knew she would feel loss, if not for herself then for Elin and Kaleb, but she had no room for it now. She was trying to stay alive for her children so they didn't suffer what she had suffered. Two dead parents.

She wondered where Elin and Kaleb would go if she died. With their cousins, she hoped. She tried to focus but her fear for her children kept pulling at her. All this ran through her head in a flash because it only took a second for Lucas to answer Noah.

"I can kill you, too," said Lucas. "I can shut the hidden entrance in your house, and I can shut the door to the bomb shelter. Cover it with a bookcase. Seal everything up airtight. All of you will disappear and no one will know where you are."

"That's not true," said Katie. "Sandra told the book club women about the bomb shelter. She told us about the wine she stored in there. Everyone knows about it."

Lucas lowered the gun. It had to be heavy. He could only hold it up for so long. "Another lie, Katie. You're a fucking liar. Sandra and I promised each other we wouldn't tell anyone about the bomb shelter because we didn't want it to get back to Hannah. And it hasn't. Nobody knows. That's why they won't find your bodies. Sandra and I promised each other to keep it secret. We *promised* each other."

"Well," said Katie. "I don't think Sandra or Jack were very good at keeping promises."

She looked again at the dead lovers, conspirators, liars. She swung her eyes back to Lucas. She had to keep him talking. He was reasoning things out, she guessed. Could he really get away with killing four people? Did he even want to get away with it?

"Lucas," said Katie, "thank you." She saw a question in Lucas's eyes. "Thank you for doing what had to be done. And I agree with your plan. It will work *if* you let Noah and me go. Because then the story will be Jack and Sandra ran off with each other. He was in trouble with the SEC and FBI."

"I know he was in trouble. Who do you think told the SEC about his fabricated data?"

Katie was stunned. With Jack and Sandra dead on the floor and her life being threatened, somehow there was more room for her to be shocked. "What did you say?"

"Jack asked me to look at the data once to see if it would hold up to scrutiny. He did that sometimes. Hired me as a consultant. Made me sign an NDA. Said it was important to get an outside opinion when what he was really doing was hiding fraud from his own board of directors. But I agreed to look at the testing data for his new battery. The math was right, but the numbers were wrong."

"What does that mean?" said Katie.

"It means the arithmetic was right. But the numbers he plugged in were fake."

"How could you know that?"

"It's what I do. It's called Benford's law of anomalous numbers. I can spot fake data a mile away. What he showed me was a joke." Lucas took a moment to catch his breath. "I've known plenty of Jacks in my life. Mean bastards. It's about time one got what was coming to him."

Katie thought, *Keep his focus on Jack* and said, "Jack and Sandra were all set up to run away together. He drained all our cash. It makes perfect sense. Everyone will believe that's what they did. But if you kill Noah and me, that won't make sense. No one will believe I ran away from my children. No one."

Lucas considered Katie's words. He looked down then over toward dead Jack and Sandra and said, "I have let other people tell me what to do for too long. I'm sorry, Katie. I can't take the chance that you'll walk out of here and go straight to the police. You might not deserve it, but that's the way it has to be." He raised the gun.

Noah threw the knife. Lucas turned and crouched to protect himself. The knife struck Lucas, but bounced off. Katie heard the clang of metal hitting concrete. Lucas lifted the gun and pointed it at Katie. The fury in his eyes returned. He wasn't thinking—he was reacting—like a rabid dog. Katie sent a silent goodbye to Elin and Kaleb and mouthed the words *I love you*.

Lucas's eyes darted to Katie's left. She heard a gunshot ring in her left ear and saw a flash from Lucas's gun. Another gunshot and Lucas staggered back. Two more quick shots and Lucas Dahlstrom fell. Katie felt the weight of a body pressing against her calves.

· CHAPTER 57 ·

Had Katie been shot? She felt no pain. No burning. Nothing. "Noah!" She looked down, but it wasn't Noah who had rolled against her legs. "Adam?" said Katie, as if she were in a dream. As if something impossible had happened. How had Adam Ross appeared in Jack's secret bunker?

His eyes were open. He held a hand over his ample belly and managed a smile. Blood stained his teeth. "Katie Ecklund," he said in a voice far from his usual bravado.

Katie looked behind her to see if Noah was okay. He seemed to be, though his complexion was ashen. She was shocked to see Makeena standing next to him, her gun still pointed at Lucas Dahlstrom.

"Katie," said Adam. "I bought it for you."

"What?" said Katie. She knelt down and held Adam's free hand, the hand that wasn't covering the gunshot wound in his abdomen.

"The beer," said Adam, "at the hockey game. I bought it for you. It was from me. It wasn't from Jack. I was so stupid." He coughed. Blood splattered his lips and chin. "I was so damn stupid. I pointed at Jack and meant to say I'm here with my friend but you thought I was just the messenger. The delivery boy. Jack's delivery boy. Because I didn't say the right thing. You thought he bought you the beer. But it was me. But when you saw Jack, your eyes . . . those weren't eyes for me."

Makeena walked over to Lucas, knelt, and placed two fingers on his neck.

"Adam," said Katie, "I'm so sorry."

Adam managed a head shake. "Don't be. It wouldn't have worked out between us." He smiled again, and this time Katie could barely see his teeth through the blood. "I'm not really a salesman. Never was." He winked. "I am in a less reputable line of work."

"Somebody call 9–1–1, please!" said Katie.

"Already did," said Noah.

Katie hadn't heard Noah on the phone. Maybe he'd left the bunker to get a better cell signal. She had no idea. Her focus was on Adam Bagman Ross. She felt like part of her had left her body and was looking down from above. Jack was dead. Sandra was dead. Lucas Dahlstrom was, most likely, dead. People she had known for decades. But it was Adam Ross who had her attention. She squeezed his hand. "Help is on the way, Adam."

"It's okay, Katie. No hope for me anyway. Ratted 'em all out. Every single one of 'em. Even my father. No way they wouldn't find me. All the organizations. Working together. I couldn't hide anywhere in this world."

Katie saw the color leaving Adam's face. She placed her free hand on his cheek.

"They'll hide you, Adam. The FBI will. Right, Makeena?"

Makeena said nothing. She just looked at Katie for a fraction of a second then broke eye contact.

"You were always kind to me, Katie." Adam took a breath. And then another. Katie wondered if he was done. He shut his eyes and took another few breaths. Then his eyes opened. Katie felt him squeeze her hand. "Jack was such an asshole. Sometimes I wondered if he married you just because he knew I was in love with you. That's why I stayed away so long. I hated him. Hated him enough to kill him. But I couldn't do that to you. Or your kids." Adam withdrew his hand, brought it to his lips and then looked at it. He saw the blood. Bright and red. He smiled. "At least I get to say goodbye. I didn't think it would be like this. But this . . . This . . . This ain't bad. I don't deserve this good of an exit."

Katie began to cry. For Adam. For her children. For all that had happened in the bunker. She sobbed and her chin fell to her chest. She pulled her hand away from Adam's cheek to hide her face, as if she were ashamed to cry in front of him. In front of Noah and Makeena. Her grief knocked the wind out of her. She gasped for air. When her breathing steadied, she reached again for Adam's face.

Adam Bagman Ross stared at the concrete ceiling. Still. Blank. Gone.

· CHAPTER 58 ·

The Country Club neighborhood was a place where neighbors took note if you hopped in an Uber, if your lawn had dandelions, if a package sat on your front step for more than twenty minutes. So you can bet they were all out in their driveways to witness the fleet of law enforcement vehicles, FBI, and Edina PD, along with two ambulances and four vans from the Hennepin County Coroner, and several news vans from local TV stations. Those who had left for Christmas vacation would soon regret it.

Katie FaceTimed Elin as soon as she emerged from the basement. She wished she could fly down to tell her children and Gwen in person, but there was nowhere near enough time. Katie was sure the kids had received texts from their friends asking what was going on inside the house.

It took a few minutes for Elin to gather Kaleb and Gwen and then Katie looked at her two children on her phone's screen. They wore pajamas and had sleep in their eyes. "I'm sorry I'm not there to tell you this in person," Katie started, "but I want you to hear it from me . . ." Even before she finished her sentence, Gwen stood then sat down again between Kaleb and Elin, put an arm around each one, and pulled her grandchildren in tight.

Katie stayed on the phone with them for nearly an hour, consoling and counseling, recalling the language her grandparents had used to tell her. She wished she could say Jack died in an accident and then tell the truth when she saw them, but that news wouldn't keep, either. And so she told them everything. About the secret room. About Jack's affair with Mrs. Dahlstrom. About Mr. Dahlstrom killing them. She could wait to tell them about Noah and the two of them going into the safe room together, and about Adam and his role. They wouldn't hear about that from their friends. So she saved those pieces of the story.

When Katie finished, she told Elin, Kaleb, and Gwen that she'd be on the next flight down in the morning. Gwen interrupted and said that wouldn't be necessary. They'd cut their trip short and get on the first plane tomorrow, whether it was private or commercial. Katie saw something change in her mother-in-law. Gwen had grown stronger, tougher, as if in an instant. Katie had never seen strength before in Gwen, but maybe it had always been there. The girl from the Iron Range had reemerged, pushing out the pampered wife who'd relinquished control of her life.

An hour after talking to her children, Katie sat in her living room with Noah, Makeena, two officers from Edina PD, and two agents from the FBI, led by Special Agent Charlotte Nevins, who even sitting, looked tall. Her short-cropped hair created no diversion from her unblinking eyes, and Katie felt their full intensity.

Agent Nevins and her colleague had taken their statements individually. The three survivors. Katie, Noah, and Makeena. Then she asked them to gather in the living room.

"We'll have to wait for ballistics to confirm your story. But what you say is consistent." Agent Nevins consulted her notes. "Jack Kuhlmann and Sandra Dahlstrom were in the safe room, sitting on the bed." Agent Nevins pronounced it S-and-ra and Katie felt no impulse to correct her. "Katie Kuhlmann and Noah Byrne entered from the laundry room of this house." Katie did want to correct *Katie Kuhlmann* to *Katie Ecklund* but felt it wasn't an appropriate time. "Katie had a crowbar. Noah had a chef's knife. Sandra pulled a pistol from her purse. There was some conversation. Then Lucas Dahlstrom entered from the bomb shelter of the Dahlstrom residence. Without speaking, Lucas Dahlstrom shot Jack Kuhlmann and Sandra Dahlstrom with a large caliber handgun, killing them each with one shot.

"Lucas Dahlstrom then threatened to kill Katie and Noah. Katie and Noah tried to talk him out of it. Noah threw the chef's knife at Dahlstrom. It struck him but with the handle. Dahlstrom raised his pistol but he saw someone to his right."

Katie was hearing the full story for the first time, stitched together by her, Noah, and Makeena. She wasn't sure of the events that happened next—that information had come from Makeena and/or Noah—Katie only knew the aftermath.

"What Lucas Dahlstrom saw was two persons: Adam Ross and Makeena Chandler. Adam Ross and Lucas Dahlstrom fired at each other simultaneously, each striking their target. Adam was shot in the abdomen. Lucas was shot in the chest. He did not go down immediately and Makeena Chandler shot Lucas Dahlstrom two more times, killing him.

"Adam Ross was still alive. He and Katie spoke. When paramedics and police arrived, Adam Ross was DOA."

"There's something I don't understand," said Katie. "How did Makeena show up with Adam? How did that happen?"

Agent Nevins looked at Makeena and nodded.

Makeena said, "When I took off to follow Adam after he thought he wasn't being tracked, I called my FBI contact to tell her Adam had fled. She told me to back off. And I said, *What? Why would I back off?* She then told me that Adam Ross was no longer considered a threat by the FBI. And that was all she could say. I responded with some choice words that I won't repeat here.

"My contact said she was confused. She thought I'd take it as good news that Adam Ross was no longer considered a threat. I explained what happened at the house with Adam pounding on the front door and taking off, leaving one of the trackers on the front step. Then I explained what you said, Katie, about the hidden safe room behind the laundry cage. Then she put me on hold. Next thing I know, Adam pulls into a service station. I follow him. He stops at a gas pump, opens his car door and comes out with his hands up. He starts walking straight toward me.

"I don't know what to do. A hired killer is walking toward me, and my FBI contact still has me on hold. I withdraw my gun, keep it in my right hand, safety off. Adam must have sensed my concern because he moved his hands behind his head and interlocked his fingers. He walked right up to the car that way. Then I relaxed a bit because I was at a gas station. Lit up like daytime. Cameras everywhere. And Adam knew there were cameras everywhere. I rolled down my window."

Katie pictured Adam walking up to Makeena, making Makeena feel safe, and her eyes blurred with tears.

Makeena said, "Everything Adam said in the safe room was true. He told me the same thing and then some. When the snowmobile picked him up on Lake Minnetonka, he went to a house on the lake, where he told the FBI who he worked for and what he did for those organizations. He had put it all on a thumb drive, so the interrogation didn't take long as far as interrogations go. He returned to the house to get his things. Then Noah and I showed up here because you weren't responding to our texts and calls. Adam told me he thought Noah and I were hired shooters who had befriended you in order to get to him. That's why he took off the way he did.

"The only reason he pounded on the front door was as a *fuck you* to me and Noah. Adam was headed into house arrest in the witness relocation program. He called the FBI from the car to explain what had happened, and I called my informant. It was just dumb luck that the agents sat near each other at HQ. They put two and two together and told Adam who I was. So he pulled over. When I explained that Noah and I were trying to help you, Katie, and that Jack was up to some bad shit, Adam was concerned for your safety going into that bunker. So he left his car at the gas station and we drove back here.

"We went straight to the laundry room and into the bunker, and when Adam saw Lucas pointing that gun at you looking all crazy and that there were already two dead people on the bed, he shot Lucas. And Lucas shot him."

Katie felt Noah's hand on her shoulder. He had said nothing since they'd gathered in the living room. She felt a wave of regret for how she had treated him after he'd admitted that Sandra had set them up to meet on the ski trail. She chastised herself for thinking Noah was using her to get info about Jack. He wasn't a class action lawyer—she was just being paranoid. She regretted so much in that moment and silently berated herself for needing to catch Jack and Sandra together. And for suggesting to Lucas that Sandra and Jack were having an affair. Katie hated that part of herself. If she had let it all go after Noah had told her about the setup, if she had walked away, Elin and Kaleb would still have a father. He might be in prison but he could have apologized to them. He could have told them he loved them.

Sandra would have been alive, too. She would have had to face the consequences of her affair with Jack by most likely losing her husband, the respect of her daughter, the respect of their neighbors, and of course, she would have lost Jack, to prison.

Most of all, Adam Ross would still be alive, trying to atone for his sins. Adam had told the FBI everything. Names. Dates. Structures of criminal organizations. The Justice Department couldn't give him immunity—but they promised to keep him out of prison where he, without doubt, would have been killed.

Katie reached up to her shoulder and took Noah's hand. He let her, but his hand did not respond with a reassuring squeeze or with anything, really. It was just a hand, and Noah, it seemed, wanted it to communicate nothing. Or maybe to communicate everything. He seemed no longer interested. How could he be, thought Katie, after what he'd just experienced in the secret bunker under the backyard?

Agent Nevins asked Katie more questions, mostly about the FBI and SEC gaining access to Jack's personal computer and phone. She granted them permission to do whatever they wanted.

At 2:30 A.M., the county coroner carried four sheet-covered bodies out the front door, loaded them into vans, and drove away. More press had joined the neighbors, and thanks to social media, especially the Nextdoor app, so had people who lived miles away. When the coroner vans pulled out of the driveway, the onlookers parted like a school of tuna bisected by sharks.

Shortly before three A.M., Agent Nevins said, "We can continue this conversation later today." She looked at Katie. "You going to spend the night here?"

"God no," said Katie.

"Wise. They'll be working downstairs through the night. Now, I don't want you to be alone."

An awkward silence, then Makeena said, "She won't be."

CHAPTER 59

Noah stepped outside. The neighbors and rubberneckers had thinned to a small herd, and the journalists huddled in their warm cars and vans. The news-van doors flung open when Noah exited the house, but he made it to his 4Runner before they could attack with cameras and microphones. Katie opened a garage door for him, and Noah pulled the 4Runner inside, the closing door behind him sending the journalists back to their vehicles.

The FBI loaned Noah a magnetic light bar to put on top of his 4Runner, which gave it the appearance of a law enforcement vehicle. Makeena sat in the passenger seat. Katie got in the backseat and lay down. Noah engaged the light bar, opened the garage door, then backed out of the driveway.

They drove for a few minutes and then Makeena said, "You can sit up now." Katie did. "I'm just going to be blunt here because it's late and I'm tired. You want to stay with me or you want to work out where you're staying with Noah?"

"I can work it out with Noah," said Katie.

"All right, then. That's good. I don't have to buy groceries. Noah, head to Northeast. I live near the corner of 8th and University."

"I have no idea where that is," said Noah.

"It's six blocks from your place. Head home and I'll give you directions from there."

Katie said, "Did you really not know where Makeena lives?"

"I still have no idea where she lives."

"And how does she know where you live?"

"Ask her. If she's still awake."

Makeena said, "I'm awake, asshole." Katie could hear the smile in Makeena's voice. "I don't accept a job from anyone unless I run a full background check on them. What else you want to know about Noah? I can tell you how many parking tickets the man has and the VIN on this 4Runner."

Katie reached from the backseat and put a hand on Noah's shoulder. "Truth?"

"Truth," said Noah. "I'm not making that mistake again."

Makeena directed Noah to her place. She got out of the car. Katie did, too. Makeena gave her a hug and said in Katie's ear, "Be good to yourself about this. Be real good."

"Thank you," said Katie.

Makeena broke the embrace, turned, and walked to her front door without saying another word. Katie sat in the passenger seat and shut the door.

Noah looked at her. Katie felt his eyes on her and said, "Can we please try this again?"

They walked into Noah's apartment. Katie went into the bathroom, brushed her teeth, and emerged wearing shorts and a T-shirt. She crawled into Noah's bed, and ten minutes later, he joined her. Katie glanced at the clock on Noah's nightstand. It read 3:45. She rolled onto her side and faced him.

The blinds were closed but city light found its way around them. When Katie's eyes adjusted to the low light, she could see Noah clearly.

Katie said, "I'm sorry I was so upset about you not telling me

Sandra set us up. I think some part of me knew things with Jack and Sandra were about to blow up, although I never imagined anything like tonight was possible. I thought maybe whatever was going to happen could have been avoided if I'd known the truth."

"I don't blame you for being upset," said Noah.

"I understand why you didn't tell me. The ironic thing is, if I'd let it go, I would have ended up in this bed hours ago, and four people would still be alive. One of them my children's father. And one of them a lost soul who still had a chance for redemption."

"Adam did redeem himself. He saved your life. And mine."

"I hope he felt that way. At the end."

They stared at each other for over a minute. Katie placed a hand on Noah's cheek and kissed him. Noah looked like he had something to say.

"Tell me," said Katie.

He set the back of his hand on her cheek. "I don't want your memory of our first time together mixed with the rest of what happened tonight."

"I do," said Katie.

"I'm not sure what to make of that," said Noah.

Katie smiled. "When I learned my parents and brothers died, I cried until my eyes could no longer make tears. I went up to my little room at the farmhouse and tried to fall asleep but every time I shut my eyes I saw their faces. So I went to my desk and put a drop of slough water on a slide, and I saw a Pediastrum."

"Sorry." Noah smiled. "History major."

"It's a type of microscopic freshwater algae. Cells cluster into star shapes. Kind of like snowflakes. They're beautiful."

Noah touched Katie's snowflake-like pendant.

Katie nodded. "It's my one good memory from that day. And

because it's surrounded by so much pain, it stands out in a way it wouldn't otherwise. Do you understand?"

Noah nodded. Katie kissed him and kissed him again and rolled on top of Noah Byrne.

· CHAPTER 60 ·

Katie was still awake at five A.M. when she received a text from Gwen.

> *Will land at MSP, Terminal 2, at 7:00 this morning. We will get through this together. Much love. Gwen.*

It took some time for the truth to come out, but it did.

Adam Bagman Ross was who he told Jack he was. And then some. He was employed as a killer for hire, mostly working for his family, but he was also loaned out to other organizations.

The night Adam was picked up in the snowmobile on Lake Minnetonka, he told the FBI everything. He was a hunted man and turned to his old college friend, Jack Kuhlmann. Adam really did want to borrow $300,000 from Jack so he could flee the United States and set up a new life as an expat, probably on a small island off the coast of Scotland, but plans changed when he thought Noah and Makeena might be killers and he was their target. His suspicion came from Jack's accusation that Katie was cheating on Jack. Adam thought that was impossible—cheating wasn't in her nature—but he knew a good con could go a long way, even when perpetrated against a highly intelligent person. Maybe Noah was someone other than who he claimed to be. If you live your entire adult life as a killer, you suspect anyone could be a killer.

Adam assumed his assassins had found him, and with nowhere else to go, he turned State's evidence. If his family and their business partners would not let Adam go in peace, he would take them all down with him, and that's what he did. Adam started his confession by admitting to a list of mob hits, all victims were criminals themselves. Even murderers can have moral codes, and Adam did.

It wasn't until after Adam had confessed everything to the FBI that he learned Noah and Makeena were not hired killers.

Adam had nothing to do with Rebecca Wong's death. That apparent accident was revealed to be a deliberate act when two white men in their mid-twenties were caught committing another crime against an Asian American. It was a hate crime, pure and simple, inspired by labeling COVID-19 the Kung Flu. The men had beaten a dozen Asian Americans and killed four of them.

The Justice Department subpoenaed the construction company that had built the remodel/addition to the house on Browndale. The general contractor admitted to Jack paying him half a million dollars in cash under the table to build an un-permitted safe room. With the house covered in tarps and the yard torn up, with several Bobcat mini-bulldozers pushing dirt around every day, no one noticed what was happening.

In the process of digging out the safe room, the builder ran into the Dahlstroms' bomb shelter, which had crossed the property line underground into the Kuhlmanns' backyard. That's when Jack paid the contractor an extra $50,000 to connect the two. According to the contractor's affidavit, he surmised that Jack and Sandra were having an affair before Jack broke ground on the remodel/addition.

Katie guessed Jack wanted his safe room connected to the Dahlstroms' bomb shelter more as a means of escape than as a way to rendezvous with Sandra, and that Jack and Sandra's relationship was built on Sandra wanting her share of old Minnesota money, and Jack wanting a partner who would help him justify his financial hocus-pocus. But no one will ever really know the truth.

Jack wiped out the family fortune, forging Katie's signature to drain them of their savings and investment accounts. Katie sold the house on Browndale to a successful screenwriter who moved back to his hometown. He and his partner had no problem that four people had recently been killed in the house—just the opposite, they found it *super cool* and *deliciously dark* according to an article in the real estate section of the *Minneapolis StarTribune*.

All monies from selling the house and its contents went to pay restitution for Jack's financial crimes. The government seized Jack's offshore account where he'd been stashing away the money he'd stolen from his business and family. Katie was left with no savings. But she had her job at General Mills, and borrowed from her 401K for the down payment on a new house.

She, Elin, and Kaleb all legally changed their last name to Ecklund. They did not move far away from the house in Edina where Jack was killed, but they crossed the border into Minneapolis and transferred to Minneapolis schools. The kids also wanted to legally change their names from Elin and Kaleb to Neil and Blake. Elin loved the name Neil for a girl and found dozens on Facebook when making her case. Elin and Kaleb wanted to change their first names partly to honor Katie's promise to herself that she'd name her children after her brothers—and partly to hide their identities and their connection to the most sensational murder in the suburb of Edina since a woman was killed eight years ago, and the murderer covered the crime scene in hundreds of bags of vacuum cleaner dirt.

Katie appreciated both motivations for her children legally changing their first names, but thought the change might be too jarring for them along with their new neighborhood and house and last name. She asked them to wait at least until they were sixteen to make that decision.

Gwen had given Jack power of attorney for her estate, and upon his death, learned that he had wiped her out, too. She was so ashamed of what her son had done to his family and to her that she sold her condo to amass some cash, and upon Katie's invitation, moved into the modest house in southwest Minneapolis with Katie, Elin, and Kaleb. Gwen also gave up her country club membership and helped take care of her grandchildren while Katie was at work, becoming a far better co-parent than her son had ever been.

Hannah Dahlstrom's young life sadly paralleled Katie's. Hannah lost her parents and went to live with her maternal grandparents in Richfield, a first-ring suburb that bordered Edina. Katie reached out to Hannah several times, hoping she could help Hannah navigate her tragic loss, but Hannah never responded to Katie's calls or texts. Katie hoped one day Hannah would change her mind and get in touch.

One day, about three months after the killings, Katie answered a knock at the door. A woman in her mid-sixties stood on the front step. Katie smiled. "Pastor Marilee. Please come in."

EPILOGUE

In the months after four people died in the underground safe room, Katie took solace in her children, her mother-in-law, Terri Ackerman, skiing, and Noah Byrne. Noah made a deal with her. To give Katie the space and time she needed, he told her he would not initiate anything, but she was welcome to initiate anything at any time. To go skiing. To meet for coffee. For a walk. For dinner. For lunch. For sex at his place.

She was tempted to sneak him into the house at night after the kids were asleep, but didn't want to risk one of them coming into her room. She never shut her bedroom door—it was important to Katie that the kids felt they had access to her at all times. She knew what they were going through.

Perhaps Jack's greatest gift to his children was his detachment and unreliability, which made it easier to deal with his death. Katie was especially worried about Kaleb. How would he cope without a father? If Jack had been someone else, more involved with his son, more of a role model, more loving, Kaleb would have struggled. But Jack had been so absent and preoccupied the last year of his children's lives, things didn't seem that different when he was dead. Katie felt this would be the case when they divorced, but was surprised to experience it even after Jack had been shot in the chest with a .357 Magnum.

A few days before Christmas Eve, just shy of one year after

the killings, Katie sat the kids down in their small living room and said, "I'd like to invite a friend over for Christmas Eve."

"A friend?" said Elin, her eyebrows raised. "I'd like to meet him."

The kids had not met Noah nor did they know he existed.

"Why are you talking like that?" said Kaleb. "Mom, why is Elin talking like that?"

"You're too young to understand," said Elin.

"Am not," said Kaleb.

"He is a friend," said Katie. "A very good friend. And his name is Noah."

"What does he look like?" said Elin.

"You'll find out when you meet him."

"I want to know now. Show me a picture, please."

"I don't have a picture," said Katie, which was not true. She did have a few pictures of Noah tucked away in a secret spot on her phone. She looked at them when she missed him.

"Then show me his Instagram," said Elin.

"I don't know if he's on Instagram."

"Mom, be serious."

"Describe him," said Kaleb, who sensed that his mother's friend was more important than just a regular friend but at nine years old, couldn't quite work out how.

"You'll meet him on Christmas Eve *if* I get your permission to invite him."

Katie and Noah married on December 28th, one year and four days after Kaleb and Elin met Noah. He moved into the house in southwest Minneapolis, and a new sort of family blossomed. It took a while—Elin and Kaleb were so used to the man in their house being detached that they didn't know how to relate to Noah.

He did not push the issue, and after a few years, genuine father-child relationships formed.

It helped when one of Noah's daughters, Carly, moved to Minneapolis to attend medical school at the University of Minnesota. She and Noah modeled a healthy father-child relationship for Elin and Kaleb. Noah's daughter embraced her younger stepsiblings, and by the middle of Elin's junior year in high school, the family had gelled to the point where Noah and Elin fought about Elin's inability to turn off a light.

Gwen moved into a nearby apartment when Katie and Noah married, but she visited frequently, embraced Noah in a son-in-law sort of way, and remained active in the kids' lives, driving them to activities and staying with them when Katie and Noah traveled.

Katie and Noah celebrated their tenth anniversary in a rented house on a golf course in Nisswa, Minnesota. It was December, and they were surrounded by miles of cross-country ski trails. The house had five bedrooms and all were occupied. Elin had one—at twenty-four, she worked on Wall Street. Kaleb had one—at twenty, he was in his second year at St. Olaf College. Carly had one—at twenty-nine, she was finishing her residency as an orthopedic surgeon in St. Louis. Samantha had one—also twenty-nine, she worked as a librarian in Larchmont, New York. Samantha shared her room with her husband and six-month-old baby.

Eight inches of snow fell while the family prepared and ate dinner then watched *Napoleon Dynamite* before dispersing to their bedrooms.

Katie curled her back into Noah and said, "These flannel pajamas doing anything for you?"

"I was nine years old the first time I fell in love. She was a model in the Sears Christmas catalog. So yes."

"I'll always regret not meeting you earlier," said Katie.

"I don't know if you would have liked me when I was nine. My teeth were too big for my head."

"Let me finish. I will always regret not meeting you earlier. But we're ten years in, and if these ten years are the only ten years we have together, they'd be worth more than fifty years with someone else."

"Right back at you, woman."

Katie looked at the window. Snow gathered between the panes, softening right angles with parabolic curves of white. Winter really was the most beautiful season, she thought. She said, "Do you think life balances out? Joy and sorrow? Pleasure and pain? Our worst experiences drive us to achieve our best? Or do you think we just see it that way to justify the hard times? Or to feel worthy of times like this?"

Noah kissed the back of Katie's neck. "That's a question for a smarter person than me, which is why I keep you around."

"You're a grandfather, Noah. You're supposed to be wise."

"I just said I'm keeping you around. How much wiser can I get?"

Katie reached back, found Noah's hand and considered the souls in that house, their lives, their futures. She wrapped Noah's arm around her, held his hand under her chin, and shut her eyes. Katie Ecklund felt a peace she had not known since she was a child.

ACKNOWLEDGMENTS

The neighborhood of Country Club in Edina, Minnesota, is a real place. It's lovely, and so are the many people I know who live there. Places that remind me of it are Hancock Park in Los Angeles; Summit, New Jersey; Clayton, Missouri; and that Chicago neighborhood where Kevin was left behind in *Home Alone*.

Country Club's yards really are dandelion-free when the surrounding area is rampant with them. And I swear this is true: those weed-free yards are the sole inspiration for this book. That's what an overactive imagination can get you.

I want to thank my agent, Jennifer Weltz, and my editor Kristin Sevick at Forge. They've been kind and patient as I stumble forward. And a shout-out to everyone at the Jean V. Naggar Literary Agency and Forge for all the hard work they do on my behalf.

And I want to thank *My Good Family*. The one I was born into and the one I helped create and the one I married into. I've been a rather lucky guy in that department, and I'm grateful for every damn one of them. Especially my wife, Michele, who sees me at my worst and is nice to me despite not having her own home to escape to.

ABOUT THE AUTHOR

New York Times bestselling author MATT GOLDMAN (he/him) is a playwright and Emmy Award–winning television writer for *Seinfeld, Ellen,* and other shows. Goldman has been nominated for the Shamus and Nero Awards and was a Lariat Adult Fiction Reading List selection. He lives in Minnesota with his wife, two dogs, two cats, and whichever children happen to be around.